D1006232

"A heartwarming collaborative debut."

— PUBLISHERS WEEKLY

"*The Sweet By & By* is the flowing story of a family struggling across the generations for redemption and reconciliation. The women in this novel are sometimes funny, sometimes serious, but always interesting. I was hooked from page one."

— HOMER HICKAM
best-selling author of *Rocket Boys*
and *Red Helmet*

". . . witty dialogue, believable characters and a page-turner of a plot. Just what I look for in a good book!"

— CASSANDRA KING
author of *The Same Sweet Girls*

"Conveys a meaningful message about forgiveness."

— CBA RETAILERS +
RESOURCES

"Beautifully real characters shine in this even more beautiful story. A wonderful first novel."

— EVA LONGORIA PARKER
actress and model

"Wow! I am completely inspired by this book. I have always admired Sara's ability to tell stories through her music, and now I can say wholeheartedly that she is able to make a great story sing on the pages of this book. This is a beautiful, breathtaking novel full of redemption, reconciliation, and grace. I fully recommend it!"

— ROBIN MCGRAW
#1 *New York Times*
best-selling author

Softly & Tenderly

Other Books By Sara Evans with Rachel Hauck

The Sweet By & By

Other Novels by Rachel Hauck

Lost in NashVegas

Diva NashVegas

Sweet Caroline

Love Starts With Elle

Dining with Joy

SARA EVANS

WITH RACHEL HAUCK

THOMAS NELSON
Since 1798

NASHVILLE DALLAS MEXICO CITY RIO DE JANEIRO

Published in Nashville, Tennessee, by Thomas Nelson. Thomas Nelson is a registered trademark of Thomas Nelson, Inc.

Thomas Nelson, Inc., titles may be purchased in bulk for educational, business, fund-raising, or sales promotional use. For information, e-mail SpecialMarkets@ThomasNelson.com.

Scripture quotations are taken from the KING JAMES VERSION. Public domain.

Published in association with the literary agency of Alive Communications, Inc., 7680 Goddard Street, Suite 200, Colorado Springs, CO 80920.

This novel is a work of fiction. Any references to real events, businesses, organizations, and locales are intended only to give the fiction a sense of reality and authenticity. Any resemblance to actual persons, living or dead, is entirely coincidental.

Library of Congress Cataloging-in-Publication Data

Evans, Sara, 1971–
    Softly and tenderly / Sara Evans with Rachel Hauck.
      p. cm. — (Songbird ; bk. 2)
    ISBN 978-1-59554-490-2
    1. Illegitimate children—Fiction. 2. Domestic fiction. I. Hauck, Rachel, 1960– II. Title.
PS3605.V3765S64 2011
813'.6—dc22   2010040269

Printed in the United States of America

10 11 12 13 14 QG 1 2 3 4 5

*To my mom, my granny,
and all the women out there just
trying to live a little stronger.*

One

Along the first of spring, when winter began to ease its grip on Whisper Hollow mornings, the word *barren* began echoing over the shadowy recesses of Jade's mind.

"You're quiet." Her mother-in-law peered at her from the passenger side of Jade's truck. She looked out of place perched on the faded red, torn vinyl seat wearing a haute couture pink suit.

"Thinking." Jade forced a smile just as the tires hit a bump in the road, jostling the passengers from side to side.

June grabbed the dashboard. "Mercy me."

"Sorry . . ." Jade urged the truck up the hill to Orchid House, her husband's childhood home. "You feel everything in this truck. No matter how new the shocks."

Truck shocks aside, Jade had managed to hit all the holes today. Holes in the road. Holes in her business. Holes in her heart. With a slow exhale, she propped her elbow on the door and pressed her fingers against her forehead.

Today it seemed that every woman, *every* woman, who came into Jade's downtown shop was pregnant. Nearly picked clean her retro maternity clothes. She'd been folding and hanging the remaining items when June called and asked Jade to give her a ride home.

"It's beyond me why you still drive this old bucket of bolts, Jade. Why don't you just buy a new truck?" June brushed a piece of foam from the crumbling ceiling off her skirt. "You're a Benson now. A successful business owner in Whisper Hollow and riverfront Chattanooga. Surely you can afford a vehicle better than this. Max would buy you one if you asked. I'm quite sure he—"

"Your pink suit is beautiful. Did you get it on your girls' shopping trip in Atlanta?"

June cut Jade a glance. "Paris, last spring. I figure I could risk wearing it another season."

"Do I get dibs when it's out of season in twenty years?"

"Shug, this thing will be completely out of vogue in three months. And by the end of summer, sold at the club auction." June ran her hand along the three-quarter sleeve, finally smiling. Ever since Jade had picked her up from the Read House Starbucks, she'd been fuming beneath a stone face.

"So Rebel got tied up with a case or something? Couldn't bring you home?" Jade asked. June had yet to say why she was stranded at Starbucks, and so steamed.

"Oh, who knows? That man. He can be so self-focused. I specifically told Rebel that Honey Andover could not drive me up to the house when we returned from Atlanta. Her granddaughter's birthday party is up in Knoxville, so she wanted to get back on the road. So . . ." June fiddled with the air-conditioning vents. "Rebel agreed to meet me at Starbucks."

"The truck doesn't have air, June."

"Well, why not? Mercy, Jade, buy a decent truck. What's this thing, a hundred years old?"

"Thirty-eight. So what happened with Honey? What's got you riled?"

"Nothing happened with Honey. She dropped me off at the Read House Starbucks like we planned, right by Benson Law, right by my husband's office, where he agreed to be. But Rebel's nowhere to be found."

"You tried his cell?"

"I'm angry, not addled, Jade. I called his cell and his office. Gina didn't know where he was—and if she doesn't know, he's gone. Vanished into thin air." June twirled her hands in front of her.

"Maybe Reb hit the golf course, taking a break from the class action suit the firm's been handling. That case has Max preoccupied and bleary-eyed."

"Nice try, Jade, but Reb hasn't *worked* a case in years. He just *oversees*. Charms. Asks a few tough questions in court when they want to intimidate someone." June snatched her handbag from the seat and stuffed it into her lap. "He's probably schmoozing someone in the governor's office, hoping he'll get a special appointment should one ever open up."

"Reb has political aspirations?" Jade crested the hill and rounded the bend toward the Bensons' white brick estate.

"Jade, have you learned to tune out his ramblings already? Reb wants to run the universe from his throne on the moon."

A fawn suddenly leaped onto the road from the cluster of trees tucked into the curve of the bend. Jade hammered the clutch and brake.

"Sake's alive." June smacked the dashboard with her Gucci bag.

Stiff-arming the steering wheel and mashing the brake, Jade winced as the truck drifted into a blinding patch of sun. Anticipation drilled a hole between her ribs.

When there was no impact, breath exploded from her lungs. Just beyond her windshield, a black-eyed doe and her two spotted fawns crossed the road into the woods on the other side.

"My heart is thumping in my throat." June spanked the dash grit from the smooth leather of her handbag. "Can you imagine if you'd not seen?"

"I wouldn't have been able to sleep for a week." Jade watched the doe as she led her young to the other side, her head high, her steps neat and sure. Jade pressed the clutch and shifted into first with a final glance at the creature.

In the grass, just beyond the trees, the doe turned and fixed her polished gaze on Jade. *Yes, I know* . . . A motor roared, and the doe dashed into the tress the moment a car whizzed around the bend.

"Farrel Lawrence," June said. "She's got a lead foot."

Run, girl. Run. Jade eased off the clutch, and the truck chugged up the last few feet of the hill, the heart of the doe and the sensation of beauty resonating within her.

~

The Bensons' foyer was cold. Jade shivered as she followed June inside, carrying a few of the bags and boxes her mother-in-law had collected from three days of shopping in Atlanta with Honey.

"Constance?" June clicked on the table lamp. The soft yellow light caught the gloss and glimmer of the polished mahogany. The wood grain matched the banister of the sweeping, curved staircase that spilled from the second floor into the Italian marble foyer. "You here, Constance?"

Jade dropped the packages at the base of staircase, rubbing the bend of her arm. "What did you buy? Bricks?" She peered into the Neiman Marcus bag. "Christian Louboutins? Don't you have, like, four pairs already?" Jade sat on the bottom step and lifted the lid off the shoe box, inhaling at the sight of dark red patent leather heels. "Wow."

"And now I have five pair." June scouted the formal living room for signs of life. "I bought them for the club's Christmas ball. Reb? Constance?"

Barely emerging from winter's gray, and June was already planning for Christmas. Jade could learn something here . . . What, she wasn't sure, but the moment sure felt teachable.

"How much?" Jade dug around for the receipt.

"Didn't your mama teach you it's impolite to ask how much? Get your nose out of my bags." June gazed into the family room on the other side of the foyer. "Well, the place looks tidy."

"Six hundred dollars?" Jade dropped the shoe back into the box and let the receipt go, fluttering into the bag. "You can buy a lot of food for the poor with that kind of money."

"For Pete's sake, Jade, don't preach to me. Reb and I give plenty to the poor." June turned for the kitchen, her low heels beating a rhythm against the marble. "Why don't you call Max and have supper here? Run quick to pick up your mama too. Mercy, I pay Constance for a full day's work and I want a full day. Whether I'm here or not. Constance!"

"Max is working late." Jade sauntered into the kitchen. "Mama's still recovering from the last round of chemo. Why don't we try for another time?"

"Well, if you're sure, fine . . . another time." June stood in the middle of the arching, stainless steel kitchen looking disconcerted.

Jade leaned against the ivory and green island. The kitchen was like a structural hug, cozy with June's Southern hospitality and dabbled with yellow and gray Smoky Mountain sunshine dripping through the skylight.

"How about we get Reb to fire up his grill this weekend?"

"He'd love that . . . We can thaw the kobe steaks." June opened the fridge and then closed it without looking inside. "I am sorry Beryl's not feeling well. Tell that mama of yours I'll be over tomorrow for a game of hearts."

"She'd like that. June?" Jade peered into her pinched eyes. "Are you okay?"

"Of course I'm okay. I've just been shopping for three days. Now, how about some hot tea? The house is freezing." June walked over to the basement door. "Constance?" June shoved the door closed. "That girl . . . I'm docking her pay a whole day."

5

"Why don't you hear her out first?" Jade slipped onto one of the island chairs and watched June fill a kettle with water and drop it onto the stove with a clank.

It was nearing five. Jade would have to leave after this cup of tea to get Mama's dinner. The latest round of chemo had zapped her energy more than the previous treatments. She slept most of the day, eating only when Jade urged her. Leukemia was a cruel taskmaster.

June set two mugs in front of Jade. "So what's new with you in the three days I've been gone? Have you and Max made any decisions?"

June never hesitated to dig around in Jade's life, prying open internal windows. Didn't Honey empty June of all her idle words? Didn't the woman just want to relax in a hot bath, order a Mario's pizza, and curl up with Rebel and a good TMC movie?

"A decision? In three days? I've hardly seen him." Her sorrow over the plethora of pregnant shoppers at the Blue Two this afternoon surfaced, gasping for air.

Perhaps June had a right to know if she would ever be a grandmother. Or not. Jade's private life with Max was private. And if Jade was . . . barren . . . then she needed to deal with that first, on her own, without her mother-in-law peering into her heart.

"What about a surrogate? The Bidwells had great success."

Or without offering myriad unwanted solutions.

"June, please, Max and I have talked ad nauseam about the options." Jade pressed her fingers into the taut muscles along her shoulders and propped her elbows on the light-kissed granite countertop. "I can get pregnant; I just can't stay pregnant. And I'm sorry, but I'm not open to using another woman's womb. It would be like . . . like having an affair, inviting another woman into our marriage. Either Max and I make a baby together, or we don't have a biological child."

"Then you'll adopt." June set tea bags and sweeteners on the island.

Jade exhaled. "If and when we decide. You can't just pick up a child like a Jiffy Mart stop for a gallon of milk and loaf of bread." Didn't she just have this conversation with Max the other night? His response and tone had been almost identical to June's. Matter-of-fact, devoid of an emotional response or commitment. But the Bensons made things happen. There was a fix for everything. "Why can't a family just be a man and his wife? Do children validate us? Prove we make love? Make us more complete? What if we're happy . . . just Max and me?"

"Are you?" The kettle rumbled from its perch on the gas flame. June reached for it and filled the cups. "If you're happy, then I'm happy." She smiled. "But every time we talk about children, I can see the pain in your eyes, hear the longing in your words. You want what you never really had growing up. A family."

"I have a family. You and Reb, Mama, Aiden and Willow." Jade tore open a packet of sweetener and dumped the white powder into her tea.

"Is that good enough? Max wants children, Jade. He doesn't care if they're biological or not."

"June." Jade fired her name with a caustic edge. "We'll have children if we are meant to have children. Maybe Max and I aren't meant to be parents. What if God doesn't find me trustworthy? Why would He give a child to a woman who . . ."

"Why would God decide you aren't . . ." June dipped her head to see into Jade's downcast eyes. "Oh, I see." Her spoon tapped out a beat against the ceramic mug as she stirred her tea. "You think God would choose you out of all the women in this world who've had abortions to say, 'No baby for her; she blew it'?"

"Feels like it sometimes." Jade sipped her tea to hide her emotion. She ignored the yearning most of the time. But it had been stirred today, by the pregnant women, by the doe with her fawns. If she could finally carry a baby to term, not miscarry again, she'd feel like her past was truly forgiven and God was smiling.

"You're young, Jade. It'll happen." June's words brought little comfort.

"Sure, I know." Jade sipped her tea.

"I've got just the thing for you." June motioned for Jade to pick up her tea and follow.

Jade carried her tea up the stairs behind June, whose narrow hips swung from side to side. She'd spent her entire marriage, the past two and a half years, trying to convince herself that children didn't matter. Max completed her. God, as she was beginning to know Him, completed her. But a child . . . one of her own. Jade could imagine the joy.

She'd lost their honeymoon baby after ten weeks. It was a long eighteen months before she got pregnant again, only to lose the baby last summer, two weeks before Mama came down for a short visit.

But her August visit never ended. Mama's leukemia symptoms had intensified since Jade had seen her the Christmas before, so she refused to let her return to Iowa to live in the old farmhouse, alone.

Between managing the shops, the Blue Umbrella in Whisper Hollow and the Blue Two in downtown Chattanooga, Jade cared for Mama, driving her to doctor appointments and chemo treatments.

Into the crisp, golden fall and blustery holiday season, the busyness of the shop and town celebrations kept Jade's yearning for babies at bay. When she discovered she was pregnant at Thanksgiving, she laid awake that night in bed, pools in her eyes, crunching her fingers around Max's fisted, sleeping hand. The God of mercy bestowed favor on her.

"So, June, where are we going?" Then she had her third miscarriage in January. "What's this *thing* you have for me? Stuffing envelopes for the club's Spring Life Auction and Dance? Or licking stamps?"

"Jade, really, no one licks stamps anymore."

At the top of the stairs, June stopped short. Jade nearly sloshed her with tea.

"What's wrong?" Jade peered around her mother-in-law's shoulder. The pink hue of her suit brightened the dim light of the landing. The media room door was ajar with an eerie blue tint emanating from the flat-panel TV screen. "Is someone here?"

"Constance?" June thudded toward the door, a matronly authority in her stride. "You best not be napping. I warned you . . ."

"June." Jade hurried behind her, hoping to cushion the clash between Constance and her mistress. "So what if she fell asleep? It's not like she ignored her chores. The house is immaculate."

"I don't pay her to sleep." June raised her voice as if giving Constance one last chance to wake up and feign dusting before June crashed through the door and flipped on the light. "Constance Filmore?"

Jade hung back. Constance didn't need an audience when June reamed her out. *Be awake, Constance . . .*

"Oh my, oh, oh?" June crashed backward into the door, her teacup toppling to the plush cream and beige carpet. The golden-brown liquid spread through the fibers, sinking into the pile, creating a sprawling stain.

Jade surged into the room, accosted by the pungent scent of day-old cologne and sweat. As she stooped to pick up June's mug, her gaze strafed a topless woman standing on the other side of the U-shaped sofa. Her tangled, bleached hair stood high over her head and her unfastened jeans rode low on her hips. Surprise shoved the woman's name through her lips.

"Claire?"

Wasn't she one of June's best friends? *What's going on?* Jade averted her eyes from Claire's form and glanced at June.

Her mother-in-law's high, rosy cheeks faded beyond pale, her eyes fixed, and for an insane moment Jade wondered if she was even breathing. "June," Jade whispered, gathering June's cup by the tips of her fingers.

"June . . . we didn't know . . ." Claire Falcon tugged on her cotton top, then hunted around for her shoes. "We thought you were—"

"We? Who's we?" June's blank, unblinking gaze matched her monotone.

"I gotta go." Claire peered down at the sofa before darting for the door, her bra, socks, and shoes clutched to her chest. A sour bile burned at the base of Jade's throat as she moved aside for Claire to exit.

Suddenly, there was Rebel, standing, smoothing his hair, fixing his belt, and fastening the bottom buttons of his blue shirt.

Jade dropped June's mug, barely having the presence of mind to set hers on the edge of the wall table just inside the door. *Rebel?* Her knees buckled.

"Maybe you should go, Jade." Rebel stepped around the couch. "I'm sorry you had to see this."

"In my own home, Rebel?" June's tone sent chills over Jade's skin. "My. Own. Home."

"You weren't supposed to be here." Rebel casually walked between the women and out the door.

June dashed after him as he descended the stairs. "Don't you *dare* walk away from me." She smashed her fist into his back.

Flinching, Jade tucked in behind the wall. For a short moment she was eight again, watching her daddy leave their Iowa farm in the middle of the night, Mama hollering after him.

But June and Rebel? The benevolent king and queen of Whisper Hollow?

"My . . . own . . . home."

The smack of June's hand against Rebel's cheek shocked Jade's heart. Tears swelled in her eyes. She expected infidelity from her mama, but not from the refined and dignified Bensons. Rebel was a church deacon. June chaired the women's auxiliary.

"You disrespect me so much you bring your filth into my home? Forty-one years, Rebel, I've been faithful and—"

Back to the wall, Jade slid down until her bottom hit the hardwood.

"Forty-one, June? Are you sure you want to stick with that number?" Jade waited for Rebel's chest-rumbling "Ah, June bug," paired with a contrite apology. She listened for his tender begging, pulling her into their room to talk in private. But instead he spoke as if June railed on about petty things: a towel on the bathroom floor, a forgotten dinner date with old friends.

"I don't deserve this, Rebel, not in my own home. Where's Constance?"

"I sent her home. Didn't need her interfering."

"Never again, you hear me?" June's voice rose with command. She would be obeyed. "Never. In my home. Do you hear me, Rebel Benson?"

Dread filled Jade's belly. Never *again*? Max never mentioned his dad's affairs. A door slammed. Footsteps hammered down the stairs and tapped across the marble.

"Jade?" June's call carried up from the foyer and bounced around the hollow pockets of the second floor.

She couldn't move.

"Jade!"

Pushing off the floor, Jade scrambled for the stairs. She peered at June as she inched her way down.

"You might want to keep this to yourself." June gripped her hands together at her waist, squeezing her fingers.

"To myself?" The chill of the encounter lifted, but her bones rattled beneath her skin. "What are you saying? Max doesn't—"

"Jade, you heard me." June's olive-green eyes pleaded, red and swimming. "To yourself."

Two

The shower ran hot down Jade's neck and back, easing the ache from her muscles. Seven o'clock came too soon.

It'd been after 2 a.m. before she'd crawled into bed and stretched out next to her husband. After three before her thoughts settled and she finally slept.

She kept seeing the low, round curve of Claire's hip. Hearing the flat, callous response from Rebel. Feeling a spirited but wounded June trying to maintain her dignity.

Jade dumped a glob of facial cleanser in her hand and scrubbed. But no amount of soap could wash away what she'd witnessed yesterday. Sighing, she returned the cleanser to the shower caddy and let the water rinse the scrub from her face and tears from her eyes.

A bang beyond the shower door startled her. "Max?" She squeezed the water from her hair and peeked out to see her husband bent in front of the sink cabinet, hand to his forehead, his expression knotted. "What are you doing?"

"Bumping my head." He leaned to assess the damage to his face in the mirror. "I was thinking of making breakfast. You want pancakes?" His silver-blue tie hung down the starched front of his navy shirt. His slacks were Armani.

"You're in court today?" She shut off the water and reached for her towel. He always wore Armani to court. Claimed it gave his clients confidence and intimidated the prosecutor.

"Meeting with the opposing counsel on the class action case against MicroDevelopment."

"Are they going to settle?"

"If there's any good in the world, yes, oh please yes." He fell against the sink and reached for her. "Your man's been *on fire* lately." He touched his lips to hers, tugging at her towel with a teasing growl. "In court, I mean."

"Of course, in court. I didn't think you meant in bed." She kissed him, letting her towel fall around her feet, then spinning from his arms for the bedroom.

"Ouch, ow, wound a guy." He stumbled from the bathroom, clutching his chest. "And on a day I might settle a very big case. My ego, darling. My ego."

Jade laughed. "Somehow I think your ego can handle a bit of bruising from me." She tugged open her dresser drawers, selecting clothes for the day. "And you know I'm teasing, right?"

"I do know." From the middle of the room, he watched her, a yearning behind his brownish-gold wink. The burn of his gaze tempted her to press pause on the morning and reach for the buttons under his silky tie. "So where were you last night?" He moved past her for the chaise tucked under the dormer window, Jade's favorite reading place on rainy afternoons, and grazed her hip with his fingertips.

"Went back down to the Blue Two."

After the encounter between Rebel and June at the Orchid House, Jade needed distance between Mama and Max. So she drove back down to the city and attempted to bury the images and sounds by logging inventory and adding numbers.

"I had to call Sugar Plumbs for Mae to fix something for Beryl and me."

"I'm sorry." Jade snapped open her crisp, clean jeans. "I should've called." Poor Mama, sitting home alone, waiting for someone to come.

"She kept asking about you. Couldn't remember how long you'd been gone. She was starving." Max leaned forward, arms on his thighs. "What was so important at the shop you couldn't come home? Or call? Didn't you check your missed calls? I called after dinner."

"Got distracted. Sorry." Jade crossed the room to her closet with a quick peek out the window. The day looked cold, like it might rain. "The Blue Two is a mess. I should've never hired Wanda. Manager at Bloomingdale's, my eye." She took a bell-sleeve blouse from its hanger. "I spent six hours just cleaning half the storeroom."

"What about those two part-timers you hired?"

"Keri and Emma? Tweedledum and Tweedledee?" Jade returned to the bathroom to dry her hair. Why'd she promise June? Why? The secret hidden in her chest burned. "They quit. Three weeks ago. Wanda didn't tell me until yesterday."

Max, your father is having an affair.

In the mirror, she watched Max watching her wield the blow-dryer. She waited, praying he'd go downstairs, make that breakfast he talked about.

"You can close it, you know. The Blue Two."

"What?" Jade whipped around. "It's only been two years. We've got to give baby Blue a chance. Really, I've not put the work into it. It's my fault it's failing. I thought Wanda would be another Lillabeth. Wonderful and hardworking. I ignorantly left her to her own incompetent devices."

The downtown Chattanooga shop at the bend of the Tennessee River had been Jade's distraction after her first miscarriage. Remembering the riverfront property her mother-in-law had discovered before she'd married Max, Jade checked on the availability of the warehouse-turned-into-shops. She and Max signed the papers within a week.

Busy expanding her vintage business after a successful first year, Jade considered her surprise second pregnancy last summer a sign from God. *Blessed.*

Max had implored her to hire a manager. *"Let's do all we can to keep this baby, shug."*

She liquefied when he called her *shug* and became putty in his emotional hands. Lillabeth, a college girl now and married to a Marine fighter pilot stationed in Iraq, worked at the Whisper Hollow Blue Umbrella after classes. If Jade found someone to look after the Blue Two, then she'd have time to channel her energy into making a baby.

Enter Wanda, the lying manger. Blissful, naive, and focused on staying pregnant, Jade left Wanda to her devices while she dreamed of motherhood. But near the end of her first trimester, she began bleeding. After the miscarriage, Jade had planned to visit the struggling riverfront shop more often, knowing it needed her tender, loving care. But she rarely made it down the mountain. Once a quarter. Maybe.

Now, almost two years after opening the store, she'd lost a good bit of Blue Two's business credibility.

"Is it still worth it, babe? The second store?" Max watched her through the mirror, arms crossed.

"There's a lot of inventory down there. And spring is coming . . . we can make up time and money between the tourists and the festivals. But if I can't get it going again, then I'll sell it." Jade sighed, fluffed her hair with a quick sweep of the blow-dryer over her crown, then hung the dryer on the hook by the sink.

"You know I heard you. Sell it." Max's gaze flickered down, toward the cabinet, then swept upward, meeting Jade's eyes in the mirror. He smiled.

"*If,* I said *if* I can't get it going again. Wanda did a lot of damage to the inventory as well as our reputation."

"Then I guess there's nothing left for me to say, except I'll go make breakfast."

But instead of backing away, he moved behind Jade, brushing his hand over her shoulders. "All this energy to get a second shop going . . . when the Blue Umbrella is going well here in Whisper Hollow. Makes me think you don't want to *try* again."

"I thought your final word was 'I'll go make breakfast.'"

"Jade . . ." Max turned her to face him, the emotion of his question lingering in his eyes. "Do you?"

"We *tried* the other night. And it's not the Blue Two or the Blue Umbrella keeping me from getting pregnant, Max. Nor is either one the cause of the miscarriages."

An anomaly. That's what Dr. Wokowsky called her: an anomaly. But to Jade, *barren* trumpeted over her arid soul with a clarion tone. Every day more true than the one before.

"We don't know for sure, Jade. Dr. Wokowsky said rest could help."

"He made up that answer because you kept pushing him." Jade freed herself from her husband's embrace, reaching to the shelf beside the mirror for her makeup bag. "You almost gave him a heart attack, drilling him the way you did. You forget you're a noted lawyer, Max. I bet all Wokowsky heard was 'lawsuit, lawsuit.' And pancakes for breakfast are fine. Use water instead of milk in the mix. Milk makes them too heavy."

"Do you even want children, Jade?"

"Don't ask stupid questions." *And please give me my bathroom time.*

"It's not a stupid question."

"Max, I'm not on birth control. I've been pregnant three times. What do you want from me?" Jade tossed her makeup bag beside the sink. She didn't want to wear any covering today. "I can straighten out the Blue Two, Max." Socks, she needed a pair of socks. And shoes. "I *need* to straighten out the Blue Two."

"Jade." Max tenderly held her shoulders, touching her in the familiar way that only comes with marriage. Not possessive, not sexual, not harsh. But connecting. *I am yours, and you are mine.*

"I love you and will support whatever you decide to do. But I'm thirty-eight. I don't want my retirement party to compete with my son's high school graduation."

"So you've said." She dug around in her sock drawer. *Matching pair, matching pair.* "Then you'd better talk to God, because I don't know what else we can do." Jade sank to the chaise and tugged on her socks. "Is Mama awake?"

"I don't know. I haven't heard any noise coming from her room." Max perched next to her, a slice of gray light falling over the high rise of his cheeks and the smooth plane of his face. "Surrogate?"

"No." Jade swerved, hooking her knee over his leg. "I can't, Max. I have no peace about another woman becoming so intimately a part of our lives. It would be like . . . an affair. Look at the women in the Bible who tried to have children with surrogates. It was painful and deceptive."

"You don't trust me? Think I'll fall in love with—"

"Babe, another woman would be carrying your precious son. Not me."

"But it would be *our* DNA, babe. Your egg, my sperm."

"And what is the plan for all the fertilized eggs we can't or won't use?" Jade shook her head. "Once, a very long time ago, a scared and heartbroken teenager decided she had the right to take a baby's life. Max, I won't be put in the position again of deciding when and if I should have a child. If God wants us to have children, it will have to be like He designed."

She walked across the room. At the closet, Jade dug her feet into her mocha brown leather clogs. The truth of her confession anchored her drifting affections. The only way she'd ever be a mother was by divine intervention.

"We can cross that bridge when we come to it. Hey, I'm not opposed to having ten kids. We could get, like, four surrogates, line them up, *zip, zip, zip,* implant the fertilized eggs, and—"

"Max, do you think that's funny? Because to me, it sounds rude and crass."

"I can see you have no sense of humor—except making fun of my lovemaking."

"If we're not careful, it will only be about baby making." She sighed. "Please, can we drop this and eat pancakes?"

Max came to her and cupped the back of her head, gently kissing her forehead. "I'm not looking for a fight here, babe. I just want—"

"A son, I know. What if we have a girl? Then what?" She'd need a sweater. The Blue Two's storeroom wasn't heated. And when the breeze kicked up off the water, Jade's bones ached.

"We keep trying." Max had all the answers today. "We adopt."

"Why are you always so sure?" Jade slipped her arm around his neck and gave her cheek to the pump of his chest, the steady rhythm of his heart her intimate lullaby.

"Because I have you." His hand slipped around her hip to the core of her back and bent her into him.

In these moments, doubt and fear were defeated foes. All other times, they were formidable and fierce.

"If it's right, Max, we'll adopt. But these are human beings we're talking about, not a plea bargain for a two-bit druggie."

"No plea bargain for a two-bit druggie." He brushed back her hair and touched his lips to hers. "What can I do to give you hope?"

"Make breakfast?" She liked when she made him laugh from the belly, a surprised, joyful melody.

"To the kitchen." He backed toward the door, spearing the air. "To the griddle and batter."

"One more thing, babe. What did you need in the cabinet?" Jade jerked her thumb toward the bathroom. The only thing under the sink was cleaning supplies and towels. And the only person who used the space was Tammy, their cleaning lady.

"Nothing . . . I thought I'd put my, my mouthwash there."

"Mouthwash is in the closet."

"Right, right." Max snapped his fingers, his expression molding to remember.

Mouthwash. Jade glanced into the bathroom and stared at the cabinet doors as if the answer would leap out at her. "I can't go through this with you again. I'm not your mama."

"Go through it? Babe, there's *nothing* to go through." Max paused at the door. "See you downstairs."

In the midst of the baby debate, she'd shoved aside the uneasy scene of Max at the cabinet, jerking his head up so fast he crashed against the counter. Her gut told her she wasn't the only one with a secret this morning. But his eyes were clear, a good sign he wasn't using again. His energy was high, and his back hadn't bothered him in months.

Jade snatched up her purse, glancing around to see if she'd forgotten anything. Max couldn't be stashing pain meds again. Not after a month in rehab last year and six months clean. How could her brilliant lawyer husband be so stupid?

She stood in the bathroom doorway, starting at the cabinet. *Just open it and see. Look, Jade.* Instead she backed away. Trust didn't begin with snooping around after him. He said he wasn't using, she had to believe him.

Or all of this—marriage, babies, and happily ever after—was for nothing.

She'd been counseled not to coddle or baby him. If Max wanted babies, he'd best not be popping Percocet for phantom back pains.

One trouble of being a noted Tennessee lawyer? It was easy for a man to find whatever he wanted.

"Jade?" Mama's call floated down the hall. "What's burning?"

"It's Max, Mama. He's making pancakes."

Three

On a yellow and blue Saturday afternoon, Jade lured Keri and Emma back to work at the Blue Two. They were giggly and ditzy, but they could sell the heck out of retro clothes and music.

Sunday afternoon while Mama slept, Jade and Max holed up in their bedroom to work on, well, future projects, to the rhythm of the rain falling against the windows.

Max hoped for a boy. Jade for a girl. Really, either one. Max seemed adamant about a son. But just wait until a tiny angelic daughter wrapped her wee hand around his finger. Jade knew he'd be a goner.

Now, Monday morning, Jade waited for Mama at the bottom of the stairs. She glanced at the grandfather clock in the hall. Eight thirty.

"Mama? You ready?" Jade sounded more impatient than she intended, but her to-do list suddenly felt like an elephant on her back. She had phone calls to make, ads to place, estate sales to scout.

"Where's the fire?" Mama gripped the banister as she descended the ancient, carved staircase.

"In my bones." Jade offered Mama a hand. "How are you feeling? Sure you want to come to the shop? I'm going down to the city, not over to the Blue Umbrella."

"If I stay inside another day, I'm going to pull out what's left of my long, gray braid." Mama's narrow frame swam beneath her clothes. Her jeans pooched out in the front, and the collar of her top exposed the bony curve of her shoulder. "Glad to be done with Rituxan for a while."

"The doctor didn't promise. He said maybe."

"Well, I say I am." Mama looked pretty, despite her sallow skin and the gray patches under her eyes. "Leukemia can knock me down but can't keep me there. I'm a teamster, for crying out loud."

Jade lifted Mama's sweater from the foyer coatrack. "Is this sweater going to be enough? It's chilly today."

"Stop treating me like a baby." Mama snatched the sweater from Jade's hand. "Or like I'm insane. I'm a dying woman, 'tis all. Battling leukemia, not brain damage."

"Are you sure you're not brain damaged?" Jade anchored the strap of her purse on her shoulder, then slung on her backpack. "If you get tired, please tell me. I'll bring you home."

"Would you just get going? I'm still your mother. So behave yourself." Mama brushed her hand down Jade's back as she crossed the threshold. "I'll let you know if I'm tired."

A year ago, if someone had told her she'd be caring for her ill mother—the woman who abandoned her, Aiden, and Willow when they were kids, left them to live with their granny while she drove trucks and partied with her friends—Jade would've scoffed.

But it was Mama's compassion and wisdom that gave Jade perspective when she miscarried, then when Max confessed his drug problems. She'd been with them less than a month when he checked himself into the hospital to detox.

Last fall held no pleasant memories for Jade.

Steering Mama into the garage, Jade opened her door and helped her into the cab. "Max drives a Mercedes, for Pete's sake, and here you are tooling around in a beat-up old pickup. It's because it's like Paps's old truck, isn't it?"

"You and June, bugging me about my truck. My baby." *Baby* pinged against her soul. The future, with all its promise, still remained unsure. But the old truck was a faithful constant in her life. One that was not subject to miscarriages, dying mothers, or addicted husbands.

Yes, she loved the truck because it was like the one Paps drove, like the one that still sat in the old barn under the hayloft. Climbing in behind the wheel, Jade gripped the cool, thin steel.

"It makes me feel connected with Paps and Granny, with our roots."

"Rotten roots, if you ask me." Mama's laugh trailed her words, but she reached for Jade's hand. "It reminds me too."

"Put on your seat belt." Jade cranked the engine, shifted into reverse, and fired out of the garage. Recent healing in their relationship aside, the woman never ceased to be both a pain and a comfort.

Jade liked the feel of the road that came up from the tires through the driveshaft into the steering wheel. She loved the whine of the engine and grind of the gears.

If she had a new truck, she'd fret every time she loaded something heavy or awkward, fearful of giving the truck its first ding. With her old International baby, the dents, dings, and scratches simply enhanced the pickup's character.

Mama reached for the radio knob, then sat back. "Ding, dang, dong—the least you could do is get the radio fixed."

Jade peered at her sideways, frowning, then snickered. Mama chuckled.

"You taught me to drive in Paps's truck. I'd think you'd love this old thing"—Jade kissed the wheel with the heel of her palm—"as much as I do."

"That was a wild afternoon. You darn near killed me."

"I only scared you half to death. There's a difference." Jade shifted into third and took the curve toward town. As she rounded the bend, the scene before her changed and suddenly she wasn't driving the willow-treed, hilly terrain of Whisper Hollow. Her memories drifted back to a sunny afternoon many years ago when Mama taught her to drive, cruising along the flat stretch of highway just north of Prairie City. A dry, furnace-like air whipped through the cab's open windows, tousling the ends of Jade's hair and scattering Mama's cigarette ashes over the dash.

"Up and over, Jade, up and over." The gears of Paps's old pickup moaned as fifteen-year-old Jade drove north on Highway 117, mashing the clutch and working the gearshift with trembling hands.

"I know, I know. Stop making me nervous, Mama." The truck splashed through the sun and shade spots—light, dark, light, dark—that drifted down from the cotton-covered sky.

"If you know, then do it. For Pete's sake, this side, this side . . ." Mama grabbed the wheel, jerking it to the right, pulling the International pickup back across the yellow line. Her cigarette dangled from her lips, barely holding on to a long, loose ash. "*This* is our lane. The right one."

Jade narrowed her eyes and slowed the truck down to forty while hanging onto the wheel at 10 and 2, driving steadily between the white and yellow lines.

"Oh, fine . . ." Mama flicked her ashes so they blew across Jade's face. "All I was trying to do was keep you from drifting across the line. Now look at you. You'd bite off your nose to spite your face. You're so rigid, girl. One of these days, you're going to have to break out of the mold, take a leap, live a little. You can't go through life so cautious. I'd be nowhere if I'd followed all the rules."

"But you might be somewhere if you had a few rules. Huh? Maybe one. Or two. Think you could handle two rules?"

"Ah, teenage angst. Finally aimed at me."

Jade knew that she, Aiden, and Willow would be better off if Mama lived by some standard other than which-way-is-the-wind-blowing. She cut a sideways glance at her mama. She wanted Jade to break the rules. Her heart revved up as she pressed on the gas, surging the truck forward, the chassis rattling.

"Woo." Mama angled forward with a pop of her hands. "Now you're talking."

Ever so gently, Jade eased the truck into the southbound lane, inch by inch, the sound of her pulse roaring in her ears.

"Jade-o, don't be stupid." Mama stopped laughing. "Here you go, biting off your nose to spite your face. Don't think you're scaring me. I've jumped out of a moving truck more than once."

"Then jump." Jade gritted her teeth and gunned the gas, fully committed to the southbound lane. "Go ahead." Gone three months driving a truck for Carlisle's carnival, leaving behind Aiden, Jade, and Willow, Mama had returned home last week ready to mother her children, deciding *she* was the one, not Granny, who should teach Jade to drive.

The truck whined as Jade revved the engine at the top of second gear, then coughed and lurched as she worked the clutch, shifting to third.

Mama's hair flapped in the breeze—a coalition of horses' tails.

"You should condition your hair. Or cut it," Jade snapped.

"That's what you're going for? Insulting my hair? Ooo, ouch, hurt me." Mama grabbed the ragged ends and fluttered them in Jade's face, then propped her foot on the dash. She flicked her cigarette out the window, half the ashes sailing back inside.

The truck surged over a small rise in the road, still careening along in the left-hand lane, the speedometer shimmying just shy of the 75 mph tick mark.

A farmhouse winked at them from between two fields of August corn.

Heat waves zigzagged along the horizon's line. A dark spot shimmied toward them.

Jade swallowed. Another truck was speeding southbound. Grille to grille.

Mama lowered her foot. "Jade-o?"

"Scared, Mama?" Jade doubled down on the gas. Adrenaline soaked her thoughts. Mama would flinch first. She would grab the wheel. Deep down, everyone who runs is a coward. Mama and the Lion had a lot in common.

In the meantime, the black spot of the oncoming truck formed into defined blue lines.

"Jade." Mama's voice spiked as her hand gripped the top of her door. "That truck is closing in fast."

"Then jump." Jade held on to the wheel as the speedometer ached to touch 85. Was she biting off her nose to spite her face? Pressing the gas pedal despite her own heart's warning? Danger. What did it matter? Jade never cared much for her skinny nose.

Mama swore and grabbed for the wheel, but Jade blocked the move with her elbow. "Don't mess with me; I'm driving. Doing good too."

"Doing good? You're playing chicken with a bigger, newer truck at eighty-some miles an hour." Mama's posture froze, her hand on the door handle, her gazed fixed on the windshield. "This is crazy."

"Wooo, this is great, huh, Mama? I'm breaking the rules." Jade's heart bounced in her chest like a Super Ball. She was beyond terrified. But she'd show Mama. "I'm not so rigid now, am I?" Jade turned up the radio volume on Paps's old truck just as the Eagles came over the speakers.

Life in the fast lane.

"Jade, get in the right lane." Mama tried for the wheel again, but Jade smacked her hand away.

By now the blue truck was fully formed and in clear view. Golden light glinted off its deep blue sheen. *Oh my gosh* . . . Jade tried to brake, but she hit the clutch instead. She wasn't slowing down . . . she wasn't slowing down.

Brake, brake. Purple and gold spots blinded her as the sunlight bounced off the silver grille of the approaching truck.

Dustin Colter. It's Dustin Colter.

In a wash of panic meeting mind-numbness, the muscles in Jade's arm surrendered before her hands received the brain's command to move the heck over.

"Jade, get in the right lane. Now!"

She meant to veer right, really. But without so much as a conscious thought, Jade veered *left* off the road, careening headlong into Tank Victor's ripened corn, swishing, crunching, popping, mowing down.

Mama expressed her pleasure with a string of four-five-and-six letter words.

Every cell of Jade's body quivered as the truck jerked to a stop about twenty corn rows in. She inhaled the power of the navy Dodge speeding past. *Just keep going. Just keep going.*

Heat and the Eagles' harmonies filled the cab.

"Jade Freedom Fitzgerald, I swear I'm going to—" Mama's face was the color of a bull's-eye.

"What? Ground me? That'd be a first." Her words came out strong and cool, but poker-hot adrenaline challenged every syllable. The small hairs on the back of Jade's neck clung to her skin with terror-induced perspiration.

"Don't be smart with me, Jade Fitzgerald." Mama raised her hand, her fingers arched back and her palm stiff.

Seeing Mama flinch, Jade ducked, smashing her bottom lip against the sharp chrome of the steering wheel's center. The sting ran along her jaw and up her cheeks until the pain filled her eyes. "You were going to hit me." Mama had never hit her. Ever. Granny had wielded the stinging wooden spoon, but not Mama.

"No. But I was tempted." Mama snatched her cigarettes from the glove box, flicking the lighter over and over, swearing when it wouldn't work, knocking the Bic against her thigh. "Look at me, I'm trembling." Mama extended her hand. "And you ruined Tank's crop." She flicked the Bic again. A small flame shot up, and the fragrance of burning mentholated tobacco meshed with the scent of crushed corn and moist soil.

The odor slipped through Jade's nostrils, down her throat, through her lungs, and settled in her belly. Cigarette smoke was Mama's perfume.

"Tank won't be mad." The crater-sized sensation filling Jade's chest began to shrink. "If he does, you can sleep with him to pay off the debt."

"Keep it up, Jade. I'll slap you silly. And you'd deserve it." The cigarette paper crackled as Mama took a long drag, and the atmosphere of the truck cab settled down. "If this is how you plan to drive, Jade, I'm not so sure—"

"It's not how I plan to drive. You just make me so mad. You go off with Carlisle and your friends, leaving me, Aiden, and Willow with Granny. And when you are here, working for Midwest, you're gone all the time, doing who-knows-what?"

"Earning a living, I'll have you know. I make good money driving for the carnival. Better than Midwest Parcel, I'll tell you that. Who do you think provides food and clothing?"

"Granny."

"If I were a man, no one would say a word about me being gone, traveling, seeing the country, earning a good wage to support my family. I don't see your dad here offering to help out. Nor you complaining about it."

"Because you drove him away."

"He left."

"And you said good riddance. I saw you burning all of his stuff."

"Did you now?" Mama clicked her thumbnail against her middle fingernail, letting her cigarette burn and swirl smoke. Sweat beaded on her brow. "You were supposed to be asleep."

"And to this day you curse him whenever you hear a Fleetwood Mac song."

"How long have you been storing up this conversation?" Mama nursed her cigarette, then blew a thick stream of smoke out the window. "What are we going to do to get out of here?"

The rhythm of swishing corn caused Jade to twist around to peer into the now-crooked side mirror. *Oh no, no, no.* She slouched against the seat, ducking below the window. "Mama," she hissed, "get down." Jade hit the radio button.

"Why, what are you?"

"You guys all right?" Dustin peered through the driver's side window, his clear blue eyes focused on Jade as she crumpled against the seat.

"We're fine." Mama flicked her wrist toward Dustin with a shower of gray ashes. "Sorry to have scared you half to death. Jade-o must be getting her period, acting all psycho, driving on the wrong side of the road."

Mama! She couldn't stop her gasp if she wanted. *Just kill me now.* The magnet of embarrassment sucked every drop of blood in her veins to her cheeks and burned like a homecoming bonfire. She pressed deeper into the seat, not daring to look into Dustin's ocean blues.

"Glad to know you two are okay." Dustin propped his arms on the top of the door, but when Jade braved a peek, there was a bit of a blush on his cheeks. And he was smiling. At her. "Your lip . . . it's bleeding." He reached toward her face.

"It is?" Jade eased upright, touching the spot where her lip had smacked the steering wheel.

"Got a napkin or towel?"

"I think so." Mama popped open the glove box and handed over Paps's old grease rag. "It's clean."

Dustin took the cloth and brushed it lightly against Jade's lip, setting her entire body aflame. "I've had a lot of busted lips wrestling and playing football. It's just a small cut, but it's going to swell. Put some ice on it when you get home."

Dustin handed back the cloth and then stepped back, assessing the damage. "Your tires are in the mud pretty deep, but I think the boys and I can get you out."

"You're a life saver, Dustin." Mama leaned over Jade, smiling at Dustin, while her scoop top drooped and revealed too much of her flesh. Jade shoved her back.

"Can you handle the clutch, Jade? You back out, and we'll push."

"S-sure." Perspiration broke out on Jade like a kiss from poison ivy.

"Coop, Hartline, Brill." Dustin rallied his troops. "Jade, when I tell you, ease off the clutch and slowly back out. Feel the tires grip before you really hit the gas. Got it?"

"Got it." She had *no* idea what he meant.

"Well, well, look who's got a crush." Mama smiled as she wadded up the rag and stuffed it back into the glove box.

"Shut up, Mama." Jade squared with the wheel, fired up the engine, and mashed the clutch, her gaze on Dustin and his football buddies. She could do this. She *would* do this. The popular boys at PCM high school were about to rescue her. She'd remember this day for the rest of her life.

"Okay, Jade, back out . . . easy." Through the windshield, she felt Dustin's piercing gaze.

The engine's rumble beneath her hands was like an extension of her heart. Jade eased off the clutch, gently pressing the gas . . .

"Do you want me to do this, Cinderella?"

She mashed the clutch to the floor and jerked her gaze around. "Mama, don't embarrass me."

"Me? You're on track to do that all by yourself. I'm just offering to help."

"Jade, everything all right?" Dustin leaned around the truck, peering at her. "You ready?"

"Ready." Giving the engine a bit of gas and easing off the clutch, the truck's heavy, worn pistons struggled like an old man working his way out of an easy chair.

Jade checked the rearview. All clear. Except for a bunch of mowed-down corn. Jade licked her lips. Dustin winked, giving her a thumbs-up.

"Go easy now."

Oh, why didn't she love the clutch more? Why didn't it love her? Ignoring Mama—who was blowing smoke rings Jade's way—she eased off the clutch, her calf taut. Less clutch. More gas. Her foot slipped. The clutch popped. The truck lurched forward and the engine stalled.

Yelping, the boys scattered into the corn.

"Reverse, Jade, reverse," Dustin hollered, his laughing smile a palette of white and ruby red on a canvas of Iowa-browned skin.

Perspiration broke out on top of perspiration. "Sorry." She buoyed her voice, sticking her head out the window. "I'll try again."

One more snicker from Mama and she'd pelt her. Consequences be darned.

Jade fired up the rusty, rattling, once-red beast after three tries and humiliated herself further by grinding her way through the gears to find reverse. Mama didn't even try to be coy or quiet. She burst right out in loud guffaws.

Dustin stepped away from the truck, motioning toward Hartline. *Great, they're leaving.*

"Move over, Green Eyes." Dustin pulled open the door, tapping the side of her arm with the back of his fingers. Fiery tingles consumed her. Where was all the air?

Mama sat up right as Jade slid to the bench seat's center. "Bless you boys for helping us out. Come by the house later. We've got cake and pop."

"Thanks, Mrs. Fitzgerald."

"It's Mrs. Ayers, technically, but you can just call me Beryl."

Dustin nodded, his eyes landing on Jade's face. "Get you out of here in a jiff."

His bare knee touched hers. Sensations Jade never experienced before crept over her skin and sank into her muscles and filled all of her hollow places. She never wanted his knee to move from hers. Ever.

Dustin wore black nylon shorts and a cutoff PCM football T-shirt. The fragrance of roll-on mingled with the warmth of summer sweat. Could she bottle it and store it under her pillow?

31

The team was in the middle of two-a-days. Big brother Aiden left the house early every morning and came home late every evening, tossing hay bales in between. Half the team did. Called it strength training.

But unlike Dustin, her brother balanced his upper body muscles on toothpick legs. Dustin was muscled all over, and as he clutched into reverse, the bulge and ridge of his thigh pumped up over his kneecap.

Jade swallowed to keep her heart between her ribs. Otherwise it was going to thump right out of her throat.

"Cooper." Dustin stuck his head out the window. "Check the road."

Cooper's blond head dashed past and returned in a second, calling all clear.

"Hang on." Dustin twisted around to see out the window, his nose a breath away from Jade's. Mama's sharp elbow dug into her side. Jade dug back. One more move and she'd pop her, right here and now.

"Ready?" he asked, giving her another grin.

"Yes." Her eyes searched his. What lived in his soul beneath the blue and the white? Oh, please let it be her name, flitting across his heart, lurking for a moment. No, a day. A whole day.

Dustin gunned the gas, shooting the truck out of the field and onto the road, fishtailing a bit, then lining it up in the lane before Jade could inhale. "There, back on the road again."

Mama started singing, off-key, snapping her fingers. "On the road again, I just can't wait to get . . ." Jade shushed her with a glance, but it didn't stop her from speaking. "Dustin, you are a true knight in shining armor."

"Call my mom and remind her, will you?" Dipping his shoulder into the door, he popped it open and stepped out.

Jade's heart sent messages to her head insisting she come up with a reason for him to hang around. But what? Check her lip to see if it was still bleeding? See if the tires needed air? Check the oil? Check her pulse?

He was turning away, saying something to his buddies.

"Hey, Dustin?" Why was she speaking? *Be quiet, Jade. You have nothing to say.* "You drive like Steve McQueen."

Mama burst out laughing, slapping her thigh. "You drive like Steve McQueen . . . That's it? Your big line? Dustin," she hollered, "forgive her; she's a horrible flirt."

Mama. Mama. Mama. Jade slid behind the wheel. If she could drive and push Mama out the door at the same time . . .

Grinning, Dustin paused at her window. "You okay to get home, Jade?" He dropped his hand down so his fingers lightly grazed her skin. Love, she was completely in love.

"We're fine, Dustin." Mama waved him off. "Thanks again. You boys come by the house with Aiden for some chocolate cake and orange pop after practice."

"Nice to see you, Mrs., um, Beryl."

As they climbed into the navy pickup and hauled off, honking a good-bye, Jade shifted into first.

"You're welcome, Jade."

"For what?" She held the truck steady, the drop of adrenaline causing her arms and legs to quiver.

"For inviting him over as a thank-you. You'll get to see him when you're fixed up and not crashed into a cornfield." Mama raked her hand through her flyaway hair. "Young, sweaty, hard bodies. Don't it make you want to be fifteen again?"

"I *am* fifteen." Jade shifted into second and eased down the road, south, toward Prairie City.

"Well, it makes me want to be fifteen again."

"They won't come by the house."

"Sure they will. Why the heck not? Aiden is one of the most popular kids in school. And you . . . getting all tall and gorgeous. Another six months and you'll be all curves."

"Mama!" Jade tucked her arms tight against her side. "You know the boys won't come to our house."

"Why not? Jade, you're being silly."

"They won't come." She shifted into third with a fierce determination.

"Why? Because of . . . me?"

Silence. As angry as she could be at Mama, Jade hated to see her hurt. Mama was careless and wild, selfish and uncivilized at times, but at the end of the day . . . she was her mama. And all Jade had besides Granny. Her beautiful, free, flower child mama.

"Am I the Harper Valley widow?"

"Yeah, a little, I guess." Her mama, the personification of a '60s one-hit wonder. "Except you're a divorcée, not a widow."

"Too darn bad. Those boys will miss out on my excellent chocolate cake. And my gorgeous daughter."

Jade laced the loose strands of her hair behind her ears and upped the radio's volume. "How about a chocolate shake to go along with your chocolate cake?"

"Now you're talking, Jade-o. Now you're talking."

Four

Sitting in a booth at Sugar Plumbs diner, June stared across Main Street, watching the Blue Umbrella, waiting for Jade. She had something important to ask her daughter-in-law.

"You're out and about early, hon." Mae freshened June's coffee without asking. She was eighth-generation Appalachian with lean, jutted features and an uncanny ability to read people. "Can I bring you some eggs and toast? Cinnamon roll? A bagel? I hate to see a thin woman starve."

"I'm not hungry." June hid behind her coffee cup. Mae's tiny brown eyes caught nuances above and below the surface.

"Starving yourself and jacking up on caffeine ain't going to solve nothing, June." Mae sat on the edge of the opposite seat. "Want to tell me about it?"

Of course she wanted to tell. She ached to spill every sordid detail about

Rebel and his infidelities. Half the town knew anyway and probably thought "poor June" was clueless. Well, she wasn't. But a careless confession here in the epicenter of Whisper Hollow gossip would crumble June's tenuous facade, and she wasn't quite ready to be so exposed.

"Restless night is all, Mae. Don't go making a county case out of a sleepless night."

"You ought to get the doc to prescribe you some Ambien or something. Knocks me right out when I pop one before bed." Mae snapped her fingers.

"I prefer warm milk." June circled her hands around her coffee mug. "I try to stay away from meds on account of Max." She lifted her coffee to her lips. "Be an example, you know?"

"You love your son, June." Mae stood and squeezed June's shoulder. "You're all pretty in your navy slacks and matching jacket, but such sad eyes."

June forced a smile as she reached up to grip Mae's arm. "I told you, I'm fine, Mae."

And she was, finally. After hatching her plan. It'd been a torturous weekend avoiding Rebel, but she'd managed to keep busy and out of sight, sleeping in her home office. And he didn't seem to have much business at Orchid House over Saturday and Sunday either.

But he came home last night, and by his demeanor, June knew he was ready to go back to relationship-as-usual. This morning he tried to kiss her good-bye. She'd ducked under his arm and walked through the kitchen and out to her car without a word. But could she really be angry with him for trying? For following their decade-old pattern?

It always played out the same. After a few months, she could no longer contain her suspicion over his infidelity, so she'd ask a few pointed questions about his whereabouts. Within a few days, Rebel would come home with jewelry and gifts, his affections sliding over to her side of the bed—morning and night. And the affair would be ended.

June ignored her tears, letting the hot rivulets cut through her perfected makeup. How could she surrender to his passion after such betrayal? But she always did. Rebel, flawed and infuriating, was a man of magical charms. And for months, even years, June lived in the sublime of being wanted. Desired.

But this morning her alarm did more than beckon her from a restless sleep; it awakened her heart. She peered across Main Street toward Jade's shop. It was after 9:00 a.m.; Jade should be there by now . . . Oh, the Open sign hung in the door.

Reaching for her wallet, June dropped a five on the table.

"Good coffee." June called to Mae as she rose from the booth and hurried across the street to the Blue Umbrella. Sudden jitters tilted her confidence. Was she really going to do this?

"Hey, June. What are you doing here?" Jade dropped the cash drawer into the register. Along the back wall, Beryl flipped through the old LPs. When she was well enough to come to work with Jade, Beryl made sure the music never stopped.

"Beryl, darling, how are you feeling?" June embraced her friend, but she had not planned on revealing her decision with an audience. She knew it was too early for Lillabeth to be at the Blue Umbrella, and June had counted on having Jade to herself.

"Want to play some cards later, June?"

"Lovely idea, Beryl. But how about a little Glenn Miller this morning?"

"I'm in the mood, June." Beryl wiggled her thin eyebrow, chuckling. June smiled at the pun. "For some 'Take the A Train' and 'Little Brown Jug.' I think I can manage a bit of the great Glenn."

Jade headed for the office and June followed, easing the door closed behind her. "Busy morning?" She perched on the edge of the metal chair by Jade's desk, steadying herself when it listed starboard.

"Very. Got to open up here, get things going, then head down to the Blue Two when Lillabeth comes in." Jade stuck her head out the door. "Mama, did I bring in my backpack?"

"I've no idea."

"It's over there, Jade." June pointed across the room to the filing cabinet.

"Ah!" Jade snatched up the bag. "I'm losing my brain here."

June's gaze fell on Jade's organization system—green and pink sticky notes plastered to the top of her desk. In recent months, she'd expanded to using the wall.

After digging in the backpack, Jade pulled out a binder and sat, flipping through the pages. With an exhale, she looked up at June.

"How are you?"

"I have a plan."

"A plan?" Jade scanned her sticky notes. "What kind of plan?" She ripped up a line of green notes muttering, "Done. Done. Done."

"Maybe I should just go. Obviously you're busy." But she didn't move.

"June, okay, now . . ." Jade tossed the ripped-up sticky notes in the trash basket. "I'm all yours. What's your plan?"

June twisted the straps of her Birkin bag. "I want to move into the loft." She pointed over her head.

"That's your plan? Moving into the Blue Umbrella's loft? June, why don't you just confront him? Are you going to let him get away with this?" Jade dropped down to her chair with a thump.

"I'll pay a fair rent, Jade."

Jade slapped her hands against her thighs. "The Orchid House is six thousand square feet. Can't you find a place to hide from him there? The pool house is twice as big as the loft and twice as nice."

"The pool house is torn up for a remodel. Besides, I cannot stay in that house." June held Jade's gaze. "Can you blame me?"

"Not really."

"Did you tell Max?"

"You asked me not to, but it was hard. Max and I promised not to keep secrets from each other once we got married."

"But this is about Reb and me. It's not like you're keeping a personal secret from him."

"What do you think he'll say when he finds out I knew?"

"What makes you think he's ever going to find out?"

"June." Jade gestured toward the ceiling, the glint in her eye challenging. "You just asked to move into the loft."

Right. "I'll tell him I needed some space. He's aware Reb and I don't have a perfect marriage." June's morning coffee burned in her stomach. "I've never lived on my own. I went from my father's house to a college dorm to marriage. Maybe now it's time."

"You raised a clever, intelligent son, June. He's never going to accept you living in the loft as 'needing space.'"

"Then I don't care. Let him find out; let his dad tell him." She gathered herself and stood. "I'd like to move in today if I could. Hire some men to bring some furniture from the Orchid House."

"June, are you sure?"

"If I don't do this, I'll hate myself for the rest of my life."

Jade regarded her for a moment, as if she didn't buy June's forceful sentiment, but then she opened her middle desk drawer. "Here's a key to the back door. It opens the loft too."

"Thank you." June clung to the key. "I'll pay a thousand a month."

"A thousand? June, no, that's too much. Just pay the utilities." Jade jotted a set of numbers on a pink sticky note. "Here's the security code. Punch it in and hit Okay twice to confirm. Simple."

"I'll pay a thousand a month. If I don't, it's not worth it to me. And I need it to be worth it."

"Isn't it Reb's money, June?"

"Who do you think keeps Rebel and Benson Law in proper society? Who plans the parties, sends the gifts, charms the clients and colleagues?" She paused in the doorway, gazing at the key in her hand. "The money is just as much mine as his, and each month when I write you a check, I'll remind myself exactly how much every dime, every dollar, has cost me."

Standing at the kitchen sink, Jade washed up dinner dishes. For Mama, crackers and broth. For Jade and Max, leftovers. Meatloaf, green beans, and corn with a wilting salad. Being raised by her granny, a woman who grew up in the Depression, Jade learned to never waste food. Even limp lettuce.

Mama had thrown up at the shop today for no reason, so Jade had to cut short her work at the Blue Two and hand control over to Emma. If the shop stood in the morning, Jade would consider it a huge victory.

Once the shop was squared away, she'd hire a new manager. But for the moment, the Blue Two had her undivided attention.

Beyond the window, a purple wash tinted the fading March day. Jade turned the window's handle and shoved open the pane. A cold, moist breeze rushed inside, scented with the aroma of charcoal.

Jade breathed in, eyes closed. Such a glorious fragrance.

"Makes me think of home, the old farm." At the sound of her mother's voice, Jade swerved around. Mama shuffled into the kitchen, holding on to the wall and counter. "Tents pitched all over the yard, everyone sitting around a bonfire until late in the night, showering with a hose behind the barn."

"You're feeling better?"

"The broth and crackers hit the spot." Mama opened the cupboard for a cup. "Thought I'd get my legs moving and come down for my ginger tea."

Jade picked up the kettle to fill it. "It was just a bunch of naked, high hippies."

"Naked? Jade, no one was naked." Mama sighed. "Well, mostly no one."

"Daddy exploded when I caught Eclipse showering behind the barn." Mama's friend was a tall string bean of a man with waist-length hair who spoke in rock-and-roll platitudes.

"I remember." Mama lifted the top from the tea canister. "We had a big fight over that one."

"His daughter was eight." Jade gathered the wet dish towel and replaced it with a clean one. "What did you expect?"

"I'm sorry about Eclipse, Jade." Mama tossed her tea bag into her mug. The same mug she used every night. "But if you want an apology about the way I lived, I'm sorry to disappoint you."

"If I've learned anything from you, Mama, it's 'never apologize about the way you live.'"

Jade carried the damp dish towel to the laundry room between the kitchen and basement door. She paused, listening. A dog barked. A car drove past, blaring the radio. On the porch, Max paced, his heels scraping against the boards as he talked on his cell phone in deep tones.

"Is Max on the phone?" Mama peered out the door, folding her arms over her chest, shivering and hunching up her shoulders.

"Must be a client." He'd been out there for almost a half hour. Left dinner to take the call.

The screen door clicked as Max entered. "Hey." He held up his iPhone. "A friend." Max popped open the fridge, stooping to see inside. "Do we have any Diet Cokes?"

"I think there's one in there. I haven't had time to shop." Jade rounded the kitchen island, taking out a spoon and handing it to Mama. "Which friend? Mama, go on upstairs and get warm. I'll bring up your tea."

"Don't have to tell me twice." Mama inched out of the kitchen.

Max popped open the coke can. "I was talking to Rice." Blunt, to the point, without prelude.

Rice McClure had worked at Benson Law until she moved to California a few months after Jade and Max's wedding. "How's she doing? Still liking California?" Why was he standing so stiff? "Babe, it's okay if you talk to your ex-fiancée. I'm fine with it. I like Rice, remember?"

"Yeah, right, I remember." Max swigged his drink. "She said to tell you hi, by the way. And she loves California and the firm she's working for. She just called to talk shop."

"Is she coming home this summer for your high school reunion?"

"Don't think so." Max shook his head, still with his stiff posture and an air of reservation. "Reunions are not her thing."

"Not her thing? Since when? She was on every prom, homecoming, and reunion committee since ninth grade."

"I guess they're not her thing anymore. People change. Sheesh, Jade, don't make a federal case of it." Max opened a cabinet door, looking, then slammed it shut. Then another. "Where are the Duke basketball glasses? Can't we keep anything in the same place?"

"First of all, the Duke glasses are here." Jade opened the cabinet by the refrigerator. "Where they always are, Max. Second of all, I'm not making a federal case out of anything."

The kettle whistled. *Oh, Mama's tea.* Jade snapped off the burner and poured steaming water in Mama's mug. She glanced back at her husband. "Are you okay?"

"I'm fine." Max filled the Duke glass with ice, then with the remains of his soda. "By the way, Dad beeped in while I was talking to Rice and wanted to know if you'd talked to Mom. He said they were supposed to have dinner with the McClures tonight, but she didn't show."

"Haven't talked to her." Jade squeezed in a spoonful of honey into Mama's tea. At least not since yesterday when she asked to move into the loft. This morning she heard footsteps as she opened the shop, but June never showed in the Blue Umbrella.

"What's that expression on your face?" Max, gruff and loud, tugged loose his tie as if he were suffocating.

"You mean the expression of me making Mama tea?" Her heart burned inside her chest, fueled by the secret she didn't want to keep. Pulling the tea bag from the water and draining the excess, Jade welcomed the small chore as a valid distraction.

"No, the one of you hiding something."

"You concluded that from my expression?"

"Call it lawyer instincts." Max stepped around the island and lifted her chin with a touch of his finger. "Do you know something about Mom?"

"Why don't you ask your dad?" Jade met his gaze as she headed out of the kitchen with Mama's tea.

"Jade?" He followed her upstairs, then waited by the door while she situated Mama with her tea and helped her find a program to watch.

"I'll check on you in a bit."

Down the stairs, Max calmly descended behind her, rounding the staircase to meet her in the family room. She clicked on the lamp by her desk and launched e-mail and QuickBooks.

"Jade, there's no guessing now. You're hiding something." He propped himself on the arm of the club chair. Jade had bought it at an estate sale a few months ago, and Max claimed it as his favorite chair.

"Max, if I tell you, don't shoot the messenger."

"Why would I get mad at you?"

"Because it's bad news, and bad-news messengers get shot at, knocked down, and labeled all the time."

"I think I can rise above it, Jade." He waited. "We're friends. Lovers. No secrets once we married, right? Wasn't that the deal?"

She regarded his face for a long moment. She, his wife, his lover and friend, was about to scourge his treasured childhood memories by telling him his hero was a cheating scum. Forever he'd associate her with the day he learned his father was an adulterer.

Jade had grown up hearing her parents fight, listening to every accusation. She'd watched her daddy drive away at midnight never to return. Max, even at thirty-eight, clung to the idea that his flawed and imperfect parents maintained an idyllic marriage.

"No, I can't." She turned back to her computer. "I won't. Just ask your parents, Max."

"I'm asking you." He touched her arm to draw her attention. "How do you know what's going on with them anyway?"

"I was there." Jade's fingers wrapped around a pen, and she absently tapped it against her desk.

"Where?"

"At Orchid House . . . last Thursday. I picked up your mom in the city when Honey dropped her off after their shopping trip."

"What happened?" Max shoved up from the arm of the chair and stood, feet apart, arms crossed.

Jade jiggled her leg. Seeing Claire . . . hearing Rebel's cold tone . . . witnessing June's stone composure. Just what did Jade witness that evening?

"Jade?" Max grew impatient. "If you don't tell me, I'll imagine the worst thing possible."

"Go ahead." Jade exhaled a bit. What if he just guessed? "What's the worst thing you can imagine?"

Max paced to the fireplace. "I don't know . . . Cancer? Losing their home? Losing their faculties? Dad gambling the family fortune on a horse race and losing? Mom walking down Main Street naked like old man Arnold?" He watched her. "An affair?"

Jade didn't fade or lessen her gaze. Could he read the answer from her soul?

"Mom's having an affair?" Max knelt in front of her.

"Your mom? June Benson?" Jade scoffed. "When pigs fly."

"Dad?"

Jade nodded. "Not his first, from what I could tell."

He stood, hands on his belt. "You heard my dad confessing to my mom he'd had an affair? Or was having an affair?" Max's expression morphed as he spoke from surprise to anger. "You two walked into the house and Dad said, 'How was your trip, June? By the way, I'm having an affair'?"

"No. Your mom and I walked in on him . . . in the media room." Jade winced. How many details should she reveal? "He was with your mom's friend

Claire. They were . . ." If she added the visual, she'd regret it. Max didn't need to deal with that image.

"They were . . . what?"

"Half-naked." *There. Get it and stop pushing.*

Max's eyes narrowed with ire. "You and Mom walked in on Dad, at the house, with a naked—"

"Half-naked."

"Woman? Claire Falcon?"

"Yes."

He exhaled like a charging bull and bolted from the room.

Jade tapped the pen on the desk and then threw it at the doorway. "I said, 'Don't shoot the messenger.'"

Five

When June came down from the loft, the morning light had hurdled the Main Street shop roofs and landed on the Blue Umbrella's glistening floor.

Jade was in her office, so June peeked inside. "Shall I run across to Plumbs and get some of Mae's sticky buns?"

Her daughter-in-law snapped the filing cabinet drawer shut. "Max knows."

June stiffened and the light barely shining in her soul flickered. "You told him?"

"I had to, June. He asked." Jade walked into the shop with a handful of fliers and business cards for the edge of the glass-top sales counter. "Rebel called looking for you, and Max started asking questions."

"How'd he take it?"

"How do you think he took it?"

"I'm sorry, Jade."

"Are you? Really? Then why didn't you tell Max yourself?"

If June had the courage, she would've. "I'll talk to him."

Jade stooped to pick up a UPS package left by the counter. "And why have you let Reb step out on you for all these years?" She peered into June's eyes. "It has been years, right?"

"'Love keeps no record of wrong,' Jade, if I recall Scripture accurately."

"And 'Thou shall not commit adultery,' if I recall Scripture accurately," Jade shot back.

"'Forgive seventy-times-seven times.'" June watched Jade disappear into her office and come out with empty arms.

"Seventy times seven? He's cheated on you that many times?"

June crossed to her daughter-in-law. "Don't hate him, Jade. I've learned to deal with Rebel despite his flaws. He's a good man, in his way." So she'd convinced herself. "Now I'm going grocery shopping. Can I get you anything?" June slung her bag over her shoulder.

"Good man? How can a 'good man' keep cheating on you?"

June considered the question, patting her lips together, careful not to smear her lipstick. "I suppose we're back to 'love keeps no record of wrong.'"

"But where does Scripture command us to allow ourselves to be wronged over and over?"

"I'm not sure it does." Until now, June had endured Rebel's wanderings to pay the penalty for her own sin. To be sure her penance was at last complete. And when she found her payment complete, then and only then would she *not* go back to him.

At The Market, June eased her Lexus into a slot right up front. Getting out, she cleansed her soul with the crispness of the day. Noticing the grocery cart by her car, June grabbed hold and wheeled toward the store, dropping her Birkin into the kiddie seat.

She'd shop devil-may-care today. No list. No mind toward eating healthy.

June just touched the store's portico when she stopped short, her floating emotions deflating and sinking. Claire Falcon exited The Market's second door, her cart loaded, her white-blonde hair piled on her head and held in place with a pink head scarf.

Pausing to put her wallet in her bag, Claire shifted her gaze and froze when her eyes glanced over June. Their eyes met, and telepathic passion exploded between them.

Claire lurched into a hasty, sloppy run, her heels skidding over the slick, painted pavement. Her loaded cart swerved and rattled across the roadway and up the main thoroughfare. "Stay away from me, June."

"Hold up, hussy!" June dashed after Claire, her empty cart shimmying and shaking.

"Stay away, June. I'm warning you." Claire circled her Escalade and peeked at June over the hood, keeping the vehicle between them. "Come nearer, and I'll call the police." She fumbled around inside her purse, raised a small tube. "And zap you with this . . . mace."

"Do it. Zap me. Call the police. I'd love to tell my side." June stalked and circled the SUV, ramming her cart into Claire's.

"Are you crazy?" Claire backed away, tripping on the curb, losing a brown pump in the process. "June, come on, this isn't the place."

"Oh really? Then where?" June rammed Claire's cart again. "My house? The club? At the spring dance? I could have the bandleader dedicate a song to all the women Reb's bedded. How about a duel in Laurel Park? Ooo, even better, up on Eventide Ridge."

"Are you threatening me?" Claire hunched close to her cart, white-knuckling the handlebar.

"How do you have any right for indignation? I caught you half-naked with my husband, Claire."

"You could let me explain."

"Explain?" June crossed her arms and waited. *This ought to be rich.* "There's an explanation? Well, then what am I all riled about? Let's hear it, all the glorious details of how you came to be naked with my husband in my own home."

"He told me you two were . . . well, that you two had an agreement," Claire said through a clinched jaw.

"Agreement? What kind of agreement?" June shoved her cart out of the way and stepped toward Claire. "You're lying."

"Honest to heaven, June. Reb told me that you two, well, stepped out on each other once in a while. He made it sound like an open marriage. I saw it on *Oprah* once. Did you see that episode?"

"Oh my stars . . . *Oprah*? Claire, are you so stupid?" Hands on her hips, June bent toward Claire. "Do I look like a woman who'd live in an open marriage?"

"Well, no. But the prim and proper women are the ones who shock us the most. I didn't see why he'd lie to me?"

"You couldn't see why he'd lie?" Ha! "Reb got exactly what he wanted, Claire. Sex without consequences."

A couple of women heading for their cars slowed and lowered their voices as if to listen.

"Hey, busybodies, this is none of your business. Scoot, scoot." June flicked her hand toward them. They hurried past. "Claire, did you think to challenge him? And you came to my house. Did he tell you I didn't mind if he brought his whores home?"

"That's enough, June." Her faced paled, and she shimmied like an uprooted reed. "There's been a misunderstanding—"

"Misunderstanding? Adultery is a misunderstanding?"

"If you'll hear me out, June . . . I'm sorry for what happened, but I'm not a whore." Claire shoved the mace back into her bag, her hand trembling. "During my divorce from Walt, Reb was so kind to me. One night at the club he gave me advice that saved me financially. Then it seemed I saw him everywhere. We started talking one night at Diamond Joe's, and he asked me to dinner. I was flattered. I mean, Rebel Benson. I remember him from high school and thought a man like him would never go for a girl like me."

"He's *married*, Claire."

"All right, June. I get it. I was stupid. But believe it or not . . ." Her voice quivered and it angered June. She didn't want her compassion stirred. "I trusted him." A single rivulet ran down Claire's polished cheek. "I'm not proud of what I did, but Reb made me feel special, made me feel desired and wanted. He's so exciting, powerful, and handsome."

Claire's words and sentiment resonated, adding color to the reason June returned to Reb year after year, indiscretion after indiscretion.

"You are one of dozens, Claire. The latest in a list of women he's made feel *special*. Don't be foolish." June yanked her cart and started to back away, gathering her sympathies and compassion. Enough of this. She'd not feel solidarity with the woman she'd caught with her husband.

"One of dozens?" Claire lifted her chin. The wind whipped the end of her scarf against her cheek. "Well now, doesn't that make you feel all warm and fuzzy, June? Who's the real fool standing here?"

June walked toward The Market, head high, back straight, eyes swimming, heart bleeding.

Two a.m. Jade jumped out of Max's Mercedes before he came to a complete stop. "Oh my gosh." She pressed her hands to her face. *No, no, no.* The bed of a Ford F-350 protruded from the front window of the Blue Two.

A Chattanooga police officer stopped her from rushing into the shop. "Can't go in there."

"But it's my shop."

"Are you Jade Benson?" He backed her up to the parking lot.

"That's my shop." She clutched the side of her head. "What happened?"

Her shop. Her pain-in-the-butt shop. Smashed. The scene overwhelmed her. Poor Blue Two. Max's hand slipped over her shoulder along with his low whistle.

"The Blue Two has looked better, babe."

"Couple of kids were street racing." The office indicated the riverfront lane. "One of them lost control and ran right through your front door."

"Is he okay?" Max asked in such a way Jade knew his lawyer mind was churning.

"Yes, *she* is. Banged-up face and broken arm. The air bags saved her. Good thing Fords are 'built to last.'"

"Can I go in?" Jade pressed past the officer toward the gaping opening. In the light of the street, she could see jagged, heavy shards of glass dangling from the main window frame.

"The firefighters have been going in and out on the far left side"—the officer pointed—"but be careful. There's a lot of glass, ma'am. And the front is pretty unstable."

"Let me go first." Max pulled her back, following the police spotlight through the opening, clearing debris with a large stride, stepping over a support beam.

The front displays were ruined, smashed by the blow of the truck, its heavy tires resting on piles of clothes. The collection of antique jewelry boxes Jade had just found and put on display had splintered against the hardwood floor. She stooped to gather the pieces in her palm, so rare and precious.

"Such foolishness," she muttered, feeling hollow.

"I'm sorry, babe." Max ran his hand over her hair. "Is this where I say 'bad things happen for good reasons'?"

"Not if you love me." Jade walked the broken porcelain pieces to the sales counter on the opposite wall.

"Mrs. Benson, here's a copy of the report." The officer handed a paper to her, but she passed it on to Max. "Your insurance company will want it."

"In triplicate." Max folded up the report, slipping it into his pocket. "I'm going to give this to Tom, Jade. Let him deal with it. He's not Benson Law's insurance expert for nothing."

"That's great for tomorrow, but what are we going to do about this . . . now?" In the pale white street glow, Jade fit two of the largest pieces together. The delicate angel wings barely fit together. A chunk was missing in between. Jade slipped the pieces into her pocket.

Inspecting the rest of the shop, Jade was relieved to find most of the damage was contained to the front. With her adrenaline rush fading, her body absorbed the burden of weariness and concern.

Before the phone had startled her awake, she'd been sleeping well, finally, after a midnight session with Max about June and Rebel.

Max told her how he'd confronted his dad at the office, but Rebel only acknowledged that June had found him in the media room. Then Max drove up to Whisper Hollow, where his mom confirmed the truth.

"Ma'am?" The officer motioned to the middle of the shop with his flashlight. "I recommend locking your inventory in the storeroom until you can board up."

"Babe, did you bring your keys?" Max picked up a bulky display table and started toward the back, the muscles of his arms taut under his sleeves.

The whole thing was so overwhelming . . . Jade whirled around at the sound of crunching. A tow truck had disengaged the Ford from the busted window. The loose glass pane wobbled before releasing from the frame and crashed on the pavement with the tinkling of a thousand glasses.

The officer hit the opening with his light. "You got about a ten-foot hole that says, 'Thieves, come on down and help yourselves.'"

"I feel like I'm in a horror movie." Jade stooped to pick up a pile of clothes thrown from one of the smashed tables.

Max held his iPhone. "I'm texting Kip to get some of his crew down here ASAP in the morning to board up. Then see how quick he can contract and get this place fixed."

A couple of the firefighters finished knocking loose glass and debris to the ground, then joined the effort to move the inventory to the storeroom. The shop was emptied in short order, and by 3 a.m., Jade and Max were walking to his car.

Jade had just settled in her seat when her phone rang. She answered with a weary sigh.

"Jade? Sorry to call so late, or rather early, but it's Colleen Millay."

"Colleen, hey." Jade clicked on her seat belt.

"Are you home? I tried your home number."

"We had an emergency in the city. Some kid crashed through the Blue Two."

"Oh, I'm so sorry. Is everyone all right?"

"No one was hurt except the shop."

"Well then, let the bad news continue. You have an emergency at home in Whisper Hollow too."

~

If she weren't so tired, she'd fill the tub with warm water, set the jets on high, and let the gurgles and bubbles drown her tears. But she needed to put Mama to bed.

"Please, just get in bed."

"I'm not crazy." Mama shrugged off Jade's assistance as she lifted a knee to the bed. "I heard the kittens crying, and I went down to feed them."

"At three in the morning?"

"Do they know it's three in the morning? They were hungry. Their bowls were empty." Mama fell against the pillows, the hue of the lamplight revealing her pale complexion and the red rings circling her eyes.

"Why did you go out there without your coat or shoes?"

"My slippers are too warm. Aiden brought those things to me after his last trip to Alaska. A very cold Eskimo must have made them. Have you seen the lining?"

"I get it, Mama." Jade tucked the blankets in around her. "You're shivering. Do you want hot tea or cocoa?"

"You think I'm losing it, don't you, Jade-o?" Mama pressed her hand over her heart and regarded Jade with shining eyes. "I tell you, I heard them mewing. I had to make sure they were all right. Colleen Millay doesn't always keep that mutt of hers under control. I've seen him harass the kitties."

Oh, Mama. Jade crawled into bed with her, nestling Mama's head against her shoulder, kissing her cheek. "Colleen's little schnauzer isn't going to hurt the kitties. I promise."

Mama seemed like her old self now, but when she and Max whipped into the driveway, Mama was wandering in the front yard, scattered and disoriented.

"Well, then where's Roscoe? Your dog?"

"Max and I had to put Roscoe down. Remember?" Jade said. "He lived a good life."

"But now you have kittens. Yes, you have all those kittens. So innocent, kittens, aren't they?"

"That's why we made a home for the stray mama and her babies on the back porch."

"Tell me about the kittens." Mama's sigh indicated she was finding peace. "Again."

"Okay, well, as you know I was busy opening the Blue Two, wondering if I'd ever have my own baby, and one day I came home and there they were, a mama tabby and her babies. She looked up at me with those golden eyes, and I knew she came to rescue me more than to be rescued. Next thing I knew I had three or four cat families, and six big bowls of food lined up on the back porch with water and cat houses."

When she looked down, Mama's cheeks were soaked.

"Why are you crying?" Jade dried her tears with the edge of her sleeve. "The kitties are fine. We take good care of them. Got the mamas fixed and took about twelve cats to the vet last year." A day that required all hands on deck: Max, Lillabeth, and June. "Even found homes for a few of the kittens."

"I want to go home." Mama wiped her nose with a handkerchief she kept on her nightstand. "I've loved being here with you, Jade-o, but I miss the Iowa plains, the smell of sunburnt prairie grass, my friends, my home, my bed, even miss that passel of dogs Willow used to have. I'm sad now she had to give them all away. That little Jack Russell, Pepper, was something else."

"Now what are you going to do in Prairie City, rattling around that cold, creaky farmhouse? And Willow found good homes for those dogs. She couldn't go to college otherwise."

"That don't change what I said . . ." Mama brushed her hand over Jade's hair, and the confusion of the woman wandering the lawn seemed to dissipate. "You're not going to want to hear this, Jade-o, but it's time to go home to die."

"Die? What kind of talk is that, dying? You're just overtired and still worked up over the cats." Jade crawled off the bed, but Mama caught her hand.

"Jade-o." Mama gently squeezed her fingers. "I want to die at home."

Jade tugged her hand free. "I'm not going to let you live and die alone, Mama. You can't drive!"

"I can't drive a Midwest Parcel truck, but I can certainly drive Paps's old pickup."

"Does it even run anymore?" Jade dropped to the side of the bed and peered into Mama's eyes. "You can't live alone."

"Now you listen to me, Jade Benson. My mother never could tell me what to do once I came of age, and she had a hard time before too, so give it up. You're not going to keep me from dying where I choose."

It was too late, or perhaps too early, at four in the morning, to have this conversation. Jade's thin patience leaked through her skin and settled into her weary muscles.

"We'll talk about this tomorrow." Maybe.

"Linc can help me, Jade. He's always been a good help to me. And I have enough to pay him." Mama held Jade's face with her hands. "I want to go home. Please."

Jade tucked Mama's blanket around her. "We'll see." When Mama had landed in Whisper Hollow last summer, Jade couldn't wait for her to go home. Now she didn't want her to leave. They'd painted this room together—a comforting pinkish white—and shopped for new curtains and bed linens. Jade made space in her life for her mother, taking her to doctor appointments, to dinner, to movies, and to club parties. And in the course of doing what was right, Jade made space for Mama in her heart. If she went home, who would fill that hole?

"How about if Max and I drive you home once I get the Blue Two squared away, and—"

"And when would that be? No, no, I'm not waiting until you decide the Blue Two is done. I'll call Aiden to come get me."

"What?" *Stubborn old broad.* "He's in Alaska until May. And don't say you'll call Willow because she's not flying fifteen hundred miles just to drive you nine hundred miles to Prairie City." In February, Jade's baby sister had taken a hiatus from college and left for a Guatemalan orphanage, joining a humanitarian organization as a medical aid worker.

"I'll find someone." Mama nodded her head, eyes closed, chin set. "Hire someone . . . take the Greyhound."

"Take a bus? You are a crazy old woman. How about I ask Max for the company jet?" Mama hated to fly, even on a private jet.

"Why don't you just bury me alive, Jade-o? I'd enjoy that about the same." Mama clutched her fist to her chest. "My heart wants to be home. Take me, Jade, please."

All right, she heard. Mama's plea tapped her heart like the mew of the kittens. But she couldn't just load up and go. She had the Blue Umbrella and the Blue Two, which at the moment sported a big hole. Last but not least, Max's parents' marriage was in a tilt-a-whirl. Jade considered how he might need her in the coming weeks and months.

"Mama, can we go to sleep for now? Talk in the morning?" Jade stooped to kiss her cheek and clicked off the lamp. "Sweet dreams."

"I could hitchhike," Mama said in the dark. "End my days like they began, on the open road, looking for the next ride."

"Times have changed, Mama. It's not the summer of love, Woodstock, or a Washington rally. And you're not twentysomething anymore." Jade hesitated by the door. "The world's lost what innocence remained."

"Rats, I was hoping all of this was a dream." Mama's breathing ladened her words with sleep.

"Sorry, it's all reality."

"But it's been good, hasn't it? Most of it, my life?"

Jade propped against the door, her shoulder cutting into the swath of hall light, hearing what Mama was too shy to ask. "It's been good, Mama. You had a lot of adventures."

"I did, didn't I? Lots of . . . adventures. But you know the best part?"

"What's the best part?"

"You, Jade-o. You."

Six

At the sound of the bells, Jade expected to see Lillabeth coming in from her UT-Chattanooga classes, ready to take over the Blue Umbrella for the afternoon.

Instead, June's coiffed and manicured form shot through the shop followed by Rebel. Her heels resounded up the stairs.

Jade winced, softly hanging the last '70s granny dresses on the antique rack she used for special displays.

"I've given you almost two weeks." Rebel's heavy words drifted through the wood and plaster, falling into the shop. Thank goodness the place was empty except for the cloak of afternoon sun splashing through the front pane. "Plenty of time to stop being angry. What are people—"

"I've stopped caring, Rebel. Stopped. Caring." The loft door slammed.

A couple of women entered the shop. Jade smiled, hoping the rabble upstairs was settling down.

Another door slammed. A voice rumbled. The startled women gazed toward the ceiling.

"Ladies, have you seen the granny dresses? Up front, by the window." Jade motioned, smiling. When the ladies started parsing through the display, Jade scurried on tiptoe up the stairs.

Pausing at the loft's door, listening to feet shuffling over the hardwood, Jade stiffened, bracing for a . . . what? A smack? A crash? Would Reb become violent?

After a thick moment of silence, Jade knocked. "June?"

The door swung open. "The man's impossible. He refuses to listen. Has cotton in his ears. Tell him, Jade." June left the door ajar and curved around the wall into the kitchen.

Jade hesitated, not wanting to become a pawn in this game.

Rebel caught her eye. "Well? Are you going to tell me?"

Jade peered back down the stairs. "Look, Reb, this isn't any of my business."

"Sure it is. You're aiding and abetting my wife. So?" Reb jammed his hands into his pockets with jocular confidence. "What is it I need to know?"

Jade loved Reb. He had embraced her like a father from the very beginning, but she'd glimpsed his defense lawyer temperament and he could intimidate.

"She thinks you're on her like a hound on the hunt." If she'd learned anything, Rebel respected strength.

The skin around his eye crinkled, but his lips remained sober.

"By the way, you're in my shop, so keep your voices down. I can hear every word and footstep."

"Sorry to have disturbed you." Rebel's slacks gracefully fell into place as he stood. His silver and black hair was thick and neat, and his jaw had the strength of a younger man. He looked regal. Like the leader of a great Southern law firm.

Not at all like the weak man Jade had caught cheating on his wife.

"Haven't you left yet?" June appeared at the edge of the kitchen, her face locked with determination, her arms folded like an X across her middle. *Keep out.* The small loft was filled with large resentment.

"Call me," Rebel said, slightly stepping toward her as if he wanted to kiss her. Jade stared at her shoes.

"Not this time, Reb. Not this time."

With a lingering glance at his wife, Rebel passed Jade, lightly pressing her arm as he started down the stairs. "Tom tells me you're in an insurance battle. Over the downtown shop."

"Apparently the Danica Patrick wannabe didn't realize You Buy It insurance company was no longer licensed to practice in the greater Chattanooga area."

"I'll check in with Tom. See if he needs help. I've got some friends at the insurance commission."

Sure he did. Reb had all kinds of friends. "Thanks," Jade said, feeling like she was consorting with the enemy. But this wasn't her fight. It was June's.

As Rebel's footsteps faded away, June emerged from the kitchen, hot anger trailing her. "He can't find anything at the house, so he comes crying to me." She fluffed the couch pillows. "'Junie, I miss you. I can't find the popcorn. We're all out of almonds. I can't find any of the good movies.'"

Jade rested against the open door, one ear to the women still browsing downstairs. Lillabeth should be along in the next few minutes.

"Did he apologize? Give you a reason for being with Claire?"

"Of course not. He tries to brainwash me into thinking I'm overreacting. Tells me she means nothing to him. Well, it means something to me." June kicked the coffee table leg. Hard. "And I'm not going to take it anymore."

"Just how long have you been taking it?" Jade scooted down a few steps and peered under the slanted wall into the shop. The women were perusing the vintage vinyl. "My name is Jade, if you need anything, ladies."

They turned, smiled, and nodded, square album covers in their hands.

"I thought . . . if I just hung in there . . . showed him I was sincere, that I wasn't going anywhere, he'd—"

"What do you mean, you weren't going anywhere?" Jade leaned to see into June's eyes, but she kept her gaze fixed on an image not in the room.

June shook her head slowly. Strands of her blonde hair stood on end. Green eye shadow ran into the corner of her eyes. "I'm tired of paying." She lifted her hand and fiddled with the pearls of her necklace. "Simply tired."

In the afternoon, Jade picked up Mama for a doctor's appointment. The news wasn't good. The doctor wanted Mama to submit to another round of Rituxan.

She'd jumped to her feet, billowing, "No!"

As Jade steered her out of the office, Mama barked at the nurse. "No."

To the receptionist, Mama said, "No."

On the ride home, she repeated no a dozen times, and muttered against the window she was going home to Iowa no matter what.

When Jade brought her back to the Blue Umbrella, Mama greeted Lillabeth with a no. Then asked what she was doing on the weekend. "How about a girls' road trip?"

Okay, Mama, I get it.

Meanwhile, Lillabeth watched over the shop.

"Is June still upstairs?"

"She left about fifteen minutes ago. Said something about going to the club for a meeting."

All morning Jade heard June's melancholy, "Simply tired," bounding around her heart. When she prodded her mother-in-law for more, she evaded. So Jade whispered to Jesus, asking Him to help her in-laws.

Now she worked on the day's accounting while Mama played records, filling the shop with music. A half hour ago Lillabeth had taken Jade's truck down to the Blue Two to load up with inventory.

The shifting sunlight glinted off the pieces of the shattered porcelain jewelry box Jade had set on the windowsill and captured her attention. Delicate pieces with no hope of repair.

Her view was of nothing more than the alley, the back corner of Mario's Pizza, and a green swath of the trees racing down the ridge to the valley of the Hollow. She rested her chin in her hand, closing her eyes, listening to her heart.

Jade wanted Mama to go through the chemo and live. For Rebel and June to go back to being the don and dame of their small village. For Max to hold his own son. For her house to be full of love and laughter.

A ripple of peace warmed her heart. God had been good to her. Deep down, she believed He loved and forgave her. But a son for Max and a daughter for her would . . . well, redeem her past and seal her future.

"Tired?" Mama appeared at the shop door, stirring a cup of tea.

"A little."

"I'm sorry about the doctor today. Perhaps I overstated my point."

"Maybe a little. And"—Jade patted her hands on her desk—"to prove your sincerity, go for the next round of Rituxan."

"You can't kid a kidder, Jade-o." Mama perched on the edge of the metal chair, catching herself as the chair listed starboard as it always did. Despite the warmth of the shop, Mama was bundled in a turtleneck and a sweater. "I'm going home."

"Alone." Doubt tinged Jade's expression. "You're going to live alone?"

"I've got friends. Bet you didn't know this, but Carla Colter and I are good friends now. Plus, there's Linc. And I've been thinking my good ol' friend Sharon can drive down to get me. One teamster doing a favor for another."

"Dustin's mom is your friend? She's going to sit with you when you're sick? Take you to the doctor, buy your groceries? Or Linc? What'd it take him . . . a week to repair your porch screens?"

The last time Jade saw Mama and Carla Colter together, they were fighting.

Her daughter had married *Carla's* son. Illegally. Mama had shoved her bosoms toward Carla when she accused her of being a bad mother. *"Bite me."*

"Jade-o?"

"Who's going to cook? And clean? What if you have a dizzy spell and fall? Who's going to help you?"

"I'll call 9-1-1."

"How are you going to call 9-1-1 if you're on the floor? What if you hit your head?"

"If I hit my head, I'll be knocked out until Linc comes." Mama sipped her tea, the sincerity in her eyes accented by the wide base of the cup.

Jade crossed her arms and legs. Two could play this game. "I'm not taking you home to die."

"Jade, either you take me or I'll find someone. Hey, June seems to be at loose ends these days. Maybe I'll call her." Mama set down her tea. "I have leukemia, Jade. I'm not recovering from this. Refusing to take me home isn't going to prolong the inevitable. I was born in Prairie City, and dear girl, I'm going to die in Prairie City."

"You seem to be set on this." Blinking the sheen from her eyes, Jade peered out the window for a long moment. "Willow e-mailed today."

"I am. What did my baby girl have to say? Can't imagine how she's faring in the hills of Guatemala."

Jade reached for the e-mail she'd printed out earlier. Willow didn't exactly write it to her *and* Mama, but Mama didn't need to know that. Knowing Willow, she didn't even think about Mama still being in Whisper Hollow. She lived in her own universe, the one she created in her head. Willow-world.

"'Hey, Jade-o,'" Jade began reading, adding what Willow didn't. "And Mama."

Yes, I live, I breathe. But cyberspace doesn't break open over the hills of Guatemala often, so take what you get. I can just hear you complaining. "Oh, finally, my baby sister e-mailed me."

"I see she's not changed. Everything is about her." Mama sipped her tea, slowly settling against the back of the chair.

We had electricity and running water for a whole week and I wanted to declare a village celebration, but everyone was too busy washing, cooking, cleaning. Then one morning, blip, back to the Stone Age. All I got to say, no wonder the folks have so many kids. What else do they have to do at night? (And no lecture from you. I'm behaving myself.)

"Ha, I take back what I said. Maybe she has changed a bit."

"I'd say giving up a hospital position to volunteer with the Guatemalan Red Cross shows some growth, Mama. I never thought she'd give up Starbucks for humanitarian work."

Anyway, after two months, I'm still the tall, white American girl, genetically incapable of rolling her Rs as in *perro* (that's dog for you Gringos). I crave Starbucks, and you don't want to see my hands and feet. Pedi and mani first chance I get.

I'm glad I volunteered, Jade. It's good to get a taste of the real world, taking a break from my final year of school, deciding if I'm right for med school. I know my dad wants me to go, but I'm not sure. So much brainpower, and so little ambition. What's a girl to do?

Being a physician's assistant might be enough for me. Like, do I want to go to school six more years just to write prescriptions? Shoot, I can do all the fun stuff as a PA. "Drop your drawers" and "This won't hurt a bit." (Insert sinister laugh here.)

Next month I'm on a medical team going into Cuba. I thought it'd be fun to drop in on the Fidel boys and see what's got them all stingy and uptight.

"I was a Communist for a while," Mama said.

"And probably on some blacklist in Washington."

"Maybe." Mama sipped her tea, grinning. "These days you're the one probably on a list for *not* being a Commie."

"I'll remind them you're my mother."

So how's things in Whisper Hollow? How's the hunky hubby? You're lucky I didn't meet him first. I might just have stolen him right out from under you.

Mama spewed a bit of tea. "Oh Willow, always a dreamer. The kite in the breeze, that one."

Any babies yet? It's okay to ask, isn't it? I am your sister after all.

Jade peeked at Mama, whose expression revealed nothing of her heart or thoughts.

How are the shops? Is Lillabeth still married to that gorgeous flyboy? Now him I did see first. Tossed him back in and don't you know, your little Lillabeth hooked him.

Oh, here's some news. Almost forgot. This will crack you up, Jade-o. I actually went on a date. One of the women who runs the clinic here, she's from Kansas, what can I say, told me she thought I'd hit it off with this friend of hers. A local. I told her, nothing doing if he wasn't at least five-nine. She said, "Oh yeah, he's at least that tall."

The woman needs a new measuring stick. Jade, he like came to the middle of my chest. He had a bird's-eye view of my ladies, if you know what I mean. And he wanted to go dancing.

Jade laughed between words, a full picture of tall Willow and a short Guatemalan forming. Mama twittered behind her cup.

Every time he tried to put his hand on my shoulder, he had to dig his fingernails into my flesh or lose his grip. Twice his hand slipped, twice he caught my bra strap. I swear he was doing it on purpose.

So I decided. If he wants to kiss me good night (ha!), he's going to have to figure out how reach my lips without me bending over. I'm sorry, I'm sounding like a snob, aren't I?

Mama mumbled, "Yes."

He really was nice, handsome, extremely intelligent. But we looked like circus freaks walking into the movie. The man must have read my mind, or gone out on a lot of dates with tall women, because when he brought me back to the clinic, he reached around the back of his seat and pulled out . . . brace yourself, a small stepladder. I kid you not. Step. Ladder. He walked me to the front door, snapped it open, climbed the two steps, grabbed my shoulders, and went for the kill.

Jade dropped the paper to her lap, shaking. Mama's soft snicker powdered the room. Oh, Willow . . .

I held it in. I did. But he got a stiff-lipped kiss from me because, if I loosened up, I'd have never gotten control. And well, the man has feelings.

As soon as he left, I ran up to my room, dove to my bed, and laughed into my pillow for ten minutes. Felt the residuals of that one for two days. Some things really are worth the laugh.

So, what's up with Aiden? I need to e-mail him, Mr. Shove-My-Religion-Down-Your-Throat. Here's news that will freak you out. If what I've written already hasn't tweaked your freak. I've started reading the Bible before going to bed at night. Don't tell Aiden, though. I'm still mad at him for giving me the stupid thing for Christmas. What kind of present is that for your sister?

Oh, look at the time. Need to run.

Mama was listening, staring at her tea. "Tell Mama hi for me, hope she's feeling better . . . and I love her."

Write me. Love mucho, Willow

Jade folded the paper as Mama leaned to see. "She did not write, 'I love her.'"

"Yes, she did." Jade opened the middle drawer and slipped the e-mail inside.

"If you're going to lie for your sister, Jade-o, at least try to sound like her. 'Tell Mama hi for me, hope she's feeling better . . . and I love her'? That's what you, my roots-in-the-ground daughter would say. My kite-in-the-breeze daughter would say, 'Tell Mama to give the doctors heck . . . and kiss, kiss, hug, hug.'"

Jade spun around. "So she didn't write it. She meant to."

"You don't have to excuse her to me, Jade." Mama rose, cradling her cup in her hand. The music had stopped. "I wasn't there for her like I should've been." Mama paused in the doorway, staring into the light-soaked shop. "It's why she calls me Beryl and gives me a hard time about nearly everything. You and Mother raised her."

"But you were there for her when I went to college."

"Some. Mother mostly. Willow hated when I married Bob." A silky laugh slipped through Mama's nose. "Turns out, I hated being married to him too." She regarded Jade with a lingering gaze. "I was born in Prairie City. Married four times in Prairie City. Gave birth to three children . . . in Prairie City. And Jade-o, I'm going to die in Prairie City."

Seven

"It's all in your mind, man. In. Your. Mind." Max gazed out of his tenth-floor office window to the blooming garden of Chattanooga's glowing streetlights.

Planting his feet, he fought his craving with his thoughts. Yet how could he deny the pain wrenching his back? Very real pain.

Today in court, when he saw he'd not convinced the jury, subtle twinges in his back had turned into a raging inferno.

One Percocet and he'd be fine. Okay, two. He'd be good for hours. Days. It didn't mean he was addicted. Just meant he had a really bad back.

He'd call Tripp, be accountable like he'd pledged when he left rehab. Then he'd pop two pills and bye-bye misery.

A sharp, fiery pain gripped his hamstring and slithered down his calf. He trolled his yesterdays trying to find the beginning of the pain. Rice's call? Jade's news about Dad and Mom? Not that he was completely surprised by Dad's indiscretion.

Office gossip flowed Max's way from time to time. He'd observed Dad's wandering eye a time or two but passed it off as harmless admiration of God's handiwork.

Max grabbed a handful of his shirt at the waist. The pain was making him nauseous. And his day was far from over. In an hour, he'd head up the firm's partner meeting with the satellite offices on videoconferencing. He needed to bring his A game. Not worries over infidelity or phone calls from ex-fiancées.

But he'd told Jade, right? *"Rice called."* No secrets there. Well, no more secrets. Just the one he'd buried before the wedding when the past-is-the-past pact mattered. But then?

Pain sank deeper into his muscle, and on reflex Max jumped toward his closet. Toward his stash.

As his hand wrapped around the knob, moisture beaded on his forehead. *God, help me here.*

Since high school football, he'd been on some kind of pain medication. During college intramural basketball, he'd torn a rotator cuff. Pain meds became a permanent part of his mental and physical landscape.

Max glanced back at his desk where his iPhone sat in its docking station. *Call Tripp.*

A knock sounded on his office door as it was pushed open. "Max?"

"Dad." He met him in the center of the room.

"Got a second?"

"For you? Sure." Max used the diversion to work past his craving.

"I received some interesting news today." Dressed casually in a polo shirt and loafers, Dad stood in front of the desk with his hands in his pockets. "I made the governor's short list to replace Judge Lewison on the supreme court."

"Really? Well, congratulations." Max gave his dad a one-armed hug and the traditional backslaps. One-two-three. "The state supreme court. And before sixty-five. You said you'd do it."

"Too early to celebrate. The other two are excellent choices, Robert Beisner and Ralph Bell." Dad walked to the window. "It's supposed to go below freezing tonight. Here we are, the end of March."

Max leaned against his desk, arms and ankles crossed, waiting. Dad didn't walk in here for a single purpose.

"I need advice." Dad rotated toward Max.

"About Mom?" *Ah!* Max jumped up, pressing his hand against his thigh. The pain made his eyes water.

"Your back again?"

Max knelt slowly to the floor, anchoring his hand against one of the chairs, taking the pressure off his back.

"Son, do I need to call 9-1-1?"

"No, I'm fine."

"You need some meds?" Dad stepped over to hold the chair as Max dragged himself up to sit. "I could—"

"In the closet. Top shelf, little toy safe in the back left corner."

Dad retrieved the safe and tugged open the plastic door. He doled out two pills. "Is that enough?"

Max nodded, then swigged them down with warm Diet Coke.

"Toy safe. Clever." Dad returned the stash to its hiding place and closed the closet door.

"You going to tell Mom?"

"About your pills or the court?" Dad sat in the wingback chair across from Max.

"The court." Max regretted giving him an ace in the hole.

"The question is, should I just come clean about the affair? Let the hoopla die down in the press before the governor decides? I can meet with him privately. I've known Matt for years."

"You realize you're talking to me about my mother. And if you weren't my father, I'd punch you in the face for what you did to her." Max eyed his father with a hard-line gaze.

"I'll talk with Clarence." Rebel rose and headed for the door. Clarence was a senior partner at Benson Law and one of Dad's oldest friends. "Don't worry about your mom and me. We've endured forty-one years of marriage, infidelities and all." He hesitated with his hand on the knob. "Think I'll make it to the court?"

"Sure, why not?" Max closed his eyes. The meds were doing their thing. "You're a Benson, one of the most enduring legal names in Tennessee."

Dad left, and Max swigged the last of his coke, staring out his office window at downtown Chattanooga traffic. His father was a confessed adulterer and a state supreme court nominee.

Tossing his empty bottle in the recycle bin, Max's gaze fell on the closet door. He was truly his father's son.

His iPhone's ring startled him. The tone was the one he'd assigned to Rice's number. Wonder what she wanted?

"Rice?"

"No, son, it's Gus McClure."

"Gus, hello, how are you?" His voice faltered, sounding weak and far away.

"I have some news, Max, some terrible news."

~

In the chilly March air, Jade waited for Max on the back porch swing, wrapped in her wool jacket, feet buried in a thick pair of socks Mae Plumb's granddaughter had made.

When his Mercedes pulled into the garage, her heart skipped. She still loved when he came home at night, his tie loose around his neck, a shock of his dark hair freed from the morning's gel and arching over his brow. His presence enveloped the house and filled her.

"Hey, handsome," she said as he came up the back walk, his left heel skipping over the concrete.

From the ground luminaries trimming the walkway, and from the lily lights she'd strung along the porch roof, Jade detected heaviness in his posture.

"Anything to eat?" Max cleared the porch steps and bent to kiss Jade's cheek.

"I thought we'd order pizza, watch a movie." Jade entered the kitchen behind him, locking the door and shutting off the outside lights. "Are you okay? How was the meeting?" She brushed aside his bangs, trying to see into his eyes. "And didn't you say you were getting a haircut?"

"Didn't go to the meeting. Didn't get a haircut." He dropped his briefcase in the middle of the floor and jerked open the fridge door. "I thought you were going grocery shopping."

"What's wrong with you?" This was not the homecoming she'd anticipated. A grouchy Max. He loved the partner meetings. Always came home in a good mood, fired up about the firm's plans and future, relaying all the stories and news from the partners. "Did something happen today? Why didn't you go to the meeting? Where have you been?"

"Driving around. Stopped to talk to Tripp." Max jerked his bag up to his shoulder and shoved past Jade as he left the kitchen. "Are you ordering pizza or not?"

"Yeah, sure." Grouch. Ruiner of plans. While he was not in a meeting, not getting his hair cut, Jade had gone into Whisper Hollow pharmacy to pick up something for Mama. The ovulation kits were on sale. As Rod Stewart so eloquently sang, "Tonight's the night."

She'd hoped to keep the news to herself, woo him with her kisses, and let nature take its course. If she wasn't pregnant next month, she'd be the only one to know.

"I don't want pepperoni. Get veggie. No olives."

"Max." Jade cupped his shoulder. "What's wrong? Look at me."

He hesitated in the foyer, his jacket dragging over the marble. When he turned, she saw the watery redness of his eyes and the sallow texture to his skin.

"Pills. You're taking pills again."

"Rice is dead, Jade." He moved toward the stairs. "Rice is dead."

"No!" She ran after him. "What happened?" Rice was too young, too full of life to be dead.

"Gus called. She was flying her first cross-country solo. Hit a storm. Her plane went down, and . . ." His first step up emulated climbing a mountain. "Rice is dead."

~

June picked at her chicken salad, unable to eat. The somber mood of the Thursday Club luncheon seemed to quell everyone's appetite.

"More water, Mrs. Benson?" The server poised a pitcher over June's glass.

"Yes, please." The plop of ice and splash of water resounded in the Lilac Room.

The server filled Jade's glass. "I loved the top you sold me the other day, Mrs. Benson."

"Good, good. I'm glad. And you can call me Jade."

The server moved around the table pouring water.

All the talk this afternoon was about Rice's death. She'd been a friend, or a friend to the daughter or son, of every woman in the Lilac Room. Several of the older women had taught her in Sunday school or at Whisper Hollow High.

"Give us the scoop, Junie? You play cards with the McClures." Penny Jo leaned over her lunch toward June. "Rice had a son? I was shocked. Did you know?"

"Penny Jo, eat your salad." June speared at her own tomato and cube of chicken.

"All I want to know is the truth. Mercy, don't get so defensive. We're all hurting for Gus and Lorelai. Missing Rice. But what about her son? He's what?" Penny Jo looked at Helen Brooks. "Eighteen months?"

"I heard he was two," Helen said.

"Nineteen months," June answered. "He's nineteen months . . . Asa McClure."

"So he has her last name." Penny Jo raised her eyebrows and surveyed the other women at the table. "No father in the picture?"

"Rice is dead, Penny Jo." June's fork clattered against her plate. "Can we please respect her memory?"

Penny Jo made a big production of wiping the corner of her lips with her linen napkin. "I just couldn't stop crying when I found out. And that poor boy."

Shut up, Penny Jo.

"I've been thinking, June. We should cancel the spring event. I'd feel like I was dancing on Gus and Lorelai's grief."

What was she doing? Stirring up trouble for nothing. On purpose. "The dance is a month away, Penny Jo. Rice's funeral is this Saturday."

The stately woman with red hair and a recent face-lift stood, determination in her brown eyes. "Ladies . . ." She tapped her water glass with the handle of her fork. "I know how much we all look to the spring dance to break off our winter doldrums, but how can we celebrate when our friends have suffered such a great loss? Most of us have served on a club or church committee with Lorelai. Our husbands golf with Gus." Penny Jo strolled slowly between the center tables, gathering emotional support. "I move we cancel the spring cotillion. We'll have the auction to raise money, but in deference to our friends the McClures, cancel the party."

"Good idea. I second." Lucy Parker stuck her hand in the air.

"Ladies, ladies." June shoved away from the table and joined Penny Jo in the middle of the room. "We are all grieving, but we can't just cancel the cotillion without discussion. We've paid deposits, ordered food and flowers."

"Then let's discuss." Helen rose to her feet. "Personally, I'd feel like I was dancing on Rice's grave."

"My point exactly." Penny Jo applauded with soft hand pats. "Where is our cotillion subchair, Claire Falcon, today?" Penny Jo's gaze fell on June.

Yes, she was doing this on purpose. "Wonder what she's up to? She never misses Thursday lunch."

"Is that the game you want to play, Penny Jo?" *Gloves off, girl. Dukes up.* June paced around the tables, catching glances before the women averted their eyes. "Let's just go ahead and get it out on the table."

Chairs squeaked. Silverware clinked.

"June, I was just funning." Penny Jo tugged at her suit jacket. Laughing. Fake. "No need to get all serious on us. This is about Rice, and Gus and Lorelai."

"June, come now." Helen spoke low and tender. "No need to air dirty laundry on club luncheon day. Let's just say we all knew Claire was gunning for some man to get revenge on what Walt did to her."

"And what was your reason, Helen? I believe you know Rebel more intimately than you should." June continued circling the room. Jade remained at their table, her expression somber. "Maybe some of you can get with Claire and form the Ex-Lovers of Rebel Benson Club. Helen, you can be president. Trudy, ducking down back there, how about vice president? And if I'm not mistaken, Annamarie, you can be secretary." June worked her way back to her table. "Be sure to recruit Penny Jo. She's wanted to be a member for a long time."

"June Benson, that's an out-and-out—"

"As for me." June strolled back to her table and slung her new handbag over her shoulder. Her belly rumbled for a burger and shake from Froggers. "I resign from this club and the committee. Do what you want. I don't care."

A collective gasp rose in the room.

"June. You can't quit."

"I just did, Helen." June motioned to Jade as she headed for the door. "One final thought, ladies. Shame on you for keeping my husband's secrets while pretending to be my friends." The smack of her heels against the tile was the perfect exclamation point.

"June." Jade whooshed out of the Lilac Room after her. "That . . . was incredible."

"Yes, incredibly stupid. I just exposed my husband to all those snippy—" June punched through the outer clubhouse doors. The mountain air cooled her hot skin.

"But they already knew."

June paused under the magnolia tree. "I used to smoke . . . Virginia Slims. I'd come out here after a dance to cool off, have a cigarette." She tipped her face toward the noon sun. "The stars would be out, floating across the night like dandelion pedals. That's when I first caught him. Leaning against Lisa Thibodeaux."

"And you never said anything?"

She shrugged. "I thought it was a harmless flirt. I thought I deserved . . . Well, what's done is done." June stepped off the sidewalk. "How about a burger at Froggers?"

Eight

The morning sunlight drifted through the stained glass of First Baptist Congregation and cast gauzy red, green, blue, and yellow veils over Rice's casket.

From the pulpit, Reverend Girden spoke of life after death. "Can we be assured there is an afterlife? Yes. Jesus told us so. 'I go to prepare a place for you.'"

Jade watched her husband with stealthy glances. He'd not said two sentences to her today. Grief, she understood, but shoving her out of his heart, she didn't. When the funeral started, she slipped her hand into his, but after a few seconds he shifted and let go.

On the other side of Max, Mama stared straight ahead with glassy eyes. Jade whispered to Jesus that now would be a good time to awaken Mama to the reality of the afterlife. She whispered loud "amens" to Reverend Girden's references to Jesus and heaven. This moment had to be hitting home for Mama.

"I'd like to take this time," Reverend Girden said, stepping down from the stage to the main floor, "to invite Rice's friends and family to share." He smiled. "I think Rice is probably watching from heaven, waiting for this part."

A soft laughter of relief rippled through the sanctuary.

"Are you going up?" Jade leaned against Max, whispering. Lines began to form on each side of the room.

"No." Flat, bordering on uncaring. Even angry.

"Why not?" She slipped her arm through his, her heart burning in her chest. She felt weak. Blindsided. Burdened and helpless.

"Because . . . Jade." He jerked away, scooting forward and propping his elbows on the pew in front of him, resting his face in his hands.

Stinging, Jade sat back. But she couldn't hold her question inside. "Max, what's wrong?"

"Rice died. What do you think?" Jumping up, he stepped over her legs and marched down the aisle toward the doors.

Mama stretched her hand to Jade. "Give him some space, Jade-o. Death hits each one differently."

Jade's pulse surged though hot veins. He acted like she was somehow responsible for Rice's death. For days she'd given him space. Ever since he came home with the news.

In the meantime, she'd lost this month to conceive. Max was edgy and terse, disappearing at odd hours, pacing the front porch with his cell phone in his ear, ending the calls when she came around.

And yesterday afternoon Jade battled with anxiety for the first time in well over a year. Was Max going to leave her? Was he back into drugs? Another woman?

Up front, Rice's best friend since first grade wept at the mic. "So we took the tadpole bowl and poured it into Mrs. Campbell's McDonald's cup during recess. She always came to school with a McDonald's Coke." The mourners laughed low. "So there she is, teaching math, and reaches down to take a drink—"

The laughter rose from the mourners and rolled through the sanctuary. Jade swerved around to the back of the sanctuary, searching for Max. He stood by the doors talking to Rice's cousin, Serena, who held Rice's son. An electric tremble traveled across Jade's torso. Her stomach constricted.

Facing forward again, she tried to listen to the stories and memories of Rice. Her thoughts melded into her emotions, sinking, sinking, sinking into a mental mire.

Burnt amber tainted her thoughts and swirled with purple ribbons. She felt loose, ungrounded, like she floated above the rhythm of her quickening pulse. Little by little, she faded from the room.

Miniscule thoughts wandered over deep, wide doubts. *Is God real? What if it's all a lie and Rice is locked in a box, six feet under. Forever.*

Breathe. Think of something excellent. Praiseworthy. Good. Reverend Girden had taught her to use Scripture to battle the beast. Jade scrambled to remember, to align her thudding heart with the truth of the Word.

Peace . . . of Jesus . . . guard my heart . . . my mind. Do not have a spirit of fear . . . do not have . . .

The first-grade friend tiptoed past, catching Jade's attention. Stopping, she leaned into the pew, wrinkling her brow. "I'm so glad Asa has Max. He's going to need his daddy." She squeezed Jade's shoulder. "And you too, of course. More than ever now."

"W-what?" Jade's sticky palms stuck to the wooden pew seat. The sanctuary air was thin and hot, burning her lungs. And a cold reality inched down her back.

The woman's light faded. "Asa. Max's son. So sad about Rice."

Jade lurched forward, the burnt amber and purple swirl defiling her. Her heart crashed. Holding down the mounting scream, Jade gave Mama a pained glance before running down the aisle and bursting through the sanctuary doors, losing herself in the light and crisp mountain air.

~

"Your son?" The grandfather clock in the hall chimed ten. Jade threw the bed pillow across the room, aiming at Max. He flinched and ducked. "You have a son? And I don't?"

"I can't talk to you if you keep yelling."

"I'll yell all I want." Jade cupped her hands around her mouth and bent back. "My husband has a son!" She fired over to the dormer windows and shoved one open. "Hey, Begonia Valley Lane, Max Benson has a son, but his wife doesn't!"

Max jerked her away from the screen, into the room. "Stop, you're being stupid."

"Oh, I'm sorry, I thought you were the stupid one in the room. The lying cheater." Jade picked up the pillow and slammed it over his back. "Just like your father."

"I am not like my father."

Jade stared Max down. Her heart was numb. Her thoughts collided. Skin-tightening chills chased feverish sweats. The shades of burnt amber hovered in her mind. "When were you planning on telling me?"

"What do you think I've been doing the past week? Trying to figure out when to tell you. How."

"Coward. You only sleep next to me every night." Except when he fell asleep in the den watching ESPN. Which he'd done a lot since he brought home the news that Rice had died. "How? When?" She crossed her arms. "I want to know."

"Vegas."

"When did you go to Vegas with Rice?"

"The bachelor party. Burl's plane. His girlfriend and Rice went along—"

"You took your ex-fiancée on your bachelor trip?" This wasn't happening.

No to the room. No to the chair under the angled wall. No to the curtains and shades. No to the night cloaking Whisper Hollow. No, no, no.

Max was the man she had pledged to love, honor, cherish. She'd opened her hand and surrendered her heart.

And he, with his sincere golden-brown eyes and kind voice, pledged to her the same. When he kissed her in front of five hundred wedding guests, sealing their deal, he'd pressed his hands into her back, holding her so close the heat of his body fused with hers and for a moment, she couldn't tell where she ended and he began. "I didn't take her on the bachelor trip. I wouldn't . . . But when Burl's girlfriend—you remember her, Kim, the one with the cheerleader voice—found out we were going, she begged to go along. She was Rice's roommate, and they decided to have a girls' weekend. I didn't even see Rice after we landed, Jade. They went one way; we went another. Then Burl decided to break the bachelor weekend rules and hook up with Kim. Rice was kicked out. She pounded on my door, looking for a place to sleep."

"And you let her in? She couldn't get another room? Max, what did you think would happen?"

"Nothing. I thought nothing would happen. I just wanted to go to sleep. But Rice was hungry, so she ordered pizza. We started talking. Watched a movie—"

"Were you drunk?"

Max hung his head, hand gripping the top of the bedpost. "No, we weren't. I fell asleep during the movie. So did Rice. In the same bed. Jade, you have to trust me, I never intended—"

"Why didn't you tell me?" Jade sank to the edge of the chaise. "Now I know why you came home so anxious to reaffirm our past being in the past. A week before our wedding. That's why you met with Reverend Girden, making sure you could go the distance and be a faithful husband. And I bought it. Hook, line, and sinker."

"I tried to convince myself it didn't happen. Rice didn't even speak to me on the flight home."

"Well, that makes it all better, then."

"Jade, I hated myself for it. So did Rice."

"When did you find out about Asa?"

Max's expression darkened. "When he was born."

"Nineteen months ago? You've had nineteen months to tell me?" Jade wished the surreal atmosphere of their room would shatter. She spoke as if Max had simply overdrawn their checking account on a large boy-toy purchase. "We were supposed to be honest with each other, from our wedding on, Max. What happened to that pledge? Is that what the pills have been about?"

"Partly, I guess. I do have a bad back. But Rice wanted it this way, Jade. Me out of her life and his, you not knowing. She felt really bad about betraying you."

"Oh, well then." Jade stood, hurling the pillow to the bed. "I'm so glad you did things Rice's way. And what vows did you make to her before God and man, Max?"

"You think I've liked knowing I had a son?"

Her knees buckled. "I can't do this anymore." She wanted out of his sight, out of his house, away from the day-old scent of his cologne. Snatching her purse from the floor, Jade ran down the hall and down the stairs, bursting out the kitchen door, her bare feet thudding on the cold, paved path to the garage.

Nine

"Daphne, open up." Jade trembled as she pounded on her college roommate's door. Unit 502.

She'd not planned to stop here, but she'd been driving around Chattanooga for several hours, weeping, wailing, sobbing, talking to her windshield, hammering her steering wheel, and finally reaching the end of her ability to process.

"Daphneeeee . . ." She hammered the door with her fists. *Please* . . . Since she'd left Max standing in their bedroom, she'd been a cacophony of emotions—tears, words, cramps, burnt amber swirls, the shimmy of the pickup's wheel under her palm. "Daph!"

If she wasn't home, she'd drive over to Margot's, who was better than nothing, but the longer she'd practiced dentistry, the shorter and sharper her compassion. Taking advice from her hurt, like drilling a tooth without novocaine.

"Jade." Daphne wore a pair of faded orange Vols sweats. Her auburn hair was sleeked back and gathered in a ponytail. Green goop covered her face.

"You look like that and opened the door?" Jade barged past her. "What if I was a Titans football player or Brad Paisley?"

"Actually, I thought it was the guy across the hall. He keeps asking me out." She grabbed Jade's shoulders. "What the heck happened to you?"

"A very bad day, Daphne."

"Is this about your friend Rice's funeral?"

"Ha, if only." Jade walked the length of the loft, stopping at the window to peer toward the lights of Ross's Landing.

She caught her reflection in the glass. Burnt amber and purple swirls dotted her reflection. Her body floated—her hands, her feet, her hair. In the next instant, she didn't recognize her image cast against the darkness. The beating of her heart echoed in the hollow chamber of her soul. She had no beginning, no end. Her thoughts scrambled, reaching for solid ground.

Who stared at her? What was her name? She must have a name. A banging rang in her ears like the call over a canyon. Fear trickled down her spine. Her pulse surged. Who was she? She gripped her hair in her fists.

"Jade, which one?"

She whirled around at the sound of Daphne's voice. "What?" Jade. She was Jade.

"Coffee or tea?" Her best girlfriend peered at her from behind the counter of the loft's kitchen. "Or cocoa. I have cocoa, and cookies. I just bought cookies. I had a hankering for cookies today. This new diet is killing me. My publicity shots are next week and afterward I'm going straight out for a Big Mac. Did you say coffee, tea, or cocoa?"

"W-whichever." She studied her hands, then her reflection. Jade Benson, yes, she was Jade Benson. And Daphne had been her college roommate.

As quickly as the instant came, it faded. But the fear of "when again" teased her heart, wrapped around her ribs, and coated her throat.

"So I told them, 'Look, you hired me to help people with their problems; I'm not going to sensationalize just for ratings.' Our sponsors agreed, and I got a raise."

Jade smiled, or tried to anyway. "So, a raise? Good, good." Sitting on the arm of the couch, she focused on Daphne. Panic, she understood. It gripped her for a few seconds, holding all of her senses captive. But this . . . terrified her. It was as if all of her senses died. She didn't recognize herself.

"Believe you me, I needed it. This loft set me back a pretty penny, and as you can see, I'm still decorating. Okay, I've decided. How about my famous pulling-an-all-nighter coffee and cocoa concoction?"

"Max has a son." The words fell off the edge of Jade's lips and crashed to the floor.

The movement and noise of the kitchen ceased.

Jade stood, because sitting was suffocating. She leaned against the window and hooked her thumbs over her jeans pockets. With every blink, her eyes both burned and watered. Every muscle ached.

"A son?" Daphne came around the kitchen counter, arms folded, watching Jade. The green mask was starting to crack. "You can't be serious. Not Max."

"Rice is the mother." Jade raised her hand to the base of her throat. Her fingers felt around for Paps's praying hands medallion. Old habit. But the medallion was not tied around her neck. It lay at home in a cedar box.

"Rice? No . . ." Daphne pressed her hand over her heart, her eyes were like blue marbles on a golf green. It was hard to take her compassion seriously with her face plastered. "W-when? How? Hasn't she been in California for the last two years?"

"Yes."

"Then how can Max be the father? Did he go out to California on business? Run into her at a convention?"

"The son is nineteen months old. Remember the Vegas bachelor party?"

"Yeah, what about . . . Oh. She went on his bachelor weekend? The one where his friends kidnapped him and flew him out on some guy's plane?" Daphne pulled out a high ladder-back chair from under the counter and sat.

"Yeah, Burl. His girlfriend Kim was Rice's roommate. She and Rice begged to fly out with the guys for their own girls' weekend."

"Oh, Jade."

"According to Max, they split up once they got to the strip. He didn't see Rice again until she came to his room. Burl hooked up with Kim and Rice needed a place to crash."

"And found Max."

Jade slumped to the couch. "My brilliant lawyer husband invited his ex to stay with him." Jade balled her hands into fists and covered her face.

"Were they drunk? Like Ross and Rachel drunk?"

"Not even close." Jade lifted her head. Could she rewind her life a couple of years and start again? "They got pizza, watched a movie, fell asleep in the same bed."

Daphne might have raised her eyebrows, but Jade couldn't tell. "Did he initiate or Rice?"

"I don't know, Daph. Too much information. He didn't say, and I didn't ask. Already the idea of him being with her a week before our wedding haunts my mental eye."

The numbness around Jade began to wear off, giving way to nervous jitters and tired anxiety.

She snatched a tissue from the box on the end table. "He said he tried to convince himself it didn't happen. Rice felt horrible. Blah, blah."

"Didn't she do a reading at your wedding?"

"Yep." Jade blew her nose, wiped her eyes, and wadded up the tissue, looking for the trash. "What happened to your coffee and cocoa concoction?"

"Oh, right." Daphne held out her hand for Jade's tissue ball. "So, what now? How'd you leave it?"

Jade perched on a kitchen counter stool. "I ran out." She started to cry. "What a fool I am."

"Don't go there, Jade." Daphne came around the counter and gripped Jade's arms. "This is all Max. Don't wear his mistake."

"He wants to raise the boy, I'm sure of it." Jade flicked a piece of peeling mask from her friend's chin. "But why do I have to live with his problem? If I learned anything from my mama, from Rice, from June . . . I haven't even told you about June and Rebel."

"What is in the water up in the Hollow?"

"Poison. You know, Daphe, I think I have to live the life I've been handed my own way." The confession released a bit of pressure.

Daphne went around and set out mugs, then opened a bag of Famous Amos cookies. Jade dug her hand inside the bag. She wasn't hungry, but she wanted to believe Max hadn't robbed her of the basic necessities.

"Which means what, Jade? You're going to leave Max?"

"I don't know, Daphne. But I know I can't stay."

Ten

At the smack of the front door, June dropped her cards to the bedspread and glanced at Beryl. Was it Max bringing in his son, or Jade returning from who knows where? According to Max, Jade had left last night and never came home.

June spent the first part of the card game bringing Beryl up to speed on Max, Rice, and the son who wasn't meant to be. But what joy comes from sorrow. Asa was a pure sweetheart and Beryl would love him, simply love him.

And she'd be a grandma too. Before she, well, went back to Prairie City.

Beryl set her cards aside. The pallor of her skin had faded to an ashen tint during the last hour or so. In the middle of a hand, she drifted to sleep. When she was awake, she struggled to concentrate.

By the light in her eyes, June understood her motherly thoughts. *What are we going to do with what we've got here?* Wasn't going to be easy for Max to fix this. The moms would have to lend all their support and wisdom.

"Jade or Max?" June asked.

Beryl lowered her chin as she listened, then pressed her hand to her chest. "Jade." She gazed at June. "It's my Jade-o."

Footsteps thudded on the front stairs followed by a *thump*. Then footsteps down the hall accompanied by a *thump-bump* rhythm.

"Mama?" A few moments later Jade appeared in the room. "Hey, June, I didn't know you were here. Your car's not out front."

"She's in the shop for her annual physical. Ol' Alfred puts her up on the lifts, and—" June smiled at her gynecological reference, but Jade responded with a steely glare. "Alfred drove me over, so I'll need one of y'all to take me home."

"Well, it won't be me. Sorry, June. Mama, you're getting your wish."

"My wish? To kiss Robert Redford before I die?"

"Ooh, didn't you just love him in *The Way We Were*?" June slapped Beryl a tender high five.

"Get packed. We're going to Prairie City."

June glanced at Beryl, then followed her daughter-in-law down the hall. Beryl shuffled slowly along behind her.

"Just like that, you're leaving?" June asked. "Why aren't you at the Blue Umbrella?"

"Lillabeth will open the shop this afternoon. We've been slow this spring, so I don't care if we're only open in the afternoons for a few weeks." Jade tossed a soft leather Italian travel bag onto the bed. One of the wedding gifts June and Rebel had given the kids. "Mama wants to go home, so I'm taking her."

"I thought you were concerned about her living alone." June walked to the center of the room so Jade would have to address her as she moved from dresser to suitcase. At the moment, she was stuffing things randomly into the bag. Underwear, then jeans, then socks, back to underwear again.

"She won't be alone. I'll be with her." Jade stepped around June for the closet. "Mama," she hollered over her shoulder, "your suitcase is in here."

"You don't have to shout, Jade." Beryl eased down to the armchair by the door. "We don't have to go right now. We can wait for you to sort this thing out."

"The train is leaving in an hour. All aboard if you want to go to Prairie City." Jade tossed a couple of pairs of shoes toward the bed. "Max can deal with his own mess. No offense, June."

"Jade, please, you know how much he loves you. He's been looking all over for you this morning. Where were you?"

"Stayed at Daphne's. And if he loved me, he'd have been honest with me. A one-night stand a week before our wedding is bad enough, but having a child—a living, breathing human being—is a whole other universe. He purposefully deceived me." Coats, sweaters, a hat. Jade carried the outerwear to the bed and reached down for the second suitcase. "Mama, are you going to wear your pajamas to Iowa? Because I'm leaving . . . How cold is the end of March, first of April in Iowa? I forget."

"Snows sometimes. Talked to Sharon the other day and she said it'd been downright freezing lately. No sign of spring in the air."

Jade disappeared into the bathroom, returning with a toiletries bag. She peered at June, then Beryl. "Can you help Mama pack? Her suitcase is right there." Jade pointed to the closet door.

"You're not going to even give it a try? Jade, he—"

"Loves me, yeah, June, I know. So you've said, and so did Daphne." Jade tossed the toiletries bag to the bed. "But would someone please explain to me how my husband hides from me his love child with another woman?" Jade smacked her forehead with her fingers. "There's a sentence I never thought I'd say. So, here I am, fat, dumb, and happy, going through life like an ignorant cow. Crying at every miscarriage, sad a few days each month when I realize another month has gone by without the hope of a child. Bearing his burden to have children."

June embraced each word. Jade was right. How did Max not love her enough to tell her? How did *she* not love her enough? Max wanted to protect her, so June had gone along. But deep down, she knew he wanted to protect himself. She recognized that part of herself in him.

So June had done what she'd always done, protected the men in her life. Covering. Denying.

"I'm coming with you." The words came without thought or consideration, but boy, they felt good. Space from Rebel would do her a world of good.

"What?"

"I'm going too." June declared her intention in a tone that let Jade know she'd not be denied.

"What a lovely idea." Beryl shoved up from her chair. "Been wanting a road trip with the girls. Carlisle and I used to have some wild times."

"There's not enough room in the truck for three, June. Mama won't be able to ride sitting up for thirteen hours."

"Jade, I can't make the trip in a day. It'd wear me out. I go to the bathroom every two hours."

"Then we'll stop overnight. But there's still not enough room in the truck."

"I've never even been on a road trip with the girls," June said. "Not even in my sorority days. I was always with my parents or my boyfriend's parents."

"Ladies, still, *not* enough room in the truck."

"You can't take Beryl to Iowa in your truck, Jade."

Jade snatched a cedar box from the top of her dresser. Lifting the lid, she pulled out a leather cord with a trinket dangling from the end and tied it around her neck. June recognized the praying hands medallion. When June first met Jade, she never saw the girl without it.

"Why not?" Jade fingered the medallion, eyes darting about the room. "I can do whatever I want. Seems everyone else can come and go as they please, but not good ol' Jade?"

"The truck is loud and smelly, not to mention uncomfortable. There's no radio. Last time I was in the passenger seat, the heat blew cold air and foam fell from the ceiling."

Jade's eyes peered into June's, and for a split second, she felt all the pain and hurt her son had inflicted on such an undeserving woman.

Oh Max, he was *her* son.

"We can take my car," June said, slow and soft.

"I'm not waiting for Alfred." Jade jerked open another dresser drawer, but instead of removing clothes to pack, she merely shoved them around. "I just need . . ." Her voice shattered. "To go . . . get . . . away . . . breathe . . . think . . ." Sobs swept over her as she slammed the drawer shut. Shaking as the first sob rolled off her shoulders and down her back and legs, Jade sank to the floor. "He has a son."

"Oh, Jade . . ." But before June reached her, Beryl came around the foot of the bed. June faded back, watching with watery eyes. Jade probably didn't want her comfort right now anyway. She was blood kin to the enemy.

A second wave of sobs collapsed Jade into a heap with her forehead against the carpet. "Not my son, his son." She pounded her fist. "*His* son."

"My baby." Beryl eased down next to Jade and smoothed her hand over her daughter's back, then gathered her sleek, dark hair into her hands.

June burned with the fire of guilt and shame, fueled by sympathy and compassion. Oh, Max, he'd wounded her so deeply. Lovely, lovely Jade.

Beryl cradled Jade's head against her leg, humming softly, finally singing low and slow, "Hush, little baby, don't say a word . . ."

She hit a sour note. June jerked, covering her mouth. Beryl kept on, hitting sour note after sour note. When she rounded the chorus a second time, Jade sat up, tucking her hair behind her ears, and wiped her face with the back of her hand.

"I think you've cured me, Mama."

"My third husband Gus used to say, 'Let Beryl sing; she'll drive everyone's blues away with laughter.'"

But June caught the watery sheen in Beryl's eyes. The off-key melody was for her heart as much as Jade's.

"Shall we go on a road trip, ladies? I have the perfect road trip car." Mercy, June had not driven the thing in years, but Alfred kept the car tuned and ready to go.

"All I know is I'm going." Jade shoved her suitcases around, assessing her inventory. "I'm going. I've got to get out of here. Ride through the plains with the truck windows down."

"Can you be ready to go by noon?" June checked her watch. It was eleven o'clock now. She'd have to call Alfred . . . Call Constance to get her going on the packing. Stop by the bank for cash.

Jade glanced at Mama. "What do you say?"

"What do *you* say?"

For a slow moment, Jade hesitated and June feared she'd change her mind. Either way, she'd take Beryl home. The idea of a road trip was like cold water to her hot, dry soul. "See you in two hours?" June backed toward the door.

"I have some stuff to do for the shop. Make it three hours. Meet at one p.m. In the alley behind the Blue Umbrella."

~

Max was standing on the porch when Jade carried out the first load of luggage to her truck. "Where are you going?"

"Where's your son?" She stepped around him, heading for the garage. She'd picked up a thread of boldness while packing.

"With Lorelai. I wanted to make sure you were okay with me bringing him home, but apparently you aren't going to be here." His slip-skip gait echoed behind her. "I've been trying to call you."

"I've been busy." Jade hoisted her bags into the bed of the truck.

"Where are you going, Jade?"

"You don't tell me things, so I don't have to tell you things. We can add this trip to our don't-ask-about-the-past-and-don't-tell policy." Her soul was on the edge, and she didn't care if she hurt him a little. Jade glanced at him as he stood in the angled light of the mid-morning sun. But only a little bit.

His weary, dark eyes seemed lost in their sockets, perched just above his unshaven cheeks. But it was his countenance that struck her the most—as if he'd met the blunt end of a Louisville Slugger.

"You're proving me right, Jade. If I'd told you about Asa, we'd be right here, right where we are now."

"We're here because you didn't tell me. Not because you did."

"And you're mad." Max stepped toward her. The breeze shook the budding tree limbs against the side of the garage.

"You chose Rice over me." Jade rubbed the tip of her nose and gazed up at the garage's wide beams. In its heyday, the structure had been a carriage house. "When I met you, Max, I said, 'Now there's one of the good ones, a man you can trust, Jade. He won't let you down. Just do your best to live up to him.'"

"You *can* trust me, Jade. This is about one night gone bad with unbelievable repercussions."

"Repercussions you hid from me." She dipped her shoulder to step around him. Mama waited inside and Jade still had to carry out her luggage. "If you'd have come home from Vegas and told me what happened, sure I would've been upset. Mad. Hurt. But I would've forgiven you."

Max walked alongside her. "And if I came to you and said Rice was pregnant?"

"It would've killed me, but I would've known about that night."

"So, if I'd known how it all played out in your head, I could've done it exactly the way you wanted. Well, I'm sorry, I played it out in my head and did what I thought was best."

"For you. What was best for you."

"I see, you're the saint and I'm the jerk?"

"Yes, you're the jerk." Jade stopped short, whirling to face him. "An arrogant jerk. Don't you dare put any of this on me."

"You're running away, overreacting."

"Overreacting? You purposefully hide your son from me, and I'm overreacting? No, Max, no. You overacted when you hid your son from me." Jade stabbed his chest with her fingers. "You should've included me from the beginning. I can walk the crooked road with you, Max. I can help bear your burdens, unless you lie to me. The only reason I know about any of this is because a woman tragically died." Her tone spiked with emotion. "When were you going to tell me? When Asa showed up on our doorstep as a teenager? On your deathbed?"

"I wanted to tell you. The timing never seemed right."

"For a brilliant man, you can be so unaware. Do you not know me?" She started for the door, then backed up. "You want to know the worst part, Max? You denied your son."

"I supported him."

"With money? Well, bully for you. Aren't you a stand-up guy? And I never saw any child support category when we went over our budget. Where'd you hide the money, Max?" She deflated. "The lies just keep on coming. Asa deserves so much better."

"Stay and make sure he gets it." His taunting didn't linger with her.

"I'm leaving." She backed away from him. "I need space, and you need to grow up and be the dad he needs."

"Where are you going? When will you be back?"

"I'm taking Mama home. And I don't know." Jade walked toward the door again. She liked the weight of the praying hands at the base of her throat. "Your mom is going with us."

"Mom? In a car for thirteen hours?"

"She volunteered to go." Max's presence tapped at the weak walls of Jade's heart. *Don't break down now, Jade-o. Hold it together. Get some distance, some perspective.* "Apparently, she has the perfect road trip car, or so she says."

Max nodded, a small grin rising. "She does."

Jade backed toward the house. "I need to get Mama's luggage."

"What about the Blue Umbrella? The construction of the Blue Two? Who's going to deal with all of that?"

Jade paused on the porch, holding the screen door open. "Kip and Tom will handle the Blue Two. Lillabeth, the shop here."

He studied her for a moment, then gazed into the sunlight.

"Look, I know you want me to just push past all this, Max, put my oar in the rapids and row with you. But I can't." Jade swung the screen door gently to and fro. "As much I want to be wise enough, spiritual enough, and healed enough, I'm not. All I know is you have a son and I have an empty womb. You share something with another woman I may never share with you. And I need space. Time apart."

"Babe, if I could change the past I would, but I can't. Don't give up on me, on us. Asa needs you. I need you, Jade. I love you. I always have. Nothing's changed for me."

"But don't you see, Max?" Her resolve dropped its final anchor. "Everything's changed for me."

Eleven

A pale pink Cadillac. June leaned against the trunk of an enormous, rectangle, ancient-looking Caddy, her legs crossed at the ankles, her arms out to her sides.

She wore, no kidding, a pair of shiny blue capris, white Keds, a cashmere sweater with a scarf tied around her neck, and bug-eye sunglasses. Jade could've sworn she'd seen the same getup on the cover of a '60s *Vogue*.

"June, this is your road trip vehicle?" Jade clapped the truck door shut and approached the car. "What is it?"

"Darling, you're looking at a '66 Fleetwood Eldorado with stereo, power steering, and heated seats. Doesn't it just scream road trip?" June spread her arms over the vehicle like a *Price Is Right* model. "Big, comfortable—"

"Does Al Gore know you own this thing?"

"We can even bundle up and drive with the top down for a while." June shaded her eyes and peered toward the sun.

"This is a land yacht, June. I can't drive this thing. I'd need a captain's license."

"Aren't you funny. Beryl, what do you think? Doesn't it take you back?" June smacked the side of the car. June had missed her calling. Interior designer? Wife of a prominent lawyer? Committee chair? No. Used car salesman. Absolutely.

"I think it's *swell*." Yes, the hippie uttered the word "swell."

"I'm in the twilight zone." Jade dropped the truck's gate and tugged out the first round of luggage. Mama arrived in Whisper Hollow with one suitcase and was leaving with three. She'd actually *shopped* with June a few times.

"Beryl, you can ride shotgun." June walked around to the front of the car. "I brought toques for us, extra coats and blankets. I know it feels springy today, but I'm betting it's still right chilly out on the open road." June held up the outerwear. "This'll be fun, fun, fun."

Fun, fun, fun? June was way overdoing it. Jade checked with Mama. "Are you okay to ride with the top down?"

"Did I tell you the seats were heated?" June plopped a wool cap on Mama's head.

"So Mama's butt will be warm. What about the rest of her?" Jade set the first two pieces of luggage by the Caddy's trunk. "Mama, are you okay to ride with the top down? And, June, don't say a word." The gray tint to Mama's skin had remained, even in the midst of a road trip and home-going excitement.

"Wouldn't be a road trip otherwise." Mama stood still as June threaded her arms through the sleeves of a ski jacket. "I remember when I first heard of heated seats. Our high school principal had an Eldorado, and how he afforded it was the scandal of Prairie City."

"This model was the first of its kind to have heated seats. And she's in mint condition. Jade, queen of vintage, you should be thrilled." June opened the driver's door and reached inside. A grinding motor sounded as the top shimmied and rattled opened, stretching toward the blue sky before settling in its "bed" behind the backseat.

Jade examined the ride. Deep, wide white leather seats, a skinny steering wheel, and a . . . "A Garmin?" She glanced at June. "Was that standard in the '66 Cadillacs too?"

"Certain modifications apply. We don't want to get lost, do we?"

"We won't get lost. I've driven to Iowa a dozen times and Mama was a teamster, for crying out loud."

"Well, there you go, sugar. All the bases are covered." June patted the Cadillac. "Perfect road trip car or I'm not June Benson."

"You pay for half the gas."

"Naturally."

Jade peered over the door toward the in-dash radio. "And Mama chooses the music."

"Fine by me." June held out her hands. "I brought my entire '60s collection." She appeared serious about having a fun, fun, fun road trip. Mama looked like a stuffed tick bundled up in red and brown ski gear.

Jade hauled the rest of their bags from the truck to the Caddy. The space was huge.

"Good grief, we could fit a Smart car in here. Or, as the case may be, most of June's luggage." Jade shoved suitcases around, making room for Mama's and hers. "Gee, June, did you leaving anything back at the house?"

"Never you mind. And would you stop complaining?"

Jade clapped the truck closed. Seeing Max earlier had set her on edge, teetering, feeling alone and abandoned.

"Jade-o, you ready?" Mama waited by the passenger door, her braids slinking out from under her wool cap, her arms buoyed out at her side.

"Let me leave the truck key for Lillabeth." Jade rolled up the driver's side window on the truck, then headed for the shop's back door.

Jade paused when she passed through the dark shop. Since opening the

Blue Umbrella four years ago, the shop had never been closed and dark in the middle of the day. The quietness screamed to Jade that things were changing. She'd come to Whisper Hollow from her Chattanooga marketing job with one idea in mind: dream dreams, open her own place. Find the balance between career and loving life.

Falling in love with Max so quickly was beyond her wildest imagination. Not a thought in her universe. She only wanted to survive her first year in business. But the God who loved her before she loved Him had already put her destiny into motion.

So, God-who-loved-her, how did she end up with a cheating husband and a marriage based on lies? *Is this Your best plan?*

The day she walked down the aisle with so much love in her heart for Max, pledging her heart to him, God knew what Max had done, and that a child had been conceived.

Jade resisted the impulse to run up the loft stairs, lock the door, and never come out. Let June road trip with Mama. Jade had been happy when she lived in the loft, running the shop, having girls' weekends with Daphne and Margot, dreaming of a "one day" love.

Instead, she stood in the dark, quiet shop, broken.

Stirring herself, Jade moved into the office, not bothering with the light, and tossed the truck keys to the desk. She'd called Lillabeth from Daphne's to let her know the plan. She'd e-mail more details from the road.

With the keys delivered there was nothing left to do but just go. Get on the road. Leave . . .

Max darkened the doorway. "Oh my gosh." Her heart jumped. "What are you doing in here?"

"I couldn't let you go away mad, hurt." He moved from the shadows, and into the pale yellow falling through the office window. He'd showered and changed into jeans and a polo. His dark hair moved freely over his forehead, accenting his hazel eyes.

"Don't, Max." She backed away. If he reached for her . . . "Can't you just give me a bit of space?"

"Space? From me?" He stepped close enough to brush the back of his fingers against her cheek. "Please stay."

Why was he doing this? Another second, she'd shatter and crumble. But she couldn't let him get away with it, could she? Look at what acquiescing had done to June's life.

"I'll call in a few days." She drew herself tight to move around him and exit the office.

"Jade, you *can* trust me." He reached for her arm. "I'm not Dustin."

"Dustin? Wow, did you just pull his name out of the air or have you been mulling over it for a while?" Jade scoffed. "You think I'm upset at you because my teenage husband walked out on me? You want to blame my disgust at your infidelity on Dustin Colter?" She leaned into him. "You spoke *wedding vows*, Max, knowing you'd already broken them." Her heels thudded against the hardwood as she walked away.

"I've never broken my wedding vows to you, Jade. Never."

Jade paused, turning to him. "Yes, you did. Once you knew about Asa, you conspired to hide your life from me. That breaks your vow to love, honor, and cherish."

Max held up his hands and trailed her out to the pink Caddy. When he got to the car, he complimented the priceless antique and then kissed his mother good-bye. When he went to hug Beryl, Jade noticed the wet sheen in his eyes. "Get well, okay?"

Mama held her hands against his face. "Thank you for last night."

"My pleasure."

"Last night? What happened last night, Mama?"

"That's between me and my son-in-law." Mama held on to June as she maneuvered into the passenger seat.

"What did you—"

Max tugged Jade into his arms and kissed her, stealing her words, cooling her anger, warming her cold heart. She couldn't help herself. She kissed him back, melting into him as her defenses crumbled. Being loved by Max, being desired by him, left her both weak and strong.

June blasted the car horn. "The road awaits. Let's go."

"See you." Jade pushed away from Max softly, brushing her hand over his chest.

He held on to her fingers. "Do you love me?"

"Max—"

"Jade, tell me, do you love me?"

"Love can't fix betrayal, Max." She crawled into the middle of the Caddy's backseat.

Max watched by the car. "Be careful, Mom, you have my precious cargo. Any message for Dad?"

"Yeah, tell him to keep his britches on." And she gunned the gas.

Jade yelped as the big Caddy fired down the alley. Oh, this was going to be a fun, fun, fun trip.

"Mercy," June uttered, gripping the wheel, mashing the brake as the car eased beyond the Stop sign. "I forgot this thing has a mind of its own."

"June, are you sure you can handle this beast?"

"Sit back and watch. I learned to drive in an Oldsmobile twice this size."

"How is that possible?"

June was gentler with the gas this time, as she turned left toward Main Street.

Turning around, Jade rose up on her knees. Max was at the end of the alley, squinting in the afternoon sun, his shirttail lifting in the breeze, his hand raised in the air.

Jade lifted her hand, responding to his silent good-bye.

~

For June, the excitement and anticipation of seeing Whisper Hollow in the Caddy's rearview was long gone. And they weren't even out of Tennessee yet.

"Are we there yet?" June viewed Jade through the mirror.

"You're driving, you tell me. What's Mr. Garmin telling you?"

"Two down, twelve to go." June smacked the side of the small box. "Tell the truth now, we're nearly there."

What was she thinking? She hated road trips. When she told Jade she wanted in on this trip to Iowa—she'd been to Paris, but not Prairie City—her daughter-in-law tried to warn her about a thirteen-hour road trip, but no, June had to surrender to the moment. She had visions of laughter and music while cruising "the strip" in her pink Cadillac. Bruce Springsteen, where was he when she needed him?

But the wind was noisy, not to mention cold. The sun's warmth had little impact while going seventy miles an hour. The engine was sound, but not quiet and humming like her Lexus. Beryl dozed against the window, and in the back, Jade stared blankly at the passing road signs.

Now what? June was about to go to sleep at the wheel when Jade appeared on her right shoulder. Thank goodness. Conversation.

"What did Rebel say when you told him you were leaving?"

"I didn't tell him." She picked up her cell. "He's not bothered to call me in days." June tucked her phone back into the Caddy's ashtray. "Truth is, now that I've left him, I feel out of sorts. Maybe I acted too hastily."

"You acted too late if you ask me," Beryl said. "June, if he cheated on you when you were home, what's he going to do now?"

June's breakfast churned in her cramping stomach. Dear Lord, help her. She still loved him.

"Okay, here's our first road trip rule." Jade held up her finger in between June and Beryl. "No more talk of men. This is girls only."

"All right, I can live with that. Good thinking, Jade." June honked the horn as she passed an 18-wheeler, pressing the gas, flying down the highway at a whopping seventy-two miles per hour. Wild and crazy was uncharted territory for her, but she was desperate to give it a go.

"I need a potty break," Beryl said, still doing a grand imitation of—what was it Jade called her—a tick about to pop?

Yet Beryl was smiling. And the sun and wind had put a bloom on her sallow cheeks.

"Jade, what about you?" June rose up to peek at Jade through the rearview. She sat hunched up with the scarf around the lower half of her face. "Ready for a break?"

"Whatever Mama needs."

"Next exit then." The Caddy floated down the highway toward the next exit.

Beryl turned on the radio and upped the volume. The Beatles joined the souls in the car, "I do appreciate you being 'round . . ."

"I had the biggest crush on Paul McCartney," June said above the wind. "You mentioned Robert Redford, Beryl, but—"

"I hung out with George Harrison in San Fran the summer of '67. He came by the Haight."

"My stars." June gasped. The car swerved a bit. "You met *George Harrison*?"

"We weren't best friends, but I said hi to him and he winked, 'Beryl, right?' He was with Patty Boyd in those days."

"Who else, Beryl? Who else did you meet?" June sat up straight as if braced for a race, gripping the wheel.

"Oh goodness . . . Grace Slick, the Dead, Bob Dylan, Joplin. And a bunch of people you never heard of, dead hippies now, most of them."

"Beryl, what a life. So much adventure."

"My cousin Marilyn dated the stage manager at the Fillmore, so we had passes to all the good shows. But in them days, Dylan and the like were *our* troubadours, *our* pied pipers. No one ever heard of them. There was no such thing as superstars."

"I was still listening to The Lettermen . . ." For a second, June peeked back at her life, trying to see the roads not taken. Her mind's eye squeezed shut. What good would pretending do? She'd lived the life she chose. She'd not have Max otherwise.

"Magical days. The world is so different. We were so naive. But we thought we had all the answers. We were going to change the world."

"You were beyond naive." Jade appeared on June's right again, tapping Beryl's shoulder. "Tell her about Charles Manson."

"What?" June began to veer off the road, the tires skidding along in the berm. "*The* Charles Manson?" Her heart murmured just imagining meeting him.

"One and the same. Tell her how you hung out with a mass murderer, Mama." Jade poked Beryl in the arm again.

"I didn't know he was *the* Charles Manson. He was just a creepy man with a lot of skinny, vacant-eyed girls following him."

"How did you meet him?"

"At a party. There was always a party at the Haight. He liked to hang around musicians, fancied himself as one. But I never saw the fascination with him." She shivered. "I did a lot of wild, stupid things, and it's hair-raising to see how close I came to danger. Now I know my parents' prayers covered me in my youth."

"Beryl." June thumped the steering wheel. "Charles Manson . . . mercy."

"He smelled. And had this sneaky, evil grin. One of the girls Marilyn and I ran around with thought he was the living end. Her father came for her just in time. Other girls weren't so fortunate. Bunch of runaways showing up in San Francisco with no money, no place to live. The vultures quickly snapped them up, getting the girls on drugs, abusing them. Men like Manson were everywhere."

"Do you regret any of it, Beryl?"

"I wish I'd spent more time with my kids." She stared out her window without even a peek at Jade. "What about you, June? Any regrets?"

"Look there, our exit." June swerved the big car toward the ramp, pressing hard on the brake.

"Come on, June. Girls' trip. Got to confess a regret."

"I wish I hadn't let my mother talk me into yellow bridesmaids' dresses." A snort slipped through her nose. "With the hairstyle of the day, my bridal party looked like a bunch of bouffant canaries."

"Bouffant canaries? That's the worst you got?" Beryl's laugh sounded like tiny bells. "That has to be right up there with meeting Charles Manson."

June merged onto the exit ramp, slowing the Caddy down in time to stop for the light. "Maybe worse."

Twelve

The Tennessee sun surrendered to Kentucky clouds by mid-afternoon. An icy chill filled the Caddy, and on the last stop, Jade insisted on raising the top.

After June talked them into an outlet mall excursion near Nashville, Jade took over driving, hoping to make up time by pushing the speed limit. Between Mama's bathroom stops and June's detour, they'd lost a good bit of the driving day.

In the backseat June dozed, exhausted from speed shopping. She purchased enough for a fourth suitcase. Mama gazed out the passenger window with a contemplative expression, freed from the ski gear.

Was she thinking of home? Of dying? In the last thirty minutes, pressure started mounting in Jade's spirit to ask Mama if she was ready to die, to stand before God. But finding the words proved difficult. New in her faith in Christ,

Jade hadn't spent much time in the witness chair. Mama seemed like a good place to start. Or not.

In the months Mama had lived with them in Whisper Hollow, she'd attended church without complaint. Sang along in worship. Followed Reverend Girden's Scripture reading with a pew Bible opened in her lap.

But she'd never confessed in Jade's hearing, "Jesus is my Lord."

Jade squirmed, inhaled, lowered the volume on the radio. *So, Mama, I was wondering if . . .*

"Dairy Queen. Look. Next exit." Mama rapped the window. Knuckle-sized imprints dotted the glass. "Paducah, Kentucky. Paducah. Pa-du-*cah*. Isn't that a funny word? Where are you from, friend? Pa-du-*cah*."

"Did I hear Dairy Queen?" June's sleepy face peered over the seat. "I haven't been to one in so long. Let's stop. Road trip food."

"Dairy Queen it is." Jade took the exit, settling her question and courage back in the box . . . for now.

The Dairy Queen was connected to a Subway, which was tucked inside a gas station. Jade filled the Caddy's gas tank while June walked Mama inside. Staring toward the western horizon and the golden hue of the traveling sun, the fragrance of the air reminded Jade of Prairie City.

It would be good to step into Granny's place. Home. Jade wondered what Max might be doing. Working? Moving in his son? She looked away from the mental image of her husband cradling the towheaded boy.

While the gas pumped, Jade pulled her phone from her jeans pocket. If she dialed him, then what? He'd start up again with how he needed and wanted her home.

Funny, in the midst of all of this, his apology and regret, he never once asked her what she needed or how all of this made her feel. She'd expressed herself, but he never reached out to her heart. What were best friends for otherwise?

With a glance back at the DQ, Jade spotted June settling Mama at a table.

Even sitting in the car wore her out. For Jade, anxiety perched on the ledge of her soul most of the afternoon, looking for a moment to jump in and gum up her peace.

The balance was precarious.

Dialing the Blue Umbrella, Jade talked with Lillabeth, ignoring the pulsing twinge in her belly. All was well at the shop. A few new consignments had come in. Lillabeth sold the miniature tea set and the set of leather-bound first editions. On Saturday, Dani Olsen agreed to cover the shop so Lillabeth could check out an estate sale in Johnson City.

"Remind me to give you a raise."

"Jade, give me a raise."

"Done." The pump clicked off. Jade lifted the nozzle and replaced it. "How much do you think you'll need for the estate sale?"

"I don't know . . . it's mostly clothes and jewelry."

"I'll budget a thousand. Call me if you find anything above and beyond."

Jade wound up the call with Lillabeth, tucking the gas receipt in her pocket. While she'd insisted June pay for some of the gas, Jade refused her help at the last stop. This trip was her gift to Mama.

With a fast glance back at the Diary Queen, seeing Mama and June talking at a table, Jade moved toward the end of the pump island and stared west into the setting sun. The cold, sharp air refreshed her worn, dull thoughts. She inhaled deep and exhaled long.

On impulse, she dialed Daphne. She was on the air, but sometimes . . .

"Hey, just a sec . . . Linda, I'm up against a break, so hang on the line and we'll see how we can help you with your relationship when we come back from the break at the top of the hour. This is the *Daphne Delaney Show*." Jade heard the commercial roll in the background, then Daphne's voice soothing her ear. "Jade, hey, how are you?"

"Standing. I'm taking Mama to Iowa. With June."

"With June? How'd that happen?"

"She wanted to go and she had the road trip car, a honking big pink Cadillac."

"Are you holding up okay?" Daphne asked.

"Still feels kind of surreal. How could he have been so deceitful, Daphne?"

"You've weathered some tough storms, girl. You'll get through this one."

Jade walked to the edge of the pump banks, her heart too sad for the lovely bluegrass evening. She reached for the medallion resting at the base of her neck. The first wave of purple panic sloshed around her feet.

"I don't want to *weather* another storm. When I married Max, the storms were supposed to end. How do I deserve this? Who have I made mad? What sin have I committed that prevents me from happiness?"

"You don't believe in karma, Jade, so don't go there. Trust in your faith. I knew you before you met Jesus and I see how much you've changed." Daphne didn't believe in Jesus, but she understood how to tap into a person's faith system. It's what made her a great psychiatrist. What won her the radio show.

"I just can't get past the idea of Max and Rice, Daph. I try, but there's a constant ache in my chest. I can't just chalk it up to one stupid night in Vegas. What happened in Vegas didn't stay in Vegas. It came alive in the bright eyes of a little boy."

"Are you struggling with panic again? Have you tried the visualizing techniques I gave you?"

"I close my eyes to imagine something beautiful, peaceful, and what do I see? Max making love to his ex-fiancée." Jade set her foot in a pothole on the edge of the pavement.

"Picture yourself forgiving him and—"

"Thirty seconds, Daphne."

"Looking past that one night. I need to go in a few . . . Hey, want to call the show?"

"Only if I can say Max's and Rice's names."

"That's my girl, moving right past the pain into revenge. Okay, quick, do this for me. Focus on a memory or place, on something beautiful."

Jade faced the warm twilight hovering over the glossy horizon.

"Are you in a good place?"

"Yes." It's what Daphne wanted to hear.

"Look deep, past the moment, past the imagery, and into the future. What do you see, Jade? Where are you and Max in a year?"

Jade narrowed her eyes, straining to see her life beyond the thin line where heaven touched earth, where the amber lights of the highway twinkled like fallen stars.

"Five seconds."

"Jade, what do you see?"

"I don't see anything, Daphne. I don't see anything."

June suggested a hotel in Paducah for the night. After the chocolate shake and burgers at the DQ, Beryl looked tired and June felt like a fading flower at the end of a long, hot summer.

She'd expected to field protests from Jade, who seemed determined to cover more road before stopping, but she'd readily agreed.

To June, Jade looked tired beyond sleeplessness. Her movements reflected her restlessness. One moment she was calm, smiling, the next fidgeting and distracted with a yearning in her eyes.

June realized she brought too much luggage. Dragging her three over-stuffed Vuitton bags down the long hall to room 315 aggravated and enflamed her tennis elbow.

When she tried to hoist her tote bag onto the luggage rack, pain fired down her arm.

"June, you all right?" Beryl watched from her bed. The old gals were bunking together while young Jade booked her own room.

"Hurt my arm. Old tennis injury." She tried to laugh, but pain tightened up her arm. "I can't raise it above my waist." Sitting on the side of the bed, June massaged her elbow and upper arm. Not anticipating this, she'd left her elbow brace at home.

"Can I do something for you?"

June laughed low, mashing her hair with her good hand. "The ride in the Caddy . . . I wanted to wash the road out of my hair, but I can't lift my arm." She tried to make a fist. "Or open a shampoo bottle."

"It's okay to ask for help, you know." Beryl headed into the bathroom. "Once in a while, sit back, kick your shoes off, relax, let someone else have a chance to serve you, June."

June swallowed two Tylenol gelcaps with a sip from her water bottle. "You mean? Oh, no, Beryl, I couldn't."

"Why not? You let the women at the Whisper Hollow Suds and Bucket wash your hair."

June laughed. "Whisper Hollow Style-n-Set. Suds and bucket. Wait until I tell Barbara Jean."

"Please, let me do something nice for you." Beryl flipped on the bathroom light. "Got us fancy bottles of shampoo and conditioner right here."

June stood in the bathroom doorway. "A good hair washing would be lovely."

"Good, let's just drop this here . . ." Beryl tucked the folded hotel towel against the tub.

"Beryl, are you afraid to die?" June reached for her arm.

"Terrified." Beryl took a second towel from the rack.

"Do you believe, Beryl? In Jesus? In heaven?"

"I'm considering my options." She laughed, but it didn't resonate with merriment. "It's just, well . . . I think I'll feel real stupid if I decide Jesus is all He claimed to be after living my entire life running in the opposite direction."

June rubbed her elbow, gazing at the small square tile floor. "I've believed my whole life and still, in some ways, ran in the opposite direction."

"Then tell me, is He true? The real deal?"

"Yes, Beryl, He is true." June glanced at her friend. "The real deal. But don't look to me and Reb as stellar examples of a Christian life. Look to Jesus."

"Here. Kneel down." Beryl motioned to the bathtub.

June started to bend her knees, but an odd bubble buoyed in her chest. "Beryl, are you sure? You don't have to wash my hair."

"And hear about road grime the rest of the trip?" Beryl sat on the toilet, leaned over the tub, and started the water. She made a pallet with the towels. "Now, be a good Christian and kneel."

"Clean hair . . ." After a second of hesitation, June knelt on the towels. "This feels so awkward."

Beryl gently guided June's head under the water. "Letting folks help makes us vulnerable."

"I suppose." The warm water cascaded over June's scalp. Relaxing chills ran down her back. She closed her eyes. "Thank you, Beryl."

"I don't have many credits of good deeds to my name." Beryl's hands gently massaged the water through June's hair. "But I've washed hair and backs, even feet in my day."

The tension eased out of June's neck and shoulders. Even the throb in her arm lost some of its grip. The shampoo was soft and silky against her scalp.

"Rebel ever wash your hair?"

June shook her head, buttoning her lips, holding a sob prisoner.

"Harlan, my first husband, loved to wash my hair for me." The tenor of Beryl's soft laugh was the kind that came with reminiscing. "I can't remember why he washed my hair for the first time, but hoo boy, it led to some passionate lovemaking."

June peeked under the water cascading over her face. "Don't get any ideas."

Now Beryl laugh-laughed. "Never did swing that way. Even in my wildest days."

June faced down again, her emotions waxing over her thoughts. Maybe she'd lived her own way for the last forty years, but she didn't have to spend the last decades of her life doing the same. She wasn't too old for some kind of Lord's work. Beryl didn't claim many good deeds. June was quite sure she couldn't either.

"I've always known about Reb, Beryl. He's a good man. A loving father. A good man."

"Are you telling me or yourself?" Beryl rinsed her hair, then shampooed again, humming softly.

"I've cried a lot of tears over him. Behind closed bedroom doors, under the cascade of a hot shower, while sitting in a dark garage bay."

As Beryl's fingers massaged June's scalp, her song grew louder. Sharper. The notes flat and sour, but lively. Lyrics whispered from her lips. "I'm gonna wash that man right out of my hair, I'm gonna wash that man right out of my hair . . ."

What in the world . . . June peered at her through the edge of her elbow. "What *did* you do with the money your mama gave you for singing lessons?"

"Spent it all on cigarettes."

A snort slipped through June's nose.

"I'm gonna wash that man right out of my hair," Beryl sang, rinsing June's hair. "Get the picture, Junie?"

She snickered, then let go a good laugh. "If only we were on an island in the South Pacific."

"I'm gonna wash that man right out of my hair . . ." Beryl shut off the water, squeezed June's hair, and handed her a towel. "I'm gonna wash that man right out of my hair . . ."

"And send him on his way." June turbaned her head with the thick hotel towel and did a jig into the bedroom. "I'm gonna wash that man right out of my hair." She spun in the middle of the room. "And send him on his way."

Truth or dare? June didn't know, but the lyrics sure felt good.

Thirteen

Eleven o'clock. Jade couldn't sleep even though her eyes and her thoughts drifted along under a permanent fog.

For the tenth time in the last few minutes, she wondered what Max was doing but kept her iPhone on the far desk so she wouldn't reach for it on impulse and call him.

They needed time apart. Space. She'd insisted. And Jade needed to pretend he was in Whisper Hollow pining for her.

Jade kicked off the covers. The boxy room was hot and claustrophobic. She'd adjusted the thermostat because the air had been chilly; now she roasted like a pig on a spit.

For the last hour she surfed the channels, bored with the same-old-same-old out of Hollywood. Was every producer or writer an overgrown geeky teenager?

She clicked off the television and tossed the remote to the end table.

Mama and June had been quiet for a while. Earlier she thought she heard them singing, but when she pressed her ear to the wall, she didn't hear Mama's pitchy melody and decided it must have been a movie.

Sigh. Now what? She had to get out of the room. Changing into her jeans and top, Jade grabbed her coat and purse and jerked open the door.

The reception desk clerk lifted his head as she passed. "Heading out?"

"Heading somewhere." Please, God, let her be heading somewhere.

Firing up the Caddy, Jade revved the engine, cranked the radio, powered the top down, and laughed with a glance toward heaven when Springsteen came over the speaker singing, "I love you for your pink Cadillac, crushed velvet seats . . ."

Divine intervention.

Springsteen's voice picked up her emotions and carried Jade back to Prairie City, Dustin Colter, and the magic of first love. Now, at thirty-one, it all seemed like a dream. Even the bad times waxed good.

She cruised the pink "boat" down Hinkleville Road, aiming toward what she hoped was the Ohio River. The midnight sky was speckled with light.

Jade sang along with Bruce, "In your pink Cadillac, in your pink Cadillac," drumming against the wheel. When her phone rang from her hip pocket, she turned down the radio to answer, and took the Y in the road.

"Hey." Max's voice filled her with warm familiarity. He sounded tired and burdened.

"Hey." On first impulse, she wanted to ask what was wrong, share in his load. But he'd done this to himself. She'd learned from Daphne over the years that people need to feel the weight of their actions and consequences. Pain invokes change.

"Y'all haven't killed each other yet?" he said after the moment of silence.

"Our mamas are having a great time."

Jade rounded a corner and arrived in a dark downtown Paducah neighborhood. Maybe she should turn around? How'd she get on this one-way street?

"Lorelai and Gus were here tonight, and—"

"Max, please. For now, I don't want to know. I want to live, for a few days, in a pretend world where my husband is faithful and honest. Where he doesn't have a firstborn son without me. Because in my real world, none of that is true. In the real world, my mama is dying. In the real world, I have a shop with a big hole as the front door."

"So I can't to talk to you? My wife?"

"Max, you're doing it again. Putting the success of us going forward on me. You're upset, so you want to talk to me. Pardon me, but I don't want to hear it. Sheesh, Max, how did you ever manage to keep Asa a secret for the last year and a half, dear?"

"It wasn't easy. Do you want me to say it? I was a jerk. A world-class jerk. Someone hand me the trophy."

"Check Rebel's office. I think it's in there." Either from the cold or the confrontation, Jade wasn't sure, but her legs began to tremble. The streetlights blended with the burnt amber glow firing up in her mind. Purple colored her emotions, and the Paducah streets began to narrow. A veil of anxiety eased down on her head. Weight from the unknown settled on her next heartbeat. She gripped the Caddy wheel tighter.

"You're making me pay for what Dad did to Mom."

"Now that's laughable. First you blame Dustin, now you blame your dad. No, Max." Jade held her phone right up to her lips. "I blame you. This. Is. All. You."

"Stop screaming."

"And stop trying to manipulate me into coming home, deflecting the fact that you brought this on." The trembling worsened. Jade whipped the car into a parallel slot next to a park.

"Excuse me for wanting you to come home and work this out with me."

"Max, I've been there for you; don't you dare imply I haven't been. I've looked the other way on your pill problem because it seemed to me that marriage is about commitment, sickness and health, for better or worse. And I loved you."

"So the stakes go up and you run?"

"Let me finish. You're the one who changed the game. Not me. So far, most of our marriage has been about you, what you want, children—"

"Who spent money to buy the River Street store? And was *happy* to do so? Who spent weekends going to estate sales with you, *gladly*?"

"Who went to benefits and banquets for Benson Law clients and business acquaintances? Who wanted children desperately, yes for me, but also for you? I wanted you to be happy, to have the family you wanted."

"You want a family as much as I do, if not more. Jade, come home. You should know Lorelai and Gus—"

Jade pressed End and tossed her phone to the far side of the big Caddy's front seat. Enough. She didn't want to listen. Neither did he. This conversation could go on all night. Until the radio waves from the phone fried her brain.

For all his great qualities, Max could be so obtuse about people. Did she have *Welcome* imprinted on her forehead? *Come in, walk all over me.* Her phone rang and lit up. Jade stretched across the seat and snatched it up, silencing the ringer.

Sitting under an amber streetlight, Jade shifted into Park. The night cold draped around her shoulders. She'd heard something about spring snow flurries on the Weather Channel as she had exited the lobby. Reaching down under the dash, left of the wheel, she pressed the power button for the top.

The cold seeping beneath her skin, Jade hit the heat sliders and revved the idling engine. The trembling in her legs had crept into her torso. But she didn't need to call Daphne to understand the nervous river flowed from within.

Closing her eyes, Jade touched the praying hands medallion and listened to the memory of Paps's voice as he tied it around her neck when she was eight years old. *"Jesus is always with you."*

The motor for the top crunched and whirred to a stop. Jade glanced up as she swerved around. The top was stuck, looking like a lazy canvas wink. "No, no, no, come on."

She hit the switch again. The motor groaned and whirred, then grunted to a stop, leaving the top sticking a foot out of its bed, mocking her.

"Oh, come on. Work, you, you, you, man-car."

Jade switched the button on. Nothing. Off. On. Nothing again. No sound, no motor groan, no movement. "Oh come on." She hit the switch over and over, on, off, on, off.

She jumped into the backseat and leaned on the top. "You can't win. I won't let you beat me." Leaning did nothing, so Jade grabbed hold and pulled, using her full body weight to free the top from its frozen mechanics. "Up, up, up, you stupid thing."

Nothing doing. The crazy thing didn't budge. Jade's fingers slipped and she toppled backward over the front seat. Muttering, she crawled behind the wheel and jimmied the switch. The motor started. She exhaled relief. "Now you're talking." The top moved. "Come on, baby. Come on."

With a grunt, the motor froze. "No!" She was on her feet, leaping over into the back. The canvas wink just grew a half foot.

"You're going up or going down, but you're not staying like this." Jade pulled, then pushed, yanked, then mashed. The top was winning.

She was warm now, but the trembling hadn't subsided. Voices coming from the darkness nabbed her attention. Shoving her hair from her face, Jade peered between the shadows and street light. Three teenage boys strolled toward her.

This wasn't good. In fact, she was downright stupid for being caught like this. Was she in a bad part of town? Did Paducah have a "bad part of town"?

The boys strolled closer. She could hear dark, fowl words followed by dark, fowl laughter. Jade grabbed the top again and leaned back with her whole body, grunting and tugging. Not one budge or *eek* from the hinges.

"Stupid, stupid top." She let go with a scream.

"It's broken." The boys gathered around the Caddy's trunk.

"Gee, you think?" Jade was too riled to be afraid, so for once, fear found no footing. Frustration and anger emboldened her. Just let them try something. She'd pummel them. Her pulse vibrated in her neck. Her abs were so taut she labored to breathe.

"The hydraulic line is probably busted. Ain't no way you're getting the top up without crawling under the car."

Balling her hands into fists, tipping back her head, Jade howled at the night. "I . . . have . . . had . . . enough! And I'm not going to take it anymore." Her piercing, high scream rolled up from the depths of her being and fired from her throat with all the force of her being. She beat the air with her fists. Stomped her feet on the wide, white seat.

The boys scrambled backward. "She's crazy, man." The boys huddled, looking ready to run.

"I'm crazy." She barked at them like her German Shepherd Roscoe used to do when strangers came to the door. "And I bite." Jade lunged at the boys.

They tried to scatter, but tripped into each other, arms raised in defense. "Hold on, lady—"

"Go home. What are you doing out this late anyway?" Jade lunged at them again. "Go, go, go—"

The teens shuffled across the pavement, dashing into the park without a backward glance.

A light flicked on in a second-story window. A silhouette of a man appeared.

"What are you looking at?" she hollered, but in the absence of rushing adrenaline, reality set in. The top was broken. Jade tugged on it again, falling back over the front seat, breaking two fingernails this time.

"I have had enough!"

A dog barked.

"Yeah? Same to you, Fido." Jade scrambled onto the top of the backseat. "If you're not going up, you're going back down."

She began to mash and jump on the top, leaning, shoving, pressing, crunching the metal ribs under the canvas.

Jump. For Max.

Jump, jump. For Asa.

Jump, jump, jump. For losing three babies in two years.

Jump. For June.

Jump, jump, jump, jump. For Mama dying.

Jump, jump, jump.

On the last jump, her ankle gave way and she tumbled forward, crashing into the backseat. Lying there, this side of defeated, she stared at the starless sky.

Under her feet, the winking top was wounded, bent and cockeyed, but still sticking a foot or so out of its bed. Jade had created a wind sail. Driving on the highway would be torturous. If not impossible.

Tumbling in behind the wheel, tears swelling in her eyes, Jade pressed her forehead against the smooth, round metal. "Jesus, I give up. I give up."

How did she get here? How did she *get here*? Hand on the gearshift, Jade mashed the brake, about to shift into Drive . . .

She sat up with a jerk. Did Max . . . ? No, he wouldn't be that manipulative, would he? She snatched her phone from the seat, powered it on, and dialed. Waiting for him to answer, she reached down to massage her right ankle.

"Jade, I've been trying to call—"

"Tell the truth. No lie this time. Asa. He's why you've been pushing to get pregnant, isn't it?"

"What? Jade . . . no . . . we both want children. Why would I—"

"Do *not* lie to me, Maxwell. When I said I wanted to wait, that each miscarriage was more painful than the last, all you did was nudge me and prod me, trying to woo me into thinking the sooner we got pregnant, the sooner I'd forget the last child."

"Where's the lie, Jade? It's true, if you got pregnant—"

"Only to lose the baby again? I've tried to talk about a life with just the two of us, without children, but you refused. It was always 'We're going to have a baby, Jade' or 'Let's run down to the Jiffy Mart and pick up a kid or two.'"

"Am I going to have to defend everything I say and do from now on? And I never referred to adoption as the 'Jiffy Mart' of children."

"I'm such a dope." Her sardonic laugh was weakened by a surge of tears. "Such . . . a dope. I believed you were the one, my happily ever after . . . children and grandchildren . . . goofy family portraits taken up on Eventide Ridge, barefoot and smiling, looking alike in stupid white tops and jeans . . . growing old together."

"I want all of that with you. Jade, I married you. I love you. I want you."

"Max, yes or no. It's a simple question with a simple answer."

"It is neither and you know it. It's a trap question."

"It's all so clear now. You pushed for children, a son expressly, to cushion the blow when you finally had to tell me you had a child with Rice."

"Jade?" His signature heavy sigh communicated his frustration. She imagined his angular, handsome face molded by a tense expression.

"Yes or no?"

"Would you stop making everything so black or white?"

"Yes or no."

"Listen to me—"

"Yes or no! You're such a coward. And your lies are making the hole deeper. You wanted to get your wife pregnant to hide your illegitimate son. Did you come up with that one on your own, or did your dad offer a few suggestions?"

"That's not fair."

"Fair." She lifted her chin so the pooling tears ran down the side of her face. "You think *fair* is anywhere near this situation? For me? Or Asa? It's one thing to not tell me about Vegas, another not to tell me about your son. But it's evil to emotionally manipulate me to help your cause."

"I want children with you. How many times do I have to say it? I've always wanted children with you. Asa or not, I'm ready for a family. With. *You.*"

"Yes or no. You were pushing to have a son close to Asa's age . . . to *cushion* the news. Whenever it came."

Sigh. "Jade?"

"Yes or no, Counselor."

"Yes, yes . . . There. Yes. Happy?"

No. Not at all.

Fourteen

The news of the broken top didn't amuse the mother-in-law. In fact, she had a conniption in the middle of the Comfort Suites parking lot.

"What were you thinking, Jade? My car, my dear pink convertible, a gift from my daddy."

"I was trying to get the top up." Then down, but really, it was all the same to June.

"So you mangled it?" June flicked her hand toward the canvas top, her expression wind-tunnel tight. "How was jumping on the top going to get it up? Where are we going to find someone in Paducah, Kentucky, to fix it? You just don't run down to Pep Boys and pick up a new '66 Cadillac convertible top."

"Now you're just talking down to me." Jade tucked her hands under her arms and shivered against the nip in the air. She'd left her jacket back in the room while they had breakfast. While she broke the news to June.

"Well, if you act like a two-year-old, then don't be surprised when you're treated like one."

"Jade, tell us again what happened." Mama stepped in between, hands up. She'd become quite the peacemaker in her illness. Dark circles traced the pale skin around her eyes. When she breathed, her chest rattled a bit.

"Once again, I couldn't sleep. I went for a drive. I put the top down. I wanted to put the top back up, but the motor malfunctioned. I thought I could force it. My friend Margot's car has a manual release on her top."

"Well, did you see a manual release? You can't just ram it up or down, Jade." June gestured wildly with her hands. "How are we going to get to Iowa now?" She folded her arms and leaned toward Jade with her eyes wide as if expecting a brilliant answer.

"I had the front desk reserve a rental car for you and Mama. A Cadillac, if you must know. Which I'm paying for." Jade pressed her hand to her chest.

"Oh?" June lowered her attitude, her blue eyes offering an apology. "Well then."

"I'll drive your Caddy to Prairie City." Never mind that the day dawned gray and icy, and the Weather Channel confirmed a spring snowstorm threat from Kentucky to Nebraska. "Linc will know someone who can fix the car."

"And who is Linc?" June asked.

"My handyman. A dim bulb, but reliable," Mama said. "Used to go around with Willow."

"This isn't any old car, y'all." June walked the length of the Cadillac, touching the side lightly with her fingertips. "You can't just drive it to the shop and say, 'Fix it.'"

"I said we'll find someone to get it *fixed*." Jade checked her emotions. She hadn't slept much. The call with Max clung to her for hours. "You want it in writing?"

"I believe I do." June made a face and tipped her head to one side.

"All right, enough." Mama flashed her palms at Jade and June. "You're both edgy and tired. June, you know Jade will get the car fixed better than new." Mama walked around the trunk and touched Jade's arm. As she did, the pickup van from the rental car company pulled up to the hotel. "Jade, we'll see you at home."

~

To: Willow Ayers, Aiden Fitzgerald

Taking Mama to Prairie City. She looked very tired and sickly today. Arrange to come home soon. More later. Much more.

Love, Jade

Who is about to drive to Iowa, in a convertible Cadillac. With the top down. Long story. Even though it's nearly April, snow is predicted. And that's just the beginning.

Sent from my iPhone at 9:30 a.m.

~

Jade saw the girl almost the moment she pulled up to the light just under the I-24 overpass. She stood at the beginning of the ramp onto the northbound highway with her thumbs hooked over the waistband of her low-rise jeans, one foot jutted forward, the wind blowing open the front of her unzipped fatigue jacket. A duffel bag sat at her feet.

For a hitchhiker, she appeared to be well groomed, in her early twenties, pretty with long blonde hair, frayed bell-bottoms, and a reddish brown headband wrapped around her brow.

Something about her captured Jade. Had she seen her before? In the hotel maybe? Wouldn't she remember? She was tired, but not that tired.

The girl turned toward Jade with a jerking motion, as if she'd just discovered she was being watched. Jade ducked behind the wheel, cracking her chin against the chrome trim. Slowly, she eased up to peek above the dash.

The hitchhiker faced forward again, and Jade returned to her position behind the wheel, rubbing her chin. She was starting to hate this car. Watching the girl for another second, Jade realized she wasn't actually thumbing. Just standing. Waiting. As if for a specific person.

"Hey, lady!" A white utility van passed her at the light, turning west off the exit ramp. "Lady . . ." The driver leaned out his window. "It's going to snow. Ain't convertible weather. Your top is down."

"Aren't you a funny one?" Jade twisted around, rising out of the seat, snarling. "Nice work, van. Glad your Harvard degree is working out for you."

He responded with a rude gesture. Jade plopped down square in the seat. *Have a nice day to you too.* It's none of his business if she's driving with the top down. But no, he has to yell his pea-brain opinion as he goes by?

The driver in the car behind Jade laid on the horn. The light was green.

Jade punched the gas, and the old Caddy surged forward, rocking from side-to-side, slow at first, then surged forward with a burst of speed. The hurried driver behind Jade rode right up on her tail.

But as Jade passed the hitchhiker, she slowed and glanced over. For an instant, their eyes met. The girl smiled and gave Jade a thumbs-up. "Groovy car."

Groovy. Jade faced the windshield, her heart exploding. She'd never heard anyone use that word seriously but Mama. Hands on the wheel, she twisted back around, trying for a final glimpse of the girl as the Caddy barreled off the ramp onto the highway.

I know her. I know her. Swallowing, brushing her hair from her eyes, Jade stared straight ahead, out the windshield.

The impatient little car honkity-honked and whipped around Jade into the passing lane. What was wrong with people?

Cold air filled the Caddy's open chassis, swirling around Jade's head and feet. She was going to need to stop for more clothes. And gloves. Definitely gloves. Where'd she put the toque June had brought?

Hot air cranking from the heater barely made it past the dash. The heated seat only warmed a certain section of Jade's body that didn't really need to be kept warm.

The image of the hitchhiker stuck to her soul, lingering like the memory of a long-lost friend. Even more, the imprint of the girl's spirit reflected something so deep and real to Jade, she felt as if she were seeing herself from another era.

Or Mama.

Pressing harder on the gas, Jade wrestled with the urge to turn around. First of all, she wasn't *Mama*. Second of all, a hitchhiker in today's world? Nothing doing. Not when Jade was alone. Turn around based on sentimental musings and end up with a knife in her gut.

A streak of sunlight cut through the pile of gray clouds, but its warmth was a long way off. Jade wasn't a risk taker. Not much anyway. She'd researched vintage shops and small businesses for two years before even considering a property hunt for the Blue Umbrella.

Baby sister Willow took chances. She leaped first and thought second when she accepted the medical trip opportunity to Guatemala. Mama always said she was the kite in the wind. But Jade was the roots in the ground.

Picking up a hitchhiker wasn't her thing. Maybe Willow's, even Aiden's. Definitely Mama's. Jade had a front-row seat to Mama's wild side. Watching her weekend tent parties from her second-story window. Enduring her affinity for husbands. Grinning behind her hand when Granny scolded Mama's zest for life. Tucking into her ribs the day she picked up a wanderer on the side of the road . . .

"Jade-o. Aiden. Let's go find us a hill somewhere." Mama's voice wound up the stairs and echoed down the hall.

Jade jumped up, nearly falling off her bed, cradling her book against her chest. Her heart thumped in her chest. *Mama, don't go yelling down the hall.*

"Jade-o . . . sledding."

She didn't want to go sledding. She peered out her bedroom window, the fat flakes falling from the soupy clouds and blanketing the earth in a thick white that looked downright cold.

Mama knocked on her door, then pushed it open. "Bookworm, let's go."

"I want to read." Jade offered her open book to Mama. "Miss Godwin said I'm in third place in the reading contest. If I read an extra book a week, I might beat everyone in the whole school. Even sixth graders."

"Well, Miss Godwin ain't your mama, and I say it's time for some fun and exercise." Mama reached for Jade's book. "Anne Rice? A vampire novel? Where did you get this?"

"Rachel's mama had it in the throwaway pile."

"If Granny saw you with this, she'd have a fit. Now come on, get your gloves and boots on. Hurry, hurry, hurry." Mama tossed the book onto the bed. "Don't come crawling in bed with me if you have a nightmare." In the hall, Mama called Aiden again. "Let's go, boy."

Jade stuck out her tongue, quick though, because she didn't want Mama to see. As mad as she could make Jade, she hated to see Mama hurt.

Sighing and crawling off the bed, Jade flipped the pages of her book. Why would a book give her nightmares? And why would Granny have a fit? She liked when Jade read. Closing the book, she tucked it under her bed and decided to return it to Rachel's house after school. The risk of nightmares and Granny's wrath was too great.

The library had plenty of stories she wanted to read. Jade opened her bottom drawer for her gloves and hat. She always read in the afternoon, after homework. Granny brought up hot cocoa, marshmallows, and graham crackers on a tray.

But when Mama came home from one of her trips with her friends or from a long run for Midwest Parcel, she made it her duty to mess up everyone's schedule.

Granny said let her be. It made her feel like she was being a good mother.

"I'm going to put the sleds in the truck." Mama poked her head around the door. "Don't forget your gloves."

Jade sighed as loud as she could, just so Mama would know she'd rather be reading. She'd never won a prize before, and she wanted this one so bad she could taste it. She'd have one trophy to Aiden's ten.

Aiden flopped onto Jade's bed. "Word is you might win the reading contest." He was in fourth grade, and even though he read as many books as Jade, he didn't tell his teacher.

"I'm trying."

"You can send a picture of your ribbon to Daddy."

Jade faced him, eyes wide, heart dancing. "Why would he want to see it?"

Aiden shrugged. "He always likes it when I show him my baseball trophies."

"I want to go to Washington to see him in the summer." Jade jammed her foot into her wooly duck boots, then yanked up the laces.

"Me too."

"Is he mad at us?"

"I think he's still mad at Mama."

A snowball pelted the bedroom window. Jade and Aiden squished into the mattress, then crawled to the window to peer down.

"Come on, you *snow* pokes." Mama lobbed another snowball at the window, laughing. She dropped to the ground, swinging her arms and legs up and down. "I'm a snow angel."

Aiden looked back at Jade. "That's as close as Mama's ever going to get to being an angel."

Jade snickered and snorted, then popped her brother's shoulder. "You're mean."

"She's the one who says she's bound for hell." He rolled off the bed.

"Just to make Paps and Granny mad." Mama wouldn't go to hell, would she? Jade heard talk of hell in Sunday school, with visions of fire and the devil haunting the sinners.

"Jade, Aiden." Mama's voice was muffled by the cold window. "Let's go . . ."

"Last one down's a rotten egg." Aiden dashed out of the room before Jade caught the last of his challenge.

"Cheater." Jade bolted through the door wrapping her scarf around her neck.

Crammed into the cab of the truck, Mama blasted the heater and cranked the radio as she drove through the snowplowed lanes of Highway 117 toward Newton and the good sledding hills.

Ten minutes down the road, as Mama rounded a bend, a dark figure appeared on the horizon. A man. Hooded. Alone. His dark silhouette scary against the white horizon. He could be a vampire, looking for lunch . . . Jade's heart raced when Mama slowed down the truck.

"Aiden, roll down your window."

"No, Mama."

"Roll it down, come on now." Mama cranked her hand in the air.

With a huff, Aiden obeyed. Big flakes drifted into the truck through the open window.

"Is that your car broken down back there?"

The stranger peered in the window. "Ran out of gas. Thought I had enough to make it to Newton." When he glanced at Jade, she ducked behind her brother.

"We're heading that way. Want a lift?"

"Mom?" Aiden glared at her. Jade knew what he was thinking. Paps said never to ride with a stranger. Or go with a stranger to a house or building.

The stranger looked at Aiden. "I can walk, really."

"Walk? It's another ten miles to Newton. It's cold and snowing. Aiden, move over." Mama reached across Jade and hooked her hand around Aiden, pulling him away from the door.

They were going to die. Jade imagined her red blood soaking the new snow.

He was in the truck. Jade's middle tightened as the door clapped closed. She burrowed into Mama, who frowned and elbowed her out of the way. "I can't drive with you burrowing into me like that."

"So, sledding?" The man sounded nice. His smile was cool. Lots of teeth. Her friend Rachel said people with big teeth might be vampires. Yep, they were going to die. "There's enough snow for it. Where do you go? Sunset Park?"

"They have the best hills around here. It's nothing like out west, like Colorado," Mama said, shifting the gears of the truck. "But we have some laughs, don't we, kids?"

"I'm Ryan." The man nodded at Mama, then Jade and Aiden.

Mama crossed her arm in front of Jade to shake his hand. "Beryl. These are my kids, Aiden and Jade."

Aiden muttered hello. Jade said nothing, but gave him a good once-over with her eyes. Now that he was closer, Jade decided he looked like the teenagers she observed when Granny took her to Sunday school.

"You're welcome to come sledding with us. I brought an extra sled." Mama motioned to the back of the truck. "There's always someone on the hill in need of a sled."

"I have to call my dad first about my car, but sure."

Mama smiled at all three of them. "Perfect."

~

A cold, wet drop of snow hit Jade's forehead. She left behind the memory of riding in the truck with Mama, Aiden, and Ryan.

Beyond the windshield, snow drifted down from opaque-bottom clouds in true solidarity with the Weather Channel's prediction and dusted the Kentucky highway.

Jade didn't have many favorite childhood memories, but sledding with Ryan was one of them. After her first swoop down the hill on her sled, she'd forgotten all about vampires and oozing blood in the snow.

Those were the final moments before Mama really went wild and disappeared for months on end. Before she married Willow's daddy, Mike Ayers. Before husbands three and four: Gig the musician and Bob the accountant.

Ryan turned out to be the seventeen-year-old son of Newton's mayor, who treated all of them to dinner and hot chocolate at Maid Rite.

Cautious Aiden ended up following Ryan around like a lost puppy, eager to be accepted by the teen. On the way home, Mama nudged him. "Connections that change your life just might be standing on the side of the road."

It always bothered Jade that Mama's careless prediction turned true. Ryan ended up as a friend and mentor of Aiden's. His love of art and photography transformed Aiden's sometimes-hobby into a fascination and lifetime pursuit. They were friends to this day.

Connections that change your life just might be standing on the side of the road.

Jade barely made the exit. She swerved the big Caddy off I-24, kissing the berm, laying on the brakes. The beast took a good bit of road to slow down.

This was nuts. Jade shivered, tapping her fingers on the steering wheel as she waited at a stop sign for a slow moving truck to gear up and move on.

Picking up a hitchhiker? Insane. But now that she was in motion to turn around, Jade had to go back. She had to see her. Talk to her.

Maybe there was a piece of Mama in the girl. Something Jade needed to see.

Backtracking down I-24, Jade shoved aside all fear. She was tired of living in fear. Tired of seeing evil in what God called good. Seeing a vampire in a big-toothed teen. Most of all, something in her gut told her she needed to peek at the eyes of the hitchhiker and see her soul.

Good thing about a '66 Fleetwood Eldorado? The car could book. Jade hung on to the wheel with both hands as she careened south on I-24, finally swerving onto the Hinkleville Road exit, wrangling the beast back from seventy to thirty-five.

Caught at the exit-ramp light, jitters slithered across Jade's belly. The light flashed green in the next second, and Jade shot off the line, only to be caught by a red light under the overpass. But now she could see the northbound ramp, and the girl was still there. Waiting.

Cool anticipation shivered beneath her skin. Jade sensed something divine in play, as if she might gaze into a mirror and suddenly have clarity.

What would she say to her? Want a ride? Hop in? Surely she'd remember Jade from fifteen minutes ago.

The girl stood with her shoulders hunched up as she did a little keep-warm hop. She'd zipped up her jacket and smashed a blue wool cap on her head. The same invisible thread between them from the first passing tugged the girl's attention toward Jade again. Their eyes locked.

This time Jade didn't duck. Instead, she rose over the windshield and waved. *Hey, I'm coming. I'm coming.*

The hitchhiker waved, smiled, even seemed eager for Jade to come. As if she'd been waiting . . . for her.

Dropping back down into the car, Jade's heart churned. She stared at the red light. *Green, green, green.*

Peering toward the ramp again, a moving van, U-Move, eased to a stop in the westbound lane and blocked Jade's line of sight.

"Hey . . ." Jade rose up and tried to wave them by. "Why don't *you* move." She stretched her neck to see beyond the obstruction, but the truck completely blocked her view.

Two seconds later the light clicked green and Jade fired forward, sweeping wide around the back of the truck. *I'm coming.* Onto the ramp, Jade eased onto the berm to pick up the girl. Gravel popped and smacked under the tires. Jade mashed the brake and threw the gear into Park.

"Hello?" Jade stood, scanning length of the ramp. "Hey—"

But she was gone. Vanished. Turning a slow 360, Jade searched the far corners of the horizon. She cupped her hands around her mouth, drew a deep breath, and hollered, "Hey, where are you? Hitchhiker?"

How could she have disappeared? The north part of the exit was empty. No cars had merged on. On the south end, traffic flowed like a spring river. If the girl had crossed the road, Jade would've seen her.

An eerie chill crawled over Jade. The first flash of burnt amber rocketed her down to the front seat. Purple swirls enveloped her, and in an instant, Jade was caught in another space, another time. She couldn't feel her body, remember her name or why she'd turned the big car around.

She'd split in two, one half observing, the other half feeling as if she'd just arrived on this strange planet. Her emotions floated in the space, detached.

Think, think . . . Blood rushed to her face and burned under her skin. Every molecule in her body was alive with awareness. She was alone.

Jade cupped her head with her hands. *Remember . . . remember.* What was hanging around her neck? Something . . . a medallion. She gripped it, holding on for dear life. The metal was familiar, a reality from her past.

Paps.

Spinning, swirling, her thoughts raced forward, colliding with her emotions. The burnt amber faded. The purple swirls lifted.

Jade. She was Jade Fitzgerald Benson. With an exhale, she collapsed against the seat. She'd returned for the hitchhiker. Snow thickened in the air as Jade positioned herself behind the Caddy's wheel and turned all the heat vents toward her.

The hitchhiker was still gone.

With a shaky hand, Jade shifted into Drive and aimed the Caddy for the highway, unable to come out from under the lingering sense that fear and hesitation had cost her something dear.

Fifteen

"June, sit." Beryl patted the bed beside her.

"And what will I do if I sit down?" June collected the thin china plate she'd used for Beryl's toast. The teacup remained half full of ginger tea. "Fall apart? Spin off into space?"

Busyness kept her grounded, distracted. She liked it. Why change now in the midst of her worst crisis?

"Sit because I asked."

"How about if I just tidy up?" June set down the dishes and shuffled around the bed, tucking in the corners and smoothing blankets.

Beryl's bedroom had been her parents' before they died. The space was old-feeling with the whispers of long-ago stories. Heavy, straight curtains hung at the window, and the thirsty hardwood was covered with a patterned carpet remnant.

"Rest, think, exhale." Beryl kept a steady gaze on June.

"This relaxes me." June fluffed the pillows. "Your handyman did a nice job preparing the house. I checked the pantry and he bought some lovely groceries. What's his name again? Linc?"

"You don't have to wait on me, June." Beryl's eyes followed her around the bed. "Yesterday your arm was in pain."

"Good as new, like I told you." Almost. Her arm had ached most of the drive from Paducah to Prairie City. "Are you tucked in and warm, Beryl?"

"First you dress me like a bloated tick." Beryl's weak smile lit her tired eyes. "Now you tuck me in like a bug in a rug."

"As long as you're comfortable." June picked up the dishes, tapping her fingernails against the bottom of the plate. Now what? Nothing to clean. No calls to make. No dinner to fix. "Want me to bring up a movie? I saw a collection downstairs."

"Don't know what happened to me," Beryl said. "I was feeling so strong, and then, *whoosh*, I became a dandelion petal in the breeze. Leukemia . . . a fierce foe." A cough caught Beryl off guard and she lurched forward.

June set the plate down and crawled on the bed to aid her friend. "I don't like the rattle in your chest, Beryl. Are you in pain?"

As she coughed, she shook her head, patting the air with her hand. "Stop fussing." Beryl collapsed against her pillows.

"Here, drink some of your tea." June held the cup to Beryl's lips. During the nine-hour drive, she'd grown weaker and paler. June regretted the short ride with the top down, even though she'd bundled Beryl in her warmest gear. Beryl's immune system wasn't strong enough to handle so much as the sniffles.

"You remind me of Mother. Always willing to lay down her needs for others, serving, helping," Beryl said weakly. June set the cup down on the saucer.

"Did your mother do it out of love or duty?" June settled against the headboard, stretching out her legs, wiggling her toes still wrapped in panty hose.

"Oh, a bit of both, I suppose. Love mostly." Beryl coughed once. She patted her chest with her palm. "What about you?"

June stared ahead at the old flowered wallpaper. "If I say duty, am I evil?"

"Do you feel evil?"

Tears flowed from her settling emotions to her eyes. "There are days, yes."

"Love is a verb, June. If you serve out of duty, isn't that a form of love?"

"Does a slave's duty reflect love? People can serve and be filled with hate, Beryl."

"There's a thin line between love and hate."

"Very thin." June brushed her fingers through her hair. "So, you grew up here? And your kids?"

"I did. Harlan and I bought a property down the road right after Jade was born. Forty acres with a house much like this one. He left when Jade was eight and I tried to hang on to the place, but it was too much for me. I sold it, put my tail between my legs, and moved back in with Mother and Paps. A real blow to my pride. Paps died two years later, and between the divorce, being a single mom, living with my own mother"—Beryl shuddered—"I had to escape or lose my mind. I hit the road. In the long run, I knew Mother would be better for the kids than me."

"And you met Mike, when?"

"A year or so later. Got pregnant with Willow after four months. Married him to give her a name. Some of Mother's morals were getting to me, and I wanted to set a good example for Aiden and Jade, give them a grid for relationships. Kids need grids."

"What was he like?"

"Mike Ayers?" The tip of Beryl's lip twitched. "Sexy."

June balked at her confession, then laughed. "I suppose that's a good enough reason to marry."

"I thought so, but we only lasted two years."

"Rebel was sexy, but he had this commanding way about him." June stopped, her mind filling with images of her husband. "I knew he would make life good for whomever he married."

"Marriage wasn't on my agenda. Then I met Harlan." Beryl laughed softly. "I didn't know I could love someone so much. Once I accepted his proposal"—she shook her head at the memory—"I never wanted to look back. Sounds square coming from a summer-of-love flower child."

"Sounds tender and sincere."

"I've done many things I'm not proud of, June, but my kids . . . I'm proud of them."

"Max always has been my pride and joy," June said. "Mercy, I had to fight the urge to smother the boy to death with my affection. It's hard with only one child. There's no way to divide up all the love and attention."

"Did you want more children?" Beryl spoke softly, eyes closed.

"We did, but—"

"You can relate to Jade's struggle."

"In some ways." June brushed her hand over the quilt's Jacob's Ladder pattern. "In some ways."

Beryl drew in a slow, fought-for breath and closed her eyes. "Bacon, coffee, toast . . . is it weird I can still smell Mother's breakfast cooking?"

"My mother's kitchen smelled like garlic." June breathed in, but the fragrance on the edge of her nose was old, warm wood and dusty curtains.

Beryl stretched for June's hand, her chest rattling, her lungs wheezing. "I admire you, staying with Rebel for Max. Never catch me with a cheater. My third husband stepped out on me with a groupie, and—"

"The musician? Please, don't tell me you expected him to be faithful."

"He said he was, so I believed him." Beryl's short laugh faded to a rattling cough.

"I knew Reb flirted. Caught him at the club a few times, talking a mite too cozy to a woman in the parking lot. But the first time I *knew* he cheated, Max was about five or so. I overheard a couple of women on my Fall Festival committee talking, in detail, about another committee member who'd recently resigned. Rebel's name was never mentioned, but every word they whispered to each other rang so familiar to me. When and where this woman had gone with her secret lover, things he'd said and done. And I knew."

"Our souls know what our minds refuse to believe."

"'Tis true, Beryl. Listening to those women, I knew I'd ignored all the signs, and the truth hit me like a belly flop into the club's icy pool. My husband had an affair."

"Did you give it to him?"

"Confront Rebel Benson, a lawyer with a reputation for tough cross-examination, with club committee gossip? He'd slice and dice my argument in two seconds. No, with Reb I had to learn how to present my case. Truth be told, I needed room to doubt."

She couldn't doubt now, could she? "Well, I'd better get to these dishes." June moved off the bed, reaching for Beryl's cup and plate.

"Jade-o here yet?" Beryl muttered, her words heavy with sleep, the congestion in her chest making her work for air.

"She'll be along," June said, then tiptoed down the back stairs to the kitchen to wait for Jade to arrive. Beryl needed to get to the doctor as soon as possible.

In the comfort of the rental car, June had found her inner Steve McQueen and made good time to Prairie City. She'd wanted Beryl home and in her bed. The handyman, Linc, had been waiting for them on the front porch and carried in their luggage, practically carried in Beryl, then returned the rental. Nice boy, that Linc.

June set the dishes in the sink and peered out the window. The afternoon was giving way to the power of twilight. Jade had called a few hours ago to say progress was slow with the broken top catching big gulps of highway breeze.

June snickered, shaking her head. What a sight. Jade trying to explain how the Caddy became mangled under her wrath.

Filling the sink with hot water, June searched the cupboard for dish soap.

She'd told Beryl more of her story than she'd told her closest Whisper Hollow friends. Lisa Thibodeaux had been a long time ago. But it was the beginning of an avalanche.

But only one knew the whole truth. Rebel. And he subtly reminded her every chance he got.

~

"The Thibodeauxs?" June tossed the decorative pillows from the bed to the floor. "Why?"

"Woody and I play golf, June. He suggested we get the wives together for some cards. Hearts or pinochle." At the closet, Rebel slipped his tie from under his collar.

"Absolutely not." She'd never out-and-out defied Rebel before.

He glimpsed over his shoulder. "Why not? You're on a half-dozen committees with Lisa."

"Are you doing this to me on purpose?" June walked around the end of the bed, the hem of her satin pajamas bottoms sweeping across the carpet. "I won't have her in my house, Reb. How dare you ask."

"June . . ." Rebel crooned as he unbuttoned his shirt, pulling the tail free from his slacks. "What are you talking about?"

"You know darn well what I'm talking about." June jumped on the bed to match his stature. "You and Lisa Thibodeaux? The gossip is hotter than a Fourth of July firecracker."

"Keep your voice down." Snapping off his watch, he stepped near the bed and placed it on his nightstand, along with his Duke class ring. "Max will hear you."

"I won't keep my voice down, Rebel Beauregard Benson. I'm not stupid." June grabbed his shoulders, then pinched his chin between her fingers. "Your sweet nothings like 'cute as a speckled pup' and 'soft as a spring rose' were as corny when you whispered them to me as they are now when you're wooing your paramours. But at least they were sweet and original when you were twenty-two."

Rebel walked over to the bedroom door and gazed down the hall before easing the door closed. "You want Max to hear you? The kid has ears like a bat."

"Are you ashamed, Rebel? Don't want your five-year-old son to know about your exploits?"

"We were discreet, June. No one knows."

"Discreet? Rebel, everyone knows."

"They know Lisa had an affair, not with whom." Rebel eased out of his slacks, folding them in quarters before dropping them in the dry-cleaning hamper.

"And how do you know?"

"A few well-asked questions. Eavesdropping on a few conversations."

"Well then, phew!" June brushed her hand across her forehead. "That's one disaster avoided. I can sleep now." From the edge of the mattress, June swung at Rebel when he walked past. "Woody is one of your best friends."

"He wasn't when the whole thing started." He took out a clean pair of pajamas, examined them in the light, then stepped into the legs. "Besides, it's over."

How could he be so callous, distant, and unrepentant? Confessing he'd slept with another woman in the same tone he discussed their weekend schedule?

"I want to know why, Reb." June dropped off the bed to the floor.

"You know why." He turned for the bathroom.

Shaking, wrapping her arms around her waist, June stared at the floor. "Is that it, then?"

He didn't answer for a long time, quiet on the other side of the bathroom door. Finally, he peered into the room. "June."

She looked up.

"That's it, then." Rebel stepped back into the bathroom and eased the door closed.

Her phone rang. June shook the water and suds from her hands, snatched a paper towel from the new roll on the rack, and hurried to the living room for her handbag.

Ringing, ringing, from her Birkin she'd left in the living room. "Hold your horses." A spot on the hardwood snagged her stockings.

On the last ring she answered. The area code was Tennessee, but the number was unfamiliar. "June Benson."

"Is this Mrs. Rebel Benson?"

"And who is this?" She didn't have the time or desire to mess around.

"This is Carissa McCown from the *Knoxville News Sentinel*." Her introduction painted a firm go-getter with a hint of charm.

"I'm a bit busy right now . . ." June walked back to the kitchen, shoulders stiff and postured for a debate.

"I understand completely. I'd just like to ask a few questions. I'll take as little of your time as possible."

"Questions about what?"

"Your husband has been nominated to the state supreme court."

"Rebel will do the court justice." She held down the quiver in her chest. Reb finally made the court? Oh my . . .

Carissa laughed a sporty laugh. "Do the court justice . . . Can I quote you?"

"I wasn't trying to be funny, Miss—"

"McCown. Carissa McCown. You have a great sense of humor, Mrs. Benson."

"I'm married to a lawyer." June walked to the sink, sank her hands into the dishwater, and pulled out the plug.

"Do you see your separation as a hindrance to his career? Mr. Benson is considered the more conservative, family values candidate."

"I'm away with my daughter-in-law. I would hardly call it a separation."

"Did you see the press release?"

The drain drank down the soapy water. Press release? "Like I said, I'm away with my daughter-in-law."

"Here, let me read it to you. 'Mr. Benson announced today that he and his

148

wife of forty-one years have temporarily separated, but he expected this development to have no impact on his candidacy for the supreme court.'"

June fell against the counter. Water slowly trickled from the tips of her fingers.

"Mrs. Benson?"

She cleared her throat. "Yes, um, so, what can I do for you, Carissa?"

"I'd like a quote from you for my article."

"Why don't you just use the quote I already gave you?" June hung her head. *Oh, Rebel. Does it all mean so much to you? Your name, your fame?*

"About being married to a lawyer requires a sense of humor? I'd like a bit more. Why the separation, Mrs. Benson?"

"Are you married, Miss McCown?"

"Engaged."

"Do you ever fight with your fiancé?"

She hesitated. "Doesn't everyone?"

"What do you fight about?"

"I don't know . . . stuff. What's your point, Mrs. Benson?"

"Well, I'd like the details to post on my blog." June had dealt with reporters before. Mostly on charity issues, occasionally on a high-profile case the firm might be handling. "Did you fight over a burnt dinner? Spending too much money? Flirting at a party with another man?"

"Mrs. Benson, my fiancé is not about to take a seat on the state supreme court."

"Perhaps not, but every day his life touches another. He gives a directive, offers an opinion. Because he's imperfect doesn't negate his ability to make wise decisions. Rebel knows the law, and he decides accordingly. Not by his own experience or beliefs."

"Did you catch him with another woman, Mrs. Benson?"

June hit End and tossed her phone onto the old Formica. The court, if he's chosen, might take Rebel further than he wanted to go and reveal more than he wanted revealed.

Sixteen

The sight of lamps glowing in the old farmhouse windows welcomed Jade home. The melody of gravel crackling under the car tires was like singing "Rocky Top" at a UT game or "My Old Kentucky Home" at the Derby.

Eleven p.m. Jade had expected Mama and June to be asleep with the lights out. It was an old reflex from growing up with Granny. Curfew was at ten thirty, and if Jade or Aiden missed it, Granny locked the doors and switched off all the lights.

Even the barn was lit with the doors shoved open. *Thank you, Linc.* Jade parked alongside Paps's old International pickup, very much like her baby back home.

Stopped, foot on the brake, Jade pried her frozen fingers from the wheel. *Oh, pain.*

Three Wal-Mart stops, six layers of clothes, eight cups of coffee, and two hours thawing by the fireplace at the Peoria Cracker Barrel, she'd made it home.

Her joints ached as she cut the engine and exited the car. Her stomach churned. There *was* such a thing as too much coffee.

"Jade-o, you're home." Linc came around the corner, his strawberry blond hair loose about his angular face.

"You're on the job late." Jade gave him a stiff and sore embrace.

"Nice hat," he said, tugging on the earflap strings of her Wal-Mart ski toque. She'd found an ugly green one in a clearance basket. Fifty cents.

"Cold drive."

The light in Linc's eyes sparked as he stepped back, hands tucked underneath his arms. "What'd you do to the top?"

"What makes you think I did anything to the top?"

Linc laughed and jostled the bent canvas frame. "You broke her good."

"Tomorrow, when I'm not a human popsicle, we can talk about where to get it fixed."

"I know somebody right here in PC. I'll give him a call."

"In Prairie City?" Jade regretted her question. She was too tired for Linc's descriptive and lengthy explanations. "Never mind. I'm going inside to take the hottest bath possible, for as long as possible, and then crawl into bed." Jade inched toward the house. "There's a twenty in it for you if you bring in my luggage."

Didn't have to ask Linc twice.

Max was out of hands. Couldn't catch one more of the fly balls popped his way even if he wanted. He was back-against-the-wall.

Gus and Lorelai were suing for custody of Asa. The other night they were to deliver his son, but instead Max opened the door to find the grim-faced McClures on his front porch, arms empty, without Asa. In a flat tone, Gus announced he and Lorelai were keeping their daughter's son and raising him as their own.

Facing his office window, Max watched the raindrops hit the pane, tapping out an erratic rhythm. As angry as he was, he couldn't shake grief's vacant look in Gus's eyes.

"Gus, this is the grief talking. You're hurting, I understand, but Asa is my son. You and Lorelai can see him anytime you want."

The porch light had given Gus's skin a ghostly aura. Lorelai had leaned against him as if she couldn't stand on her own.

"It's not the grief, Max; it's what's right. You don't know your own son. You abandoned him."

"Rice insisted on raising him on her own."

How many times had he gone over their conversation? Pieces of it invaded his sleep. He felt for the McClures. Asa was all they had left of their only child, and Max had given up rights to him for nineteen months. But while the circumstances were extraordinarily sad, he'd not deny his son again.

Gus and Lorelai could just live with it.

Max walked over to his desk. Two o'clock. What the heck was taking Cara so long? The Benson Law senior partner had left at ten o'clock for a meeting with Bradley Richardson, the McClures' lawyer. If Cara didn't show up in a half hour, he'd call her to make sure that sleazeball Richardson didn't ambush her.

Sharp and spicy Cara Peters could take him if he played by the rules. But Richardson rarely did.

"All right, here's what we got."

Max whirled around as Cara stormed into his office, slipping off her suit jacket and tossing her dossier onto a chair.

"Where have you been? How bad was Bradley?"

"Arrogant, licking his chops over the idea of besting you."

"It's going to get ugly, isn't it?"

"It's already ugly." Cara paced in a small circle, rubbing her forehead, then peered long and hard at Max. "Bradley laughed when I told him we wanted to settle out of court."

Max sighed. Figures. Could he confess his loathing for the man right now? He dug up dirt even God didn't care about—like unreturned library books, or a 7-Eleven candy bar heist.

"I thought, hoped, he'd be reasonable. After all, an innocent child is involved. But no, he played his jerk card first round. We need to lawyer up, Max, get our strategy hammered out and airtight. Bradley is going to go for the jugular, especially because this particular vein is throbbing beneath the skin of a Benson lawyer."

"If he can dish it, I can take it. Cara, this is an easy case. Gus and Lorelai are the grandparents. I'm his father. They are trying to keep their daughter alive through her son." Max twitched, and a sudden craving for meds slithered beneath his skin and overshadowed his thoughts. But this morning Max had cleaned the office of all meds. Not even an aspirin remained.

"You can rationalize all you want, but the McClures want that boy and Bradley is going to make sure they get him. He's drawn the long sword, Max, and is poised to plunge it deep." Cara leaned toward him, her expression grim. "You know I have to run all this by Rebel. Any case that's got *press* written all over it."

"I'm aware." Max sat and rocked back in his chair. The motion eased the pressure on his back. For a moment. "Let's file a motion for me to at least get custody. See if we can file under seal, try to keep this quiet."

Cara laughed. "Seal? With Bradley Richardson? Are you kidding? He'd block that motion before you could say hut one, hut two. This is a civil case, Max, come on, and there's nothing confidential enough for a seal. We won't get a sealed ruling. What we can do is pull a few strings and get this worked out in chambers rather than open court."

"And Bradley will be pulling a few strings to have the proceeding on the courthouse lawn with Channel 9 filming." He'd seen Bradley do it dozens of times.

"I have to tell you, Max, he practically sang your list of faults. Add music and he could've played on Broadway. He wants this in the public eye."

Max rubbed his tired eyes with his fingers. Sleep had not been his friend the last few nights. "I just want this to be over."

"I'm going to talk to Judge Howard today, see if she'll go ahead and grant custody to you. She's pro fathers, so we'll win this one. But, Max, how far do you want to go?" Cara sat forward, resting her arms on her knees. "The McClures are offering *nothing*. Not even visitation. I countered Bradley with, 'No way.'"

"No way? That's your brilliant rebuttal? Did he cave right away or did you have to repeat yourself?"

"Don't get smart with me. I'm on your team."

He growled, then gave her a soft gaze. "I'm sorry, Cara. Just upset, that's all. How far should we go? I want my son. Do what it takes." Overriding the grief in Gus and Lorelai's eyes was the vulnerability and innocence of one small, towheaded boy. Max needed to protect and love his son.

"We'll win this, Max, but are you prepared for all your problems to come to public light?" Cara's steel glare drove the words home. "Because they will. You need to be forming answers as to why you didn't meet Asa for the first time until he was nineteen months old. Even with a father-friendly judge, that's a hard sell, child support payments aside. You need to be prepared to explain your drug problem. Max, you're my friend and colleague. I support you, you know that, but when the facts are laid out, you're not the ideal dad. The McClures, on the other hand, appear to be Santa and Mrs. Claus with the Easter Bunny thrown in. By the way, you should consider hiring an investigator."

Max stood, sending his chair into the bookcase behind his desk. He needed to pace and think. All his problems . . . Wish he'd known this day was coming twenty years ago when he popped his first pain med. And an investigator? On the McClures?

"Barely getting started, and already we're hiring investigators?"

"You don't think Bradley is giving the McClures the same advice? And the court will order one, so we might as well have our own man on the team."

"Cara, let's just play it straight." Max faced her, hands on his belt. "The facts of the case are this: One, I'm his father. The paternity test can be entered into evidence. Two, I'm on his birth certificate. Three, I paid child support. All evidence. We argue I wasn't involved in Asa's life because Rice preferred to raise him alone and our residences were two thousand miles apart."

"The McClures are named in the will?"

"If I'm unwilling. But I'm willing." Max smacked his chest. "And able."

"Bradley will argue willing but incompetent. And abandonment. I can hear him now. 'What, you didn't hop on that fancy plane Benson Law owns and fly out to see your son? My, my, my.'" Cara made an ugly face. "Frankly, it's a great argument."

"The McClures are almost seventy, Cara. They can't raise Asa. He needs parents who can teach him to play catch, attend his high school graduation, see him through college, attend his wedding."

"People live long today, Max. It's conceivable the McClures will attend Asa's wedding and—"

"Without a cane. Or false teeth."

"False teeth and walking canes hardly paint the picture of incompetence. Bradley will subpoena your mom. Probably Jade. What's up with you two anyway? Is she coming home?"

"Eventually." He hoped. What a mess. "Be honest with me, Cara. Am I fit to be Asa's father?"

Her brown eyes held on to his face for a long, painful moment. "If you'd have asked me a few weeks ago, I'd have said no. You're selfish, Max. Driven, ambitious, focused until something knocks you off the path and you topple headlong into something stupid like addiction. I never have figured that out about you. But with Jade, I saw you overcoming. I saw her bringing out the best in you. She's a good partner. You need her to help you win this, Max."

Well, he'd asked.

"But," Cara said, standing, "I can see how much you love this boy and want to do what's right." She approached Max. "To answer your question, if you act like the man I know you to be, you will be an amazing father." She put her hands on his shoulders. "Keep away from the pills, Max. Haven't they caused enough havoc? Now, let's do some digging on the McClures, see what's swept under their rug."

"I'm not an addict, Cara." His eyes stayed fixed on her as she lowered her hands. "I have doctor-prescribed Percocet. For back pain."

"Ever doctor shop, Max? Ever take more than the prescribed dosage? Ever been to rehab? Ever lie to Tripp Bunn, your counselor?"

Each question hammered his chest. Nails in a coffin. His. If he testified—and what father worth his salt wouldn't testify in his own son's custody case?—Bradley would ask the same questions and Max would have to answer yes to each one. What a *stellar* man he'd become.

Seventeen

"Mama, how are you feeling?" Jade opened the blinds to let in the afternoon light. The March snow melted by mid-morning, and a spring balm glossed the day. For the first time since Rice died, Jade had slept through the night. It was good to be home.

"Jade-o, you made it." Mama reclined against a pile of pillows June had packed behind her back.

"You were asleep when I got in." Jade sat on the edge of the bed and brushed her hand over Mama's forehead. "Dr. Meadows is seeing you Thursday."

"That old coot? He's just going to say I'm dying. He took me off the road, cost me my job at Midwest."

"He wanted to keep you and the rest of the traveling population safe." Jade straightened the blankets around Mama. She studied her eyes for a minute. "Didn't you hitchhike once?"

"Once? Many times. Many times."

"Why did you do it? Hitchhike?" Jade pictured the girl in Paducah.

"To get from one town to another." Mama smiled. "Why do you think, Jade? For adventure."

"Did you travel alone? With friends?"

"Both. Jade, why are you asking?" Mama coughed, lurching forward, holding her sides. The fluid in her chest rattled against her ribs.

Jade crawled over her to the center of the bed, holding Mama's shoulders and rubbing her back. When the cough subsided, Jade held her water glass to her lips.

"The hitchhiker in Paducah impacted me in some crazy way."

"The hitchhiker in Paducah?"

"Yeah, the girl on the northbound ramp. She had blonde hair, a bandana, bell bottoms, army jacket." Jade set the glass on the nightstand. "Didn't you see her when you drove by in the rental car?"

"No hitchhiker that I could see." Mama puckered her lips. "I used to wear Paps's fatigues, carry his duffel bag. Even wore a bandana for years."

"She was on the right side . . ." Wasn't she? Yes, Jade saw her. She. Saw. Her.

"Maybe it was me forty years ago." Mama laughed softly, tapping her chest. "I might have gone through Paducah once. I remember going to Kentucky for a concert."

Chills gripped Jade's skin. She and Mama were caught on life's timeline; God was not. If He wanted to show Jade something . . .

"But those were some wild, crazy days." Mama rolled her head gently, side to side. "Literally the blurry years."

"When I saw her, it reminded me of that snowy day we went sledding in Newton and picked up Ryan on the side of 117." Jade tucked the image of the hitchhiker away in the treasure box with memories and snuggled next to Mama.

"Oh, Jade-o, when did we do that? I don't remember picking up Ryan on the side of the road. Aiden's friend, Ryan?"

"It was a long time ago." Jade often had different memories than Mama.

"The hitchhiker made me think of you." Tears burned in the corners of Jade's eyes. "I'm sorry I hated you for so many years."

"I'm sorry I made you hate me." Mama fished for Jade's hand and laced their fingers together. "I somehow believed I was a better mama for you kids by following my heart."

"Then tell me. What should I do about Max?" Jade suddenly craved her wisdom. "What would you do?"

"You can't do what I would do, Jade-o. I've always been the kite in the breeze like Willow. You're the solid, stable, rooted one. Like your dad."

"I don't feel so stable." Jade cradled her head deeper into Mama's shoulder. In fact, she felt very uprooted. Mama's hand felt soft and tender when she touched Jade's cheek.

"You have to live and let live, Jade-o. Don't cling so tightly."

But how could she not? Her soul constantly searched for the ground, the soft soil, a place to dig in deep. "What did you mean when you said to Max, 'Thanks for last night'?"

"Oh, he just spent the evening with me, picked up dinner from Mae's, brought me my ginger tea."

Jade brushed the trickle of tears from her cheek. "He's so confounding. Sweet and kind, so loving, then whap, he's a lying cheater."

"The answer's already in your heart. Search. You'll find it. You're so strong and capable, Jade. Don't be afraid."

"That's just it, Mama, I'm always a little bit afraid."

~

"Jade?" The bedroom door hinges squeaked. "Sugar, you awake?"

"I'm sleeping." Light from the hall cut a triangle in the darkness. Jade burrowed her face into her pillow.

"Jade, shug, it's me, June." She snapped on the bedside lamp and shook Jade's shoulder. "Darling, we have to take Beryl to the hospital."

Jade shot up, her hair fringing her face. "What's wrong?"

"She's burning up, darling. Soaked right through her nightgown to the sheet. Her breathing is shallow. I think it's pneumonia."

"What time is it?" Jade scrambled from the bed, turning in circles, grasping for her bearings. Jeans, yes, she needed her jeans. She tugged them on over her pajamas. Where was her sweatshirt? Aiming for the closet, she ran into the wall. Growling, she hammered it three times. "Who put this here?"

"The builder, I believe." June steered her to the closet. "Is this what you want?"

Jade tugged her sweatshirt from the top shelf. "Is she awake?"

"Not really. She stirs and mumbles occasionally."

"What made you check on her?" Shoes, the cold floor reminded her she needed shoes. And socks.

"I woke up a little after three to go to the bathroom and heard Beryl moaning, thrashing around. Should we call an ambulance?"

"I can take her in Paps's truck. It'll be faster." Jade dropped to her knees, searching for her shoes. "Can you get Mama ready while I bring the truck around?" What would the morning have looked like if June hadn't checked on Mama?

"I'm going with you." June darted out the door.

"No, June, I'll need the whole seat to lay Mama down." Jade tied on her sneakers. Forget socks. No time. Jade stumbled across the hall to the bathroom and scooped her hair back into a ponytail. She splashed her face with cold water, trying to douse the hovering fog.

Down the stairs, Jade grabbed her jacket from the back of the kitchen chair and the truck keys from the hook by the door, where they always stayed.

The dark morning was still with an icy thickness. Jade walked, then jogged toward the barn. She wasn't ready for Mama to die. Not when there was treasure yet to be discovered.

The engine rattled when she fired up the truck. The gears whined and the brakes squealed as Jade drove toward the back porch. Leaving the engine idling with the heater blowing, she popped loose the passenger door and ran inside.

June met her in the upstairs hall. "I put a fresh nightgown on her, her coat, socks, and a hat."

"Mama?" Jade approached Mama's side of the bed. She was so frail and small, pale and glistening with perspiration. "Mama?"

No answer.

Scooping Mama into her arms was all too easy. Her bones were discernible beneath her gown.

"Let me go along." June followed Jade down the stairs with an armload of blankets. "I can hold Beryl."

"June, please, stay here, man the phone." Jade cuddled Mama close as she exited the back door, careful not to bump her head or feet. Her heart and mind were awake, beating and thinking.

"She's going to be all right," June said, tucking the blankets around Mama as Jade settled her in the truck. "I know it."

"You don't know that, June." Jade clapped Mama's door closed and walked around to the driver's side.

"I guess I don't, but I'll be praying. I'll call the prayer team at church back home, get them praying."

Jade held on to her door for a moment, then stepped back, falling into June's arms. June hesitated, then tightened her arms around Jade's back, whispering, "Dear Jesus, dear Jesus."

As Jade fired out of the driveway, the tires crunching over the gravel, Mama moaned. Jade reached over and pressed her arm. "Stay with me, Mama. Stay with me."

The truck shimmied as Jade urged the speedometer toward eighty, flying west on route 163, gripping the wheel for control, the high beams slicing through the darkness.

Jesus, Jesus, Jesus.

Jade dropped to her knees before the gold cross perched on the wooden table of the hospital chapel. A prism of colors reflected off the gold and cascaded over the Communion table and onto the floor.

A man-made light burnt through the stained glass suspended from the ceiling behind the cross. The image captured Jade. The juxtaposition of God's work and man's.

Jade spoke to the Light she knew to be real. *Jesus. Jesus. Jesus.*

After four hours of waiting, uncomfortable in the molded plastic chairs and subzero temperature of the ER, the attending doctor finally admitted Mama.

He had to wake up Dr. Meadows for a consult, not knowing exactly what was wrong with her or how to treat her. Too much education can dull an otherwise great mind.

Now, three floors up, Mama slept semipeacefully in her room hooked to an IV, antibiotics pumping into her system.

Jade had e-mailed an update to Aiden and Willow, asking them to come. Immediately. It would take both of them several days to make travel arrangements from Guatemala and Alaska.

Then she wandered the hospital halls until she found the chapel. Jade stretched prostrate before the altar, sipping on an odd cocktail of loneliness and anxiety. Her skin twitched. Her head buzzed. Her heart hurt. She'd spent so many years angry at her mama only to discover her uniqueness at the untimely end of her life.

First grade . . . Jade remembered the long plank-walk down the gravel driveway to the bus stop. She'd stopped at the edge of the gravel and glanced back at Mama, who stood on the porch with her coffee, watching.

If Aiden hadn't been holding on to her hand, Jade would've run back to the house, crying, and buried her face against Mama's jeans.

Jade pounded her fist on the chapel floor. "God, I'm not ready to lose her." Too tired to weep, Jade's heart was soggy with emotion.

From the chairs, her phone beeped. It had been beeping for the past hour, so Jade pushed herself up to her knees and crawled toward her purse. It was probably June messaging to find out what was going on.

Lillabeth had also texted a dozen updates on the eight hundred dollars she spent on the Johnson City estate. She was quite proud of her purchases.

Jade replied: *Ya done good.*

There were messages from Daphne and Margot, checking in. One from Tom at Benson Law with an update on the Blue Two insurance debacle. Looked like arbitration was in the future. Another from Kip informing Jade he could not start working until he had money.

And three voice messages from Max.

"Jade, come on, call me back, this is stupid—" Delete.

"I need to give you the latest on Asa—" Delete.

"Jade, this is important—" Delete.

She'd asked for space. What did his lawyer-mind not grasp about that concept? Life didn't always revolve around him, surprise, surprise. Couldn't Max just grow up and see that?

From the back of the chapel, the door hinges moaned and a bright light shot into the room. Jade looked up. Who was joining her in the early morning? The phone slipped from her fingers.

Dustin Colter.

"What are you doing here?" She crawled to her feet, tucking her phone back into her purse.

"Is this a bad time?" He hesitated before coming all the way inside. His chestnut hair had lost its tight curl but grew in long waves around his ears and neck. His open jacket revealed a neat plaid shirt hanging over his crisp jeans.

"Please, come in." He looked good with his Elvis-hook smile and ocean-blue eyes.

Dustin enveloped her in his thick arms before she could exhale. She pressed her cheek against his chest like he was a warm blanket on a cold night. Seeing him made coming home complete. As if Jade had suddenly realized something was missing from her life.

"What are you doing here?"

Dustin's embrace didn't ease up. "I wanted to make sure you were all right."

"How did you know?" Jade stepped out of his arms. Leaning against him, inhaling his fresh meadow scent, brought her weaknesses and vulnerability to the surface. He'd not been dangerous when he came to Whisper Hollow days before her wedding. But the terrain of her life and heart had changed since then.

"Linc called, asked me to work on the Cadillac. I stopped by the house to give it a look. Your mother-in-law told me about your mom."

"You work on cars now?" Jade folded into one of the chairs, tucking her arms close against her body. If she stood next to him any longer, she'd meld into him, weeping, letting out weeks' worth of pain and disappointment, using him as her wall. "What happened to St. Louis and Purina, brand manager and all?"

He smiled, shaking his head, and sat next to her. "Marketing, branding, business strategies, spinning the truth . . . not me. I looked in the mirror one day and said, 'Dude, what are you doing here?' I quit, moved back into the farmhouse. Mom was about to go crazy living with Sydney and her brood, so she moved in with me. Yes, I'm a thirty-two-year-old man living with his mother; save the jokes for later. Remember Hartline?"

"Okay . . . no jokes pending. Hartline? Yeah, how could I forget?" Ben Hartline had been one of Dustin's best friends in high school. The night Jade realized her relationship, her secret marriage to Dustin, was unraveling, Dustin had been at Hartline's house flirting with his sister, Kendall.

"Yeah, right." Dustin cleared his throat. "Anyway, we were having a few beers one night out at the new place on 163, The Hoss, mellowing to the jukebox, dreaming about what we'd do if we could do anything we wanted . . ." He stopped and analyzed her for a moment. "Hey, I didn't come here to talk about me. I came to find out about you. How are you? How's your mom?"

"I'm tired, but fine. Mama has bacterial pneumonia." Jade leaned forward, resting her arms on her thighs. "They have her hooked up to a heavy antibiotic, which seems to be working. She's stable and sleeping." She held on to his gaze. So much blue hope and strength there. "She's dying, Dustin."

The first sob hit Jade without warning. She'd not been braced, so her arms slipped from her legs as she collapsed forward, shaking. *Mama, Max, June . . .* Her emotions stormed her heart's gates.

Dustin slipped his arms around her and cradled her against his chest, stroking her hair, whispering everything would be all right.

But it wouldn't be all right. *Everything* was changing. Everything *had* changed.

Jade cried against him until his arm slipped slowly down her back and around her waist. The familiar and comfortable move sent warmth through her and suddenly reminded her of what it was like to be in love with Dustin, pressed against him with his thundering heart in her ear.

Jade jumped up, breaking free, finding the tissue box up by the altar. "Sorry, I didn't mean to dump all over you." She blew her nose and wadded the tissue against her palm.

"Don't be." His voice was husky with emotion.

It felt as if the connection between them had never severed.

"So you and Hartline dreamed up a business?" She returned to her chair, sitting on the edge and leaning away from him. Looking down as she squeezed the tissue tighter in her hand, she was suddenly aware of her bare left finger. In her haste and panic over Mama, she'd forgotten her rings.

"We did. Turned Dad's equipment garage into a chop shop. We do specialized cars and trucks. It's been an interesting adventure." His smile confirmed he'd found his life's calling. "The show *Overhaul* took a look at us . . . We have a shot at being a part of a mid-America show they're creating."

"Well, look at you and Hart." Jade dotted her wet eyes with the dry edge of her tissue, then hid the wad in her purse. "You must be thrilled."

"Nothing is signed yet, but the producers love Hart's work. His designs got us the attention."

"So you can fix the Cadillac? All we need is a new top, not a new chop." She sat back with a smile.

"New top, not a new chop . . . Ha, I like it." He angled his body toward hers and brushed the flyaway hair from her eyes. The move was almost like a reflex, intimate and tender. "I already took the car to the shop. We need to look up parts, but we can have the old girl good as new in a week to ten days. The motor for the top is tricky, but doable. How did the top get so mangled?"

"I jumped on it." Jade let free her ponytail and combed her hair with her fingers.

"Interesting . . ." He laughed low. "Because?"

"Because it wouldn't go up. It wouldn't go down. And I was mad."

"Now, what did that poor top ever do to you?" He peered down at her. "It's really good to see you."

The tenor of his voice made her drink deep of his spirit. "I must be a sight," she said. He was trying to read her, figure out what drove her to trample a convertible top. Dustin knew darn well it wasn't because the top was stuck.

"A beautiful sight, if you ask me." He motioned to the hem of her jeans. "I like the pajama-trim look."

"I wasn't exactly awake when I dressed to come here." Jade lifted her foot to see her cotton bottoms poking through the end of her pant leg. "Couldn't find socks."

"I'm sorry about your mama." Dustin rubbed his hand across her back, over her shoulders. Every sleeping molecule awakened.

Jade couldn't discern if being tired, frustrated, or feeling alone made her want to curl up in his arms and never leave, but with each minute, with each touch, her pulse tugged her toward him. Dustin was her heart's first home.

And the combination of past memories colliding with present emotions tempted her to leap without looking.

"Is there anything I can do for you, Jade?"

Leave, don't come back. Close that door to your heart that remains ajar. "Well, I'm hungry, I guess."

"Breakfast, coming up." Dustin jumped up and started for door. "Let's see . . . eggs and bacon with wheat toast and a side of pancakes?"

"Some things never change."

"Some things never do." His eyes lingered on her as if he wanted her to hear what lived beneath the surface. "If you're not here?"

"I'll be in Mama's room. Three-oh-three."

As he exited, a nurse entered. "Ah, there you are, Mrs. Benson."

"Is Mama okay?" Jade stood and reached for her purse.

"She's awake, asking for you."

Eighteen

June wrapped her hair in a do-rag and carted all the cleaning supplies from the utility room and from under the kitchen sink onto the red Formica table.

Snapping on a pair of laytex gloves, she faced her image reflected in the shade falling across the kitchen window. "Germs, your days are numbered. Junie the Disinfector is in the house."

She rolled her eyes at the words. In her younger days, she was always doing something funny, urging her sorority sisters to put on plays for their house mother or their favorite fraternity men. She was the nucleus around which they all bonded.

"Junie, the Kappa Alphas from Mercer called. They're coming . . . they're coming! What should we do?" Squeal, scream, giggle, pound their feet into the floor as they turned in a circle.

But now she was sixty-something, coloring the gray out of her hair and considering Botox injections. Her only child was grown, successful at law but flailing in his relationships. And she, June Benson, spent the bulk of her marriage seeking penance and forgiving her husband's sins.

The lively June Carpenter of Wesleyan College was nothing like the stoic June Benson of Whisper Hollow.

After a second, the shadow on the window faded, taking June's reflection with it. Peering beyond the rain and dirt-splattered pane, June studied the gray clouds congregating from the northwest. Looked like fall instead of spring.

She began her work upstairs, yanking off Beryl's bedding and tossing it down the laundry chute to the basement. What a handy device, a laundry chute.

She planned to give Beryl's sheets and blankets a good hot washing, Lysol the mattress, and open a few windows to let in the fresh prairie air.

For the better part of the day, she worked with zeal, going from room to room, cleaning and disinfecting, thankful to be busy.

Jade had called to let her know Beryl was out of the woods, for now. "See, I told you." And Rebel sent one text message: *The governor is deciding tomorrow.*

Linc came around in the afternoon, and while June wrote a shopping list— she felt like baking—she had him chop some firewood. Snow was in the air.

The doorbell rang as June sent Linc off to the store. She opened to find three women standing on the porch.

"Can I help you?"

"You must be June. I'm Carla Colter. My son, Dustin, is the one who looked at your car this morning."

"Right, right, do come in, please." The one who married Jade before Max.

The ladies entered as Carla finished the introductions. "This is Sharon Watson and Elizabeth Stone. We're friends of Beryl's."

"It's lovely to meet you." June pressed her hand to her head, thinking twice about removing the do-rag. "Pardon my appearance, but I've been trying to keep busy, cleaning. Would you like some tea?"

"Yes, thank you. Can we do anything?" Carla asked, following June to the kitchen. "Cook? Shop? Help clean?"

"Pray. Beryl could use a bit of divine intervention." June filled the kettle with water and set it on the burner.

The teatime conversation was about Beryl and her health, then drifted toward friends and family who suffered illness and the mercy of God. June liked the women. She found their company refreshing, unencumbered with expectation.

They'd eaten all the Chips Ahoy! cookies (a Linc shopping choice) and sipped through a second cup of Earl Gray tea when Linc burst through the back door, his arm threaded through plastic bags of groceries. "Excuse me, ladies." He glanced at June. "Where do you want me to put these?"

"The counter is fine, Linc." She moved to help him.

Carla helped unload the few groceries while Sharon offered to write up her favorite cake recipe. Once the kitchen was squared away, Carla carried her cup to the sink. "June, we'll get out of your way, but call us if you need anything."

"I will, I will." She walked with them to the door. "Thank you so much for the company."

Linc was waiting for her in the kitchen. "Want me to bring in the firewood, Mrs. Benson?"

"Please." June was halfway through putting up the groceries when her cell went off. She answered, hoping to hear good news from Jade.

"Mrs. Benson, this is Carissa McCown."

"Slow news day?" June exhaled. "What can I do for you?"

"Can you give me a statement about Claire Falcon?"

June froze. The phone slipped in her fingers.

"She's accusing you of assaulting her in a parking lot."

"You're joking." Will the circus *ever* leave town?

"She's not filed official charges, but while speaking with a reporter—"

"A reporter? You mean you, Miss McCown?" June's fingernails made deep imprints into her palm.

"Do you have a comment, Mrs. Benson?"

Linc stumbled through the door, his arms loaded with firewood.

"No, I don't." June caught the door for Linc, holding it open.

"Can you tell me about Bill Novak?"

A gray veil dropped over June's mind. A cold chill slithered down her torso. "I—I have no idea?"

"What was your relationship to Bill Novak, Mrs. Benson?"

Linc moved past her, heading out for a second load of wood. June rammed the phone at him.

"What? Mrs. Benson, I—"

"There's a woman on the other end. Talk to her."

He wrinkled his brow. After a second, he put the phone to his ear. "Lincoln here, who's this?" He pulled out a kitchen chair and sat. "A reporter? You don't say."

June smashed through the back door, striding across the yard to the woodpile. Yanking the ax free from the tip of a round, stubby log, she stood the piece on end, raised the ax, and swung down hard—tennis elbow be darned. "Here's to you, Rebel Benson."

She whacked the piece again. Bill Novak. And again. *How could he?* Thick, ragged splinters hit the air around her. This time Rebel had gone too far.

~

He'd been summoned. To the wide corner office on the west side of the tenth floor. Max worked his way through the maze of offices and cubicles, hearing blips of strategy and planning by associates, most of it about lunch and the weekend.

Passing Cara's office, he poked his head inside and gave her a thumbs-up. "Thank you."

"You're welcome," she called after him.

She'd worked her magic and got Judge Howard to kick an injunction filed by Bradley to give the McClures temporary custody of Asa. He was awarded sole custody. For now.

"How's the nanny?"

Max stepped into Cara's office. The old man could wait a few minutes. "Mrs. Tobias? Great. A true Mrs. Doubtfire." Max had spent the last twenty-four hours hiring a nanny and buying a crib, unloading Asa's clothes and toys.

"And your first night with your son?"

"Rough. I'd never changed a diaper before. Asa kept looking at me like, *Get it right, dude.* When Mrs. Tobias arrived, he took right to her, so I think he'll have a good day."

"I heard you were summoned to The Corner." She tipped her head toward his dad's office. "What do you think he wants?"

"Probably wants to make sure I'm ready to take over when the governor appoints him to the court. Do I have a nanny? Am I working on getting Jade home? All his little fix-it details."

"You think he's going to get the court?"

Max started for the door. "I think he's done everything in his power to make sure he gets the court. Even sending out the press release."

"Your mother's too classy not to come back."

"Classy, yes. But this time, I think she's adding smart."

As Max approached his dad's office, he straightened his tie and made sure his shirttail was tucked in tight. *Bring your A game, bring your A game.*

Max rapped lightly on the door under the nameplate Rebel Benson and then entered. Dad waved him in from the other side of his desk, phone to his ear.

"Art, I need to run. We'll talk soon."

Max reclined in the chair by the desk. He looked forward to moving in here. Two walls of windows, wet bar, shower, law library, sitting area. Mom's classic taste in art and color graced every nuance of the room.

"How goes it?" Dad rose from his mocha-colored leather chair, smoothing his tie and buttoning his coat as if he were about to address a judge and jury.

"Hired a nanny. Asa seems to like her. Changed my first diaper."

"Got to watch the boys; they'll get you." Rebel moved his finger in a spouting motion as he leaned against the edge of his desk.

"So I heard." But Max knew his dad didn't call him in to give parenting advice.

"What's up with the McClures?"

"Just getting started. You know how these things go. It'll take months to bring to trial if we even get that far. I'm hoping they'll get tired of the process and let it go."

"Not if they're listening to Bradley Richardson."

Max shifted forward. "We hired an investigator. Meanwhile, I have my son." The words *my son* still felt foreign even though he'd known for nineteen months. Even though Rice called once in a while to let him know how Asa fared. Man, he'd forgotten about those talks. If he confessed to Jade, she'd have another valid weapon in her arsenal of mistrust. "You might want to stop by one night and meet your grandson, Dad."

He nodded while gazing at the floor, distracted. "I'm sorry you're going through this, son."

"You didn't call me in here to talk about my situation with Asa." Max had watched his father charm unsuspecting witnesses, gain their confidence, then tear them apart like a hungry bear emerging after a long winter. The tactic came with a certain aura, a foreboding that now stirred in Max's gut.

"No way to put this gentle, son." Rebel glared hard at him. "I'm going to turn the firm over to Clarence Chambers when, if, I get the appointment to the court."

"Excuse me?" Max leaned forward. "For what reason? This is my firm, the family firm."

"And I'm still in charge."

"Not if you go to the court. The partnership agreement states if you leave the firm or die, the next Benson in line assumes control." For seventy-five years the rules had been ironclad. Father to son, father to son, father to son. No outsider ever ran Benson Law. "I can run this place with my eyes closed."

"I've got the executive management behind me on this, Max."

Max stood, Dad's confession sinking through him, stinging all the way down. "And what's your reasoning?" He kept his tone even. Calm and cool was the best strategy with Dad.

"Simple. You're not ready, Max. You just said you could run this place with your eyes closed." Dad walked over to the wet bar and set out two glasses. "That's exactly what I'm concerned you'll do. You live by the seat of your pants, not looking before you leap, finding shortcuts, looking for the easy way. Because you're good at just about everything, your methods have worked. For you. Right now, everything around you is in upheaval. I won't let the firm move under your umbrella."

Dad dropped ice in the glasses and splashed them with Diet Coke. Pain, phantom or real, gripped Max's back. "You're taking away your own son's inheritance."

"Temporarily. Until you work through all your private battles. I assume you've considered what this case with the McClures could do to your reputation, as well as the family and the firm." Dad slid one of the glasses to the end of the bar for Max.

"What do you suggest I do? Not fight for my son? Give in to Gus and Lorelai?"

"Fight for your son, Max. But not while running Benson Law. I'd bet money that Gus is counting on you choosing the firm and your reputation over Asa."

Max picked up his glass, but he wasn't thirsty. "I won't abandon him."

"You need to learn from this, son." Dad sipped his soda. "Always carry condoms."

Max peered at his dad. Was he serious with that remark? "I'm married. Unlike you, I'm not going to cheat on my wife."

"Hear what I'm saying to you, son. Think ahead, plan, cover yourself."

More left-handed advice. "Like you did with Claire?" Max tossed back his soda with one gulp.

Dad refilled his glass. "Our clients need to know that they are valued and that the firm is looking after their interests. The future of the firm, our employees, our livelihood, depends on it. Clarence can do that well."

Max shoved the chair aside and confronted his dad. "When has my private life ever interfered with this firm?"

"Last fall when you had to leave a million-dollar case to spend a week in the hospital detoxing." Dad's steely gaze never wavered. "You don't handle stress well. Work on that." He slowly raised his glass to his lips. "Clarence will retire in a few years. You'll be ready then."

Max set his glass on the bar. "How are you going to announce it?"

"No big hoopla. Low-key. Give a call to all our major accounts. Clarence is on board, ready to go if the governor calls."

"Rebel?" A knock sounded before the door eased open. Gina peered inside. "The governor's on the phone."

"Well, what do you know?" Rebel checked Max visually. "Are you on the team?"

"Yeah." Max aimed for the door. *For now.*

Nineteen

The closet's naked lightbulb dropped a hard glare over Jade's shoulders and cast her silhouette over the old sewing box of photos.

Sitting cross-legged on the old shag carpet in Mama's closet, Jade held a black-and-white photo in her hand of Mama with long blonde hair wearing a headband and fatigue jacket. Just like the hitchhiker. Jade put the picture in her pile of things to take home with her. Her pile of one . . . so far.

Dr. Meadows called earlier to say Mama could go home in the morning. Jade had run upstairs to get clothes for her to wear home, and while digging around in the closet, she'd stumbled upon an anthology of Mama's past.

Inside the sewing box of pictures were shots of Mama with Aiden and Jade as babies, though most of the images were from Mama's commune and hitch-hiking days. Jade only recognized two people, Mama's friends Carlisle and

Eclipse. Then she found a stunner. Mama sitting two feet from a smiling George Harrison, sitting cross-legged, playing his guitar. Oh, June had to see this one.

Jade thought of the perfect frame she had at the Blue Umbrella. She'd hang George and Mama in the shop.

Next she found a portfolio of mint-condition, original show prints of bands who played San Francisco's Fillmore Auditorium between '66 and '67.

Turning over one poster advertising the Grateful Dead and Jefferson Airplane, Jade found an inscription on the back. *To Beryl, with love, Wes Wilson.*

Signed by the artist. This was an amazing find. Jade set it in the pile. How did Mama know these people? How had her experiences with them impacted her life? She guessed the poster to be worth a good bit of money. But she'd frame it and hang it on the wall next to the ex-Beatle.

In a leather suitcase, Mama had folded up several muumuu-type dresses, miniskirts and tops, and a tattered pair of moccasins. In a banged-up shoe box, Jade discovered letters to and from Granny and Paps, from the Vietnam vet Mama had fallen for when she was seventeen, concert ticket stubs, and a variety of tarnished silver and turquoise jewelry.

Pulling a letter from an envelope stamped July 1967, Jade's eyes scanned her mother's young, determined handwriting.

Dear Mother,

I'm fine. Stop worrying. Marilyn and I have met some far-out people, having a groovy time. We go home to Aunt Lillith and Uncle Dave's once a week for laundry and a square meal.

We have a cool crash pad right on Haight. Lots of the kids go there at night and it's such a serene scene.

We help the Diggers serve breakfast in the morning, and I just started help-ing at the free clinic. It's like I'm home, Mother. These people understand me. I understand them. This is the scene I was born to live in, I know it. I feel it.

I don't think I'm coming for my senior year. Why do I need to graduate high school when our boys are fighting a useless war? The government is ripping off our generation and is going to kill us all if we don't do something about it.

Jade laughed softly. Mama sipped a lot of the political Kool-Aid of her day. But Paps put an end to her plan to drop out of high school. He drove out to San Francisco and brought her home. Paps wasn't a big man, but he was powerfully built with a gentle demeanor. Until pushed. Once he arrived in San Francisco, Jade knew Mama had no choice but to come home to Prairie City. Mama was lucky. She had Paps.

Jade folded the letter, missing her grandpa, her granny, and her innocent youth. She was only ten when Paps died, but she remembered the safety of his tree-trunk arms.

"There you are." June stood in the closet doorway, her hands on her hips, her hair tied in a handkerchief. She wore flared slacks and a short-sleeved sweater-top. "Are these Beryl's clothes for tomorrow?" June stooped to pick up the slacks and blouse.

"Yeah. They should fit." Jade offered up the picture of Mama with George. "I found this stuff while going through her things. She really wanted to do something, be somebody."

June stared at the picture for a long time. "We all want to leave our mark in the world, Jade. Especially when we're young."

"I was reading her letters, and she was such a combination of wisdom and unfocused zeal. One sentence she's volunteering to feed the hungry. In the next, she announces she's not going to finish high school because the country was at war."

"That's the way it was with our generation." June settled on the closet floor by the box of pictures, curling her legs behind her. "Look, there you are, Jade. With your mama. Or is that Willow?"

"Me. My dad took these. Aiden found his Nikon when he was nine, and that's how he got started in photography."

"Hospice called." June straightened and replaced the pictures. "They'll be here in the morning."

"Oh, here's a good one." Jade handed June a picture of Mama and Daddy. A rare find.

June motioned to the poster of Scott McKenzie. "I can still hear him singing, 'If you're going to San Francisco, be sure to wear flowers in your hair.'"

"It's the right thing to do, isn't it?" Jade shuffled through another stack of photos. "Calling hospice, discussing the details of Mama dying at home."

"It's what she wants, so, yes, it is."

Talking about hospice iced Jade's sentimental journey into the past. She closed the sewing box lid. "I feel like we're just giving up. And I hate it."

"It's been a long eight years, Jade. She's tired. Most chronic leukemia patients don't live this long."

"Well, I'm not ready for her to go. I can't make up for lost time if she dies." Getting to her feet, Jade stepped over the memorabilia and passed June to exit the closet. Did the earth under her feet have to crack open all at once? "Even though I hated her at times and we weren't close for many years, she is still my mama. Daddy's in Washington, out of my life. She's my only real parent, June. And she's dying. I'm thirty-one. How is this fair?"

"I don't suppose it is. How is it fair Rice died at thirty-eight, leaving her nineteen-month-old son behind?"

"It's not fair. But don't mix issues, June." Jade peered at her through misty eyes. She slipped off the headband she'd tied around her head and carefully folded it against her palm. "I just hate the alone feeling. Even more that I'm afraid."

"Sugar, you're not alone." June stood, cradling Mama's clothes. "You got your husband, me, Willow, and Aiden."

"I'm not going back to Max, June."

"Just like that, you've decided? Doesn't he have a say?"

"He voiced his opinion when he slept with Rice."

"Jade, come on, aren't you being a bit immature?"

"If being mature means I have to endure forty years with an adulterer, then, yes, I'll be immature."

"Max is not Rebel, Jade."

"No, he's not. Yet." Jade turned out the closet light and closed the door. She wanted out of the room. The walls were inching closer, squeezing out the thin air.

"Jade, Max has always struggled with being sidetracked. He's brilliant . . . And I'm not saying that as a mother. He is. But his weaknesses rival his strengths. That's how he got onto the pain pills. How he ended up with Rice in his room on his bachelor weekend."

"I don't have to go down with him, June." Jade started down the back stairs. She was hungry. "I grew up dealing with a lot of other people's weaknesses. I'm all out of endurance."

June broke into the kitchen behind Jade. "So you judge Max?"

"Judge? No. But make a sound assessment? Yes. I won't be tread upon."

"Is that what you think of me? I'm tread upon?"

"Aren't you?" Jade jerked opened the fridge and took out sandwich meat and fixings. Beyond the kitchen window, Tank Victor plowed his field.

"Love makes us do strange things." June walked around the table and took the bread from the wooden box. She tugged a couple of napkins from the holder on the counter and got down paper plates from the top of the refrigerator.

Jade tore open the lunch meat package. "By the way, Aiden and Willow will be here this weekend."

"Beryl will be happy to hear that." June handed Jade two slices of bread.

"I hope she's still here by the time they arrive." Jade peeled off a couple of slices of roast beef and matted them into her bread.

"She's too stubborn to die without seeing her children." June handed Jade the mayonnaise jar and a knife.

"Thank you."

June walked behind Jade, her fingers gently dusting her shoulder. "Now, you want tea with your sandwich or a soda? Or pop, as you say in Iowa?"

Mama was home and settled into her bed. She fussed about Jade and June fussing, cracking on herself about her old, worn-out body. But she surrendered to her pillows without a word.

Her legs constantly rustled under the quilt. Every once in a while, she'd moan, low and long.

The hospice nurse arrived around noon and spent a good bit of the afternoon talking with Mama. Then she sat on the living room sofa with Jade and June, reviewing the medications Dr. Meadow prescribed, setting expectations and explaining the goal to keep Mama comfortable and let her live out her final days the way she wanted.

"If she wants to go outside, let her. If she wants a chili dog—"

"Mercy be, a chili dog?" On a good, *healthy* day, June turned up her nose to chili dogs.

"Yes." The hospice nurse gave June The Look. *You're not going to be difficult, are you?* "A chili dog."

"I'll bring her everything on the Dairy Queen menu if she wants," Jade said.

"Only if she wants." The nurse smiled. "I know this is hard, but the less stressed and more comfortable your mother is, the better it will be for all involved. Be prepared for Beryl to see things."

"Like what?" Jade asked. The hitchhiker came to mind, but that was her vision.

"She might see someone from her past, a parent or treasured family member, maybe an old friend. I've had patients see demons and angels, even God."

Intense. "Will she get frightened or upset?" Jade glanced at June.

"She might. Usually the patients have comforting visions. Just talk with her, help her through anything that might be disturbing." The nurse reached down for her bag. "Here's my card. Call if you need me."

June walked the hospice nurse out. Jade brought Mama her tea and set her up with the remote control and a tattered paperback.

"*Atlas Shrugged*?" Jade read the book's spine.

Beryl held out her hand. "Been on page eighty-five since high school."

"Ayn Rand? Seriously?" Jade flipped through the pages of the book before putting it on the nightstand. "They'll come take your socialist card away."

"Got to see what the other side is thinking." The bang of the kitchen's screen door echoed up the stairs along with excited female voices and laughter. "Having a party down there?"

Footsteps echoed up the back staircase and June appeared in the door. "Carla Colter is here to see you, Beryl. Sharon and Elizabeth too. They brought a passel of food. Mercy, we'll have to pawn some off on Linc."

"Well, send them on up." Mama scooped her hand through the air. Once. Her hand dropped to the quilt. But Mama never refused a party.

"Wait a few minutes, June. Then send them up." Jade stretched out next to Mama and held her hand, listening to Mama's soft and even breathing. "Are you sure you're up to this?"

"Jade, don't coddle me. The hospice nurse gave me the same speech she gave you and June," Mama said. "Carla and the girls are good friends. Though, please, go down there and make sure Carla didn't make her tuna casserole. A hideous dish, but none of us ever had the heart to tell her. She keeps cooking it and bringing it to parties."

"Doesn't she get suspicious when no one eats it?"

"Shh, we just scoop it into the garbage."

Jade laughed. "Your idea, I'm sure." Jade had eaten a lot of meals at the Colters' the year she'd been with Dustin, but she didn't remember bad tuna casserole. Yet she'd been so happy and in love, Carla could've served baked mud and Jade would have thought it was chocolate.

Above Mama's bed, the ceiling fan swished the warm air around. Daylight slipped beneath the partially drawn shades. In the corner by the dresser, the floor lamp cut a white V into the shadows and highlighted the edge of the area rug.

Below them, the kitchen was full and alive with female voices and clattering dishes. But the bedroom remained still and peaceful.

"Are you scared, Mama?"

It took a moment for her to answer. "A little." She squeezed Jade's fingers. "I want you to do me a favor."

"Anything."

"Will you call him, please?"

"Who?" Jade sat up, peering at Mama, who spoke with her eyes closed. She'd anticipated this, Mama's deathbed urging for her to work it all out with Max. Another warning from the hospice nurse: the dying become peacemakers.

"Your dad. Please, call Harlan. He's all you have."

Jade picked at a pucker in the quilt, inhaling slowly. "He's all you have" stung her heart with the same sense of loneliness she'd experienced sitting in the closet yesterday.

Several times last night she'd walked the edge of panic, the burnt amber sparking on the horizon of her soul and heart. Her heart raced as she tried to outmaneuver the bottoms-out fear.

She searched her mind for the triggers, but other than *her whole life*, there wasn't anything specific. If she closed her eyes, she could almost envision some dark thing hovering over her, spitting and vomiting its brand of evil. At least that's how she felt in those moments, like an ooze ran down her hair.

Jade hopped off Mama's bed, trying to escape the memory. On its own, it had the power to kick open panic's door. Purple swirls hung in the corners of the room waiting for their moment to descend.

"Jade?" Mama called, eyes still closed. "You all right?"

No, no, I'm not all right. You're leaving me. I'm alone. "Just stretching my legs." Jade paced, whispering, "Jesus, Jesus, Jesus" as she corralled her thoughts and spurred them away from the mire of anxiety.

Loneliness and anxiety were kissing cousins.

After a moment, peace flowed from the well she'd been digging for the past two years, since she'd met Jesus. It only took a few seconds, but seemed like an eternity. The darkness ebbed and the boundaries of her true self came into view.

"It's not a fair request, I know," Mama whispered. "But I'm a dying woman."

"Mama, we're just not meant to be, Daddy and me." Jade exhaled, sitting on the side of the bed. "He came to the wedding, and after a few e-mails, we just stopped communicating. What do you say? 'Hey, how's life been treating you since you walked out on me when I was eight?' We can't undo all the years of distance and silence. Besides, I have Aiden and Willow. And the Bensons . . . well, June." She rubbed her forehead with her fingers.

Was she destined to be alone, without a family? She was finally finding her place as a daughter with Mama, who was leaving this world. Where was the place Jade could exist where she was 100 percent home? No masks. No secrets. No addictions, or abortions, or miscarriages, or ex-fiancés and ex-husbands.

"I never asked much of you, Jade. Didn't ask you to make straight As or to . . ." Mama struggled for each word, for each breath. ". . . cheerleader . . . band, or home . . . queen." The rattle in her chest vibrated like metal dragging along the pavement.

"Mama." Jade's gaze fell on the oxygen tank, trying to remember the nurse's instructions. "Do you need the mask?" Dr. Meadows said she'd be weak.

"No . . ." Mama peeked through narrowed eye slits. "I'm fine."

Jade smoothed her hand over Mama's pale forehead. "I never gave you a chance. Never tried to understand you. You wanted me to try to see the world through your eyes, but I refused to try. I liked being resentful."

"Did the same thing to Mother . . ." Mama barely lifted her finger to point. "In the dresser . . . for you."

"Hey up there, is it safe to come up?" Carla's voice shot up the stairway and into the room.

"Five minutes, Carla," Jade called out the door, then went to Mama's dresser. "Which drawer?"

"Top . . . left."

Sliding the drawer open, Jade found a small, velvet black ring box and inside, Mama's jade ring. "You kept this?"

Jade hadn't heard the story of Daddy giving Mama the ring during a Fleetwood Mac concert in decades. "I thought you tossed this into Miller's Pond."

"I wanted to . . ." she whispered. "But we named you after—" Talking drained her strength. "Jade . . ."

Jade slipped the ring onto her pinky finger and held up her hand for Mama to see. "It's beautiful."

Mama strained to open her eyes. "Jade-o, promise me you'll talk to your dad. For me."

For Mama's sake, he'd come to Jade's wedding. For Mama's sake, she could promise to call him. "If I say no, then you'll have to keep on living."

"If you say no, I'll die with a wound in my heart."

Jade knelt by her side of the bed. "Maybe we should just let things be, Mama. They are the way they are for a reason."

"Jade, try." Mama tugged on Jade's pinky finger, the one with the ring. "Promise me."

"Aren't you the one who told me not to cling to things in life that aren't making me happy? Or benefiting me? I should move on when the moving was good?"

"Jade-o, my roots-in-the-ground girl. Moving on is not for you. You need to be stable, in the same place, day after day, year after year. Leave the wandering to me and Willow."

"I'm tired of being grounded, Mama. I get stepped on." Jade studied the ring's shades and depth of green in the light. Next to it, her ring finger was stark and barren. She'd forgotten again.

Jade brushed the tears from her cheeks.

"You pull up roots too quickly, Jade-o, and you'll wither. You need the soil, sun, and rain, even the winds. Be strong. Bloom where you've been planted."

"What if I want to uproot and bloom in a new place?"

Mama touched her cheek. "Then do it quickly. Know what came to my mind while I was in the hospital? Your sixteenth birthday party."

"Oh, please, what a nightmare."

"Nightmare? What party are you remembering? I'll give you it started out slow, but—"

"All right, it's been five minutes. We're coming up," Carla called. Footsteps announced the approach of Mama's friends.

"Well, look at you all lounging around." Carla came around and hugged Mama, Sharon and Elizabeth right behind her.

Jade settled in the corner rocker. Mama's eyes brightened as she engaged her friends. What made her think of Jade's sixteenth birthday? She'd not thought about that night in a long time. She used to, though, when the afternoon was melancholy and she had nothing pressing on her mind.

Mama was having fun with the girls. Hard to imagine she and Carla once duked it out at the Coltons' the night Dustin broke up with her.

Sweet sixteen. Spring had come early to the prairie that year, and as Jade approached her birthday, she dared to dream of a party in the barn and dancing under low lights in the arms of Dustin Colter.

~

Paps's barn was fragrant with last fall's hay and the aroma of roasting meat. The beef and pork no one came to eat. In the hayloft, Jade laid on her back, staring at the dry, gray rafters, tears slipping down her cheeks to her ears.

Stupid party. Stupid, stupid, stupid.

"Hey there, Jade-o." Mama arrived over the edge of the loft. "Mother and I wondered where you'd hidden."

"Leave me alone." Jade wiped her face, sniffling.

Mama crawled across the hay and stretched out next to her. "At least you know who your friends are, right?"

"What friends?" A fresh tide of tears washed her eyes. Tonight was humiliating. She'd invited the entire sophomore class to her birthday party. All last week kids stopped her in the hallway to tell her they were, "ready to *par-tay*."

Granny took two days off work to clean the house and prepare food. Mama came off the road from driving the truck to help clean out the barn while Aiden wired it for lights and sound, then dug a big fire pit by the western field.

There was to be music and dancing. Barbeque and chips, with beans and slaw, cans of cold pop, and cookies, cakes, and pie.

Even little Willow helped, collecting firewood for a bonfire. Granny bought all the fixings for two hundred s'mores. Jade had new jeans, top, and shoes for the evening. And this morning she went by Millie's for a cut and blow-dry. For her birthday, Jade's best friend Rachel paid for her to get a set of acrylic nails.

But then Monday morning Shannon Bell arrived at school and tossed a grenade at Jade's parade, announcing *she* was having a party this weekend, "for the heck of it." She passed out hand-lettered invitations and promised big door prizes like a CD player.

"Here, Jade, just in case *no one* comes to your party, you can come to mine." Shannon had sneered a bit when she handed Jade an invite to *her* party. Why Shannon hated her, Jade couldn't figure.

"You could've picked another night." Rachel had jumped in front of Shannon, shoving her back a bit.

"But I liked *this* Saturday night."

"Witch." Rachel called after her, but Jade dug her fingernails into her friend's arm.

"Leave her be. It's okay."

"No, it's not. She put on this party just to spite you."

"Why would she want to spite me? She's got everything—head cheerleader, homecoming court, a new car, Dustin Colter."

"Never mind her, I'll talk up your party and everyone will come. People will see right through that spineless bleach-blonde, phony, plastic . . . Besides, it's your birthday, Jade."

But by seven thirty on party night, only Rachel and Coop had arrived. By eight, Jade's girlhood friends Chelle and Lindsay showed up with David and Sticks. Being inaugural members of the Death Dragon—a club started by neighborhood bully Boon-Doggle when they were ten—they were bound by an eternal code. Initiation into the club required spending a chilling night locked in Boon's daddy's cellar. They *had* to choose Jade over Shannon. At least for a little while.

But by nine, the party that never started was over. Even Rachel went home "to go to bed."

Jade rolled over on her side and wept against a clump of hay.

"Are you crying again?" Mama touched Jade's shoulder.

"It's my party, and I'll cry if I want to."

Mama started singing, "Cry if I want to, cry if I want to," snapping her fingers. Gag, she could be so annoying. Her voice grated like sandpaper. "I really should've been in music. Maybe my next boyfriend will be a musician."

"Why didn't they come?" Mama's musical aspirations aside, Jade sought comfort in her freewheeling mama.

"Jade, you'll make yourself crazy with that question. Do you really want to be friends with kids who chose a shallow girl like Shannon over a sweet, kind girl like you? You know, I bet she stuffs her bra."

"Mama." Why did she say things like that? A snort sounded through her nose as she moved onto her back. "Supposedly she did in sixth grade." Jade covered her snort with her hand. "I just wish I could be popular."

"It ain't what it's cracked up to be. In ten, fifteen years, the cheerleaders will be fat, the star athletes bald, the nerds richer than Donald Trump, and the girls like you will be running a Madison Avenue advertising company that pitches weight-loss programs and hair-growth products."

Now that was a pretty picture.

"But you know what's sad, Jade-o?"

"What?" She sniffed.

"You were so busy crying over who didn't come, you didn't appreciate the kids who did show up. You snubbed them while you watched the driveway for more cars. With five or six of my friends, we'd throw a party to beat the band."

"I've seen your parties. And you *are* popular. People come from all over."

"Including the sheriff's deputies." Mama laughed.

"Just want to see what all the fun is about."

Mama's parties were famous. Every Fourth of July, her gypsy friends migrated to Prairie City, set up a tent village in the yard, and partied every weekend until Labor Day. People from all over the Midwest drove to the farm on weekends. They danced to their own melodies while reminiscing about James Dean, Bob Dylan, and Woodstock.

"Everything is so serious with you, Jade-o. If it's not exactly like you thought it would be, you think it's a failure. What about the spectrum of colors in between?" Mama swept her hand in the air, left to right. "You and Rachel could be getting down right now with Coop, who is downright cute if you ask me, and David or Sticks—watching him dance would be worth the price of admission—but you're up here moping."

"I wanted *him* to come." Jade grabbed a handful of hay and tossed it at Mama. Might as well confess, get it off her mind.

"Him who?" Mama watched her for a moment, then said, "Ah, our knight in shining armor, Dustin Colter. You still got it for that boy?"

"Maybe." Ever since he and his buddies rescued Mama and Jade from the cornfield, she couldn't forget him. And it'd been eight months. Then a few weeks ago he started sitting kitty-corner to her in Algebra 2.

"How did you know Daddy was the one? Or Mike?"

"Mike? The one?" Mama laughed. "He was sexy and got me pregnant. But your daddy, now he was special. He swept me off my feet. Never even saw love coming."

"Then why did it end?"

"Haven't we been over this? Don't get maudlin on your birthday. Your dad and I grew apart, Jade. Our lives became about different things."

"I don't want to ever get divorced."

"Then don't. Granny and Paps lasted nearly sixty years. He's in the ground, cold, and Mother still wears her wedding ring and refers to herself with the plural 'we.'"

"Can you know someone is right for you at sixteen?"

"Mr. Right? At sixteen? Jade-o, there you go being serious again. Why not go for Mr. Right Now? There is no love like the first love, and you're going to spoil it if you get all worked up and possessive, talking about forever or *never*. You're only sixteen once. Date lots of boys. If it's Dustin you want, go for it, but don't get serious. Have fun. You're young and beautiful." Mama brushed straw from Jade's hair. "These will be your good ol' days."

Aiden's shiny, gelled head popped over the lip of the loft. Jade knew he'd rather be at Shannon's place with all of his friends, but he'd hung around Dullsville for her sake. She'd make him pancakes and bacon in the morning.

"Dustin Colter just drove up." He grinned.

"Nuh-uh. You're lying." Jade scrambled out of the hay, shaking the yellow straw from her arms, and hung over the loft to see out the barn door. Sure enough, Dustin's truck sat in the light of an ordinary utility lamp, the bed loaded with a dozen other guys.

She couldn't breathe. Her beating heart hogged all her air. Lights trailed down the highway, turning off 117 into Granny's drive.

Jade crawled to Aiden and gathered his collar in her fist. "Did you call them? Your friends, make them feel sorry for your loser sister? I swear to goodness, if you did . . ."

"Are you crazy?" Aiden tugged her hand off his shirt. "You think I want my friends witnessing my sister's lame party?"

"Where's the birthday girl?" Dustin stood in the barn's opening, dark, curly hair flowing into his collar. His strength-robbing blue eyes swept up to the loft. "Is the party up there?"

"I'm coming down." Jade whipped around at Mama. "How do I look?"

Mama smoothed Jade's hair and straightened her top. "Perfect. Slip inside when you get a second and touch up your face."

Jade started for the ladder, but stopped before going down. "Should I let him kiss me?"

"First kiss?" Mama angled toward her with her hands on her hips.

Jade's cheeks burnt deep as she nodded.

"Then definitely. A sweet sixteen to remember. And if he don't kiss you, Jade-o"—Mama winked—"you kiss him. It's your night. The first night of many nights."

Jade paused two rungs down. "Mama, what if—"

"Jade, go, stay loose. Have fun, for crying out loud, have fun."

Twenty

June sank her hands into the hot, sudsy dishwater just as Jade entered the kitchen through the back door. Her daughter-in-law's olive eyes were bright, her sleek, dark brown hair windblown. Holding her cell to her ear, she made a face and kicked the back door closed.

"Kip, what if I write you a check to get started? We're still going after the insurance money . . . Well, right, I know . . ." Jade stopped by the table, listening and exhaling, setting a Dairy Queen bag on the table. "So, that's it, you can't get to work now for another month? No, frankly, I don't understand. We scheduled the repair weeks ago . . . Oh, come on, like we wouldn't pay you . . . Whatever, yeah, next month . . . Don't worry about my lost business, I'll deduct it from your fees. No, Kip, I'm not serious . . . but I wish I were." She tossed her phone into her purse.

"Trouble?" June turned away from the sink to face Jade, wrapping the dish towel around her hands.

"Kip took another job because he thought we weren't going to pay. So he can't start the Blue Two until late April or the first of May. It looks bad for the shop to be boarded up and closed for so long." Jade slipped out of her jacket with a sigh and draped it over the kitchen chair, then held up the DQ bag. "Mama wanted a chili dog and a chocolate shake. June, you don't have to wash dishes. I'll get them, or ask Linc to in the morning. Never could get Granny to install a dishwasher."

"What? Not do dishes? I was standing at a sink washing dishes at my own granny's house long before your parents even heard of the birds and the bees." She glanced down at the suds. What was it about the white fluffy bubbles that soothed her? "I think I can wash a few dishes. Already done it twice now."

"I'd better get this up to Mama before it melts." June nodded as Jade started up the stairs. She'd just turned back to the dishes when Jade popped back into the kitchen. "I forgot, a package came for you this morning when you were in the shower. L.L.Bean?"

"Mercy, that was fast." June dropped the dish towel on the counter and headed for the living room. "Why didn't you tell me? Is it in here?"

"On the chair by the door." Jade followed. "Since when do you shop at L.L.Bean?"

"Since my Louboutins keep getting stuck in the mud." June returned to the kitchen with the package and cut open the box.

"Heard from Rebel lately?" Jade popped the top off the shake and stirred the thick mixture.

"Now why did you go bringing up his name?" June held a pair of jeans and a short-sleeved V-neck top up to her body, and watched Jade watch her. As if she were unsure what her eyes beheld, June asked, "What do you think?"

"I think . . . not very elite Paris, but very Midwest prairie."

June refused to let the corners of her mouth slip as Jade offered moderate approval. What did it matter? June welcomed the change. "I'm going to put them on." She pulled a pair of shoes from the box. "Ever see these before? Skimmers? They look comfortable."

In her room, June slipped from her slacks and knee-highs into her jeans and top, then slipped her feet into the red Skimmers. Ah, heaven just enveloped her feet. Walking around, trying out her new footwear, June gazed out her window.

A wine-washed sky held on to the end of the spring day. The sunshine still hadn't warmed the breeze much, but the trees and grass promised spring's green.

Hanging up her Whisper Hollow clothes, June paused, listening when she heard a sound like the clap of a car door. Was someone here? Jade's voice floated down the hall from Beryl's room in a steady tone. She'd not gone to the truck for anything. And Linc had gone for the night.

Heading back downstairs, June peered out the second-floor window, seeing only the edge of Beryl's lawn kissing the fresh harrows of Tank Victor's field. Back in the yellow-and-red checkered kitchen, June retrieved a mixing bowl from the bottom cupboard.

Though Carla and crew had left plenty of food in the refrigerator and a couple of pies in the pantry, June had a taste for cake tonight.

She raised her head, listening, when a *thump* resounded from the porch. June shoved aside the curtain at the back door. No one was there. She shivered.

Back to the business of baking, June opened the fridge for the eggs. She had in mind her granny's from-scratch pound cake. And if she wasn't mistaken, she'd spotted an ice-cream maker in the barn the other day. Homemade ice cream and pound cake. Her mouth tingled.

This time the sound was definite. A knock. From the front door. June set the eggs on the counter. Must be Carla or one of Beryl's friends.

"Hello? Anyone home?"

June froze midstep. *No, please, no.*

The knock hammered the front door, intent on getting someone, anyone's, attention. June gathered her courage, crossed the room, and flipped on the porch light. On the other side of the screen stood—

"Mercy sakes, Rebel, what are you doing here?"

His tie hung at half-mast. His tan overcoat sat askew across his shoulders, and his normally politician-stiff hair was a windblown mess.

"I came up in the jet to talk some sense into you," Rebel called. "Took a cab from the airport."

"You should've called. Would've saved you the price of jet fuel." June walked back toward the kitchen. "I'm busy."

"Don't walk away from me." The screen door hinges moaned and balked. "I want to talk to you."

June whirled around. "I'll walk away from you if I want, Rebel. You can't fly up here, knock on my door, and tell me what to do."

Footsteps echoed on the stairs. "June? Is someone—" Jade bounded into the room. "Rebel, hey." She stopped cold as she hit the invisible line of tension.

"Jade." Rebel shook his coat as if he'd been standing in the rain. He ran his fingers through his hair. "You might want to know the McClures are suing Max for custody of Asa. He's in for the fight of his life over that boy. He needs you by his side."

Jade crossed her arms, then released their hold and rested her hand on the curved end of the banister. "Did he tell you to say that to me?"

"He doesn't even know I'm here." Rebel squared his shoulders, propped his hands on his belt, collecting himself, getting into character. June had observed this routine a hundred times. "I counted you as a reasonable woman, Jade. Didn't figure you for a quitter, leaving Max for an indiscretion he had before you were married."

"You figured right, Rebel." Jade fired off a couple of visual daggers. "I am a reasonable woman. A *smart* woman." She glared at June. "I'll be upstairs."

"She's foolish to leave him." Rebel's exasperated expression punctuated his comment. "Does she think men like Max hang out on street corners waiting for women like her?"

June stepped toward him. Once. "Do you think women like Jade stand around waiting for men like Max? Men like you? He's blessed to have Jade. Unless he's blown it. Now, why don't you go on home. Leave me be. What, is Claire busy tonight?"

"The governor appointed me to the court." As Rebel drew up, squaring his shoulders, extending his back, his persona increased.

"Well, Rebel." June propped her hands on her waist, slipping her fingers through the jeans' belt loops. "The pinnacle. What you've always wanted."

"We, Junie. What we've always wanted." An excited light beamed from his hazel eyes. "The state supreme court."

"What *I've* always wanted? No, you Rebel. What does the court do for me except enlarge your shadow over me?"

He took off his coat and draped it over the wingback chair. *Don't, Reb. You can't stay.* "So, that's it? I've overshadowed you? Poor June, never had a life of her own? Just all she ever wanted. The wife of a successful man. Nice house, friends, status, cars, European vacations, political and social connections, clothes from Paris."

"You forgot 'faithful and devoted husband.'" June stepped toward him, catching a whiff of his cologne. The fragrance, along with his projecting persona, nearly choked her resolve. "Rebel, I'm not sure I want this anymore." She gestured her hand in the space between them.

"Or course you do." Rebel tucked his hands in his slacks pockets, his posture for closing arguments. "Forty-one years can't end because of a woman like Claire. We belong together, June. It's only been you for me. Now, see here, the governor's wife has invited you to a tea next Wednesday. I'll be sworn in on Friday." He locked his eyes on hers. "You must be there."

"Beryl is dying. I won't leave Jade alone here."

"Jade? She's a big girl, June. She doesn't need you mothering her. Besides, where are her brother and sister?" He stepped toward her, covering her doubts with his shadow. "What do you want from me? To say I'm sorry? It'll never happen again?"

"Yes, Rebel, for all that's decent, yes." Adrenaline flowed like lava through June's veins. "I'm sick of this routine, this game. I'm sick of your infidelity, sick of being held hostage by status and, well, lack of a better idea of what to do with my life. Sick of paying over and over for my one mistake." June swore, hard bitter words. "I've had enough guilt for two people's lifetimes and I'm done, Rebel, done."

"One mistake? One?" Rebel held up his index finger.

"Yes, one." June narrowed her gaze at him, crossed her arms, and willed her thudding heart to rest. "Then you took revenge, Reb. Revenge. You've stabbed my heart over and over, and some nights I would hurt so bad I prayed you'd just leave me. Tell me, Reb, did you stay so you could punish me? Endlessly?"

"No." The word came from his throat, his lips drawn, his jaw tense. "I stayed because I loved you." His eyes searched hers.

"Loved me? Rebel, you've had dozens of affairs. Is that your idea of love? What would you have done if you wanted to punish me?"

He shifted his gaze to the ceiling, tightening his jaw so the muscle bulged. "It just got easy, that's all."

"Easy?" June collapsed onto the coffee table. "Easy . . . Do you know how many nights I cried myself to sleep when you traveled out of town, wondering if you were finding pleasure in another woman's arms? How helpless I felt to stop you? I mentally packed my bags so many times, I actually believed I'd leave you. Just like I'd planned that night with Bill, but I couldn't do it. Not to you, not to me, not to Max. I chose you over Bill because I loved you. So I was determined to find happiness, dreaming one day you'd stop cheating. But you never let up, Rebel. What was I supposed to think? If you love me, why?"

"I told you. It just got easy." He turned his back to her. In his tailored slacks and shirt, hand-tooled leather shoes on his feet, Rebel was out of place in the boxy farmhouse living room with its brown walls and yesterday's furniture.

"Does revenge taste that sweet, Reb?" Her emotions controlled her tongue, her words. "Should I try it for myself? See if Tom Carnahan would like a date? He's always flirting with me, and—"

Rebel whipped around. "You stole my son, June!" His eyes blazed with the intense heat of his confession. "You *stole* my son. I had one chance"—he jabbed his finger in her face—"one, and you robbed me of it."

"Oh, Rebel." She pressed her hand to her chest, bile scorching her throat.

He grabbed his coat and burst out the door. June ran after him. The evening was crisp and still, and the moon was not yet in its orbit.

"No, Reb, no. What are you talking about? I ended it with Bill six months before I was pregnant with Max."

"Stop, June, I've known." He draped his coat over the rail and stepped into the yard, disappearing into the shadows. "You're not the only one who knows what it feels like to be made a fool of, to have your love and trust trampled."

"Rebel." June remained with her toes lined up to the porch's edge, clinching her jaw to steady her words. "This is crazy talk."

"For thirty-eight years, I've shoved aside the nagging doubts. But with every growth spurt, I'd wonder if this would be the year he'd turn into Bill Novak. He looked so much like you, I found moments of rest, but when he took architecture in high school and sailed through with straight As . . ."

June's breath escaped her—through her nose and mouth, out every pore of her body. Blood drained from her head until she saw spots. She gripped the porch post.

"How did you know?"

"Queenie Spencer called the night you left to meet him." Rebel spoke from the outer reach of the porch lights.

June sank slowly to the steps, chilled to the bone, pressing her hand to her forehead. Queenie. One of her best college friends and an attendant at their wedding. "Reb, why didn't you say something?"

"Why didn't you?"

"She was supposed to cover for me."

"She tried. But when I told her you were halfway to her house, she splashed her oar into the river and paddled in a panic, coming up with some lame story about getting the date of your girls' weekend messed up."

June covered her face with her hands, hot shame colliding with the chill in her soul. He'd known? For thirty-eight years?

"So you kept it from me and used it against me all these years."

"It didn't start out that way, June." Rebel came up the walkway, slowly, scraping his heels over the pavement. "I fumed the entire weekend, ready to unload both barrels when you walked in the door. I'd planned to leave *you.* But when you came home, sad, guilty, broken, I knew it was over with Bill. So I stayed." Rebel sat next to her, and the porch boards creaked. "It's hell lying in bed next to your wife, knowing she's hurting, but also knowing you can't do a thing to help her."

"I hurt because of what I'd done to you. Not because I loved Bill." June clicked her thumbnails together. There were no tears for the situation. She'd cried them all. "If you'd confronted me, you would've known I broke it off with him. For good."

"I had you home with me. That was enough. I guessed it was over with Bill and you were fine with it. We were moving on. Then you told me you were pregnant, and all the anger and bitterness came flooding back. It took over."

"Do you want to know the truth?" June stared at her new shoes. "Or do you want to stay angry, cheating on me? But you should know, I'm not living like this the rest of my life."

"You tell me. Is the story worth telling?"

June clasped her hands together in her lap. Peace whispered past. "After you found me with Bill, ready to leave you, I'd made up my mind to forget about him. You were my husband, and I loved you. I knew the affair was a mistake, childish, looking for attention in all the wrong places. A few months later he started calling. He asked me to meet him. You were so wrapped up in exams and studying for the bar, and I was so lost about what to do with myself, who I was to be. A lonely wife? A part-time interior designer?"

"You never said you wanted a career."

"I didn't know what I wanted. But when a handsome, successful architect called with passion in his voice, I convinced myself being loved and wanted was better than being loved and ignored."

"I wasn't ignoring you. I had exams!"

June stifled him with a flash of her palm. "He asked me to meet him, and so I did. Queenie never was good with dates." She hated hearing the story. Foolish girl.

"I hired a detective agency to keep track of him for a year after that week-end." Rebel's confession didn't surprise her.

"We met at a hotel in Asheville. What seemed like a happy, romantic, sexy tryst turned out to be horrible. We fought. And what I remembered as sweet, passionate lovemaking was rushed and selfish. When I woke up the next morning, full of regret, panic, fear, I ran. Packed my bags and ran. All I wanted was to see you, Reb. Bill manipulated me the entire affair."

Rebel cleared his throat. "And Max?"

"Is your son, Rebel. My goodness, how can you even wonder? He may look like me, but the rest is all you, all Benson. Arrogant, competitive, yet sensitive and romantic. Smart. In fact, I'm fairly certain I was already pregnant when I went to see Bill."

"Fairly?"

"I was late . . ."

"I see." Rebel's feelings rumbled in his chest. "Thirty-eight years . . . glad we cleared that one up."

June's laugh spewed, but another looming reality sobered her soul. "Look at the path you took because of one misunderstanding. How are we going to undo a lifetime of affairs, Reb?"

He propped his arms on his knees and patted his palms. "We can't if you won't come home, June."

With an exhale, she shoved up from the porch. "Maybe, in time. You can live in the life you carved for us, Rebel, but I think there's a new road out there with my name on it. For now, I'm going inside to build a fire and make my granny's pound cake." She held open the screen. "Have you eaten?"

"No."

June opened the door wider. When the hinge squeaked, Rebel pushed up from the porch and followed her inside.

Twenty-one

Max bolted up from a dead sleep, the glass in his hand crashing to the floor. A shrill cry floated through the house. Jade's kittens. For crying out loud, he'd just filled their food bowls.

Foggy and disoriented, he angled forward with his hand against the coffee table.

The cry resounded again. Shrill. Loud. Like a baby.

Max fired off the couch, knocking his knee against the coffee table. Tomorrow, the table was out of here. He never wanted the thing in the first place, but Jade insisted. Some precious antique.

Asa's thin, high-pitched scream sliced the air. Max's heart beat at the base of his throat.

"C-coming . . . Asa. C-coming." Oh, his head. With each step, the room swam, his mind sinking into a dense fog.

The scream bounced against the fog so the noise consumed his whole being.

"H-hang on." His voice was gravelly and weak; his legs fought to gain control of his motion.

Breathing deep and exhaling as far as his lungs would allow, Max stumbled up the stairs, gripping the banister.

Three more screams. Would he ever get to the room?

On the landing, Max wobbled, letting the black-and-blue spots fade before starting down the hall to his son's room.

Asa was in his crib, naked and covered in feces—his face, his hair, the rungs of the crib, and the wall. "Asa?" Max's step landed in something warm, wet, and mushy. He lifted his socked foot. And on the carpet.

Max reached for his screaming son. "Asa, Asa, here buddy." But the baby was stuck. His wail rocketed to the ceiling, shattered, and rained down on Max.

Oh man, somehow Asa had wedged his leg between the crib rungs, his knee bent around one rod while his foot hooked another.

This time with tenderness, Max eased his son's leg free. His screams eased, but tears ran down the boy's flushed cheeks and terror lit his sloppy brown eyes.

Max patted his back, trying to clear his own head while figuring out how in the world the kid wedged his leg like that while painting the room in poop.

Asa shuddered as he sucked up his sobs. "Mess," he said.

"I'll say."

The room had the aroma of a sewer. Max ripped off his soiled sock and dropped it into the crib. Then shutting the door behind him, he carried Asa to his room.

"Let's get cleaned up." And cleared up. Max stripped Asa, then himself, and climbed in the shower.

How many Percocets had he taken? Dad's announcement about Clarence taking over the firm hit harder than he wanted to admit. When he got home he popped a couple, chasing them down with bourbon. He was flying high most of the night. Until he crashed.

Warm water washed over father and son. Asa shivered with a ghost sob, then patted the water with his pink, pudgy palm.

Lathering up his washcloth with soap, Max bathed Asa, who squirmed and tried to drink from the shower. When Max set him down on the tile, he saw the angry, brooding bruise forming on the trapped leg.

"Asa, I'm so sorry." Max cradled him in his arms to examine the purple and brown flesh. Dread flowed over him along with the warm water. Had he not heard Asa's scream?

Max collapsed against the wet shower floor, his stomach filling with disgust. He was a man with everything, yet possessed nothing. Once again, he was becoming an addict.

Everyone knew the walls of Granny's old house were onion-paper thin. Except Rebel and June.

Gripping the wheel of Paps's truck, Jade traveled along Old 163 toward the Colters'.

She'd slipped down the stairs and out the front door when Mama went to sleep. And after June and Rebel settled into a silent routine in the kitchen. Looked like he was on his BlackBerry while June stirred something at the stove.

Jade had tried not to listen, but hushed tones traveled faster and louder through the walls and thin paned windows.

So it all started with June. Complicated by Rebel's doubts. Who was Max's real father? June's pledge to Rebel didn't convince Jade one bit.

And what was that comment from Reb about the McClures suing Max for custody? That must have been what Max was trying to tell her the other night.

The news burned her with frustration. What did she have to do with any of it? She resented being a Benson dumping ground. Jesus help her, but she'd longed to marry into a strong, healthy family where she, the daughter of a hippie, could dump and disguise her gunk like weeds along the backyard fence.

Instead, she'd married into Oz. Nothing was as it appeared. Where were the Lord's faithful and righteous?

What Jade had was a *Melrose Place* script. Granny had watched that show, munching popcorn, shouting at the TV, "Don't do it . . . ah, I said, don't do it!"

Cheating husbands, an illegitimate son, a supreme court justice, a barren wife, secrets and suits.

A house appeared on the horizon as Jade rounded the bend, its golden light luring her in. Every window was aglow. Downshifting, she made the left into the Colters' drive, bouncing and bobbing over the winter-washed drive toward the back.

The barn doors were swung wide, the walls framing a square of yellow light. Jade cut the ignition and set the brake. What was she doing here?

Since Dustin's hospital visit, she'd not seen or talked to him. But then Mama brought up the story of her sixteenth birthday party and she couldn't *stop* thinking about him. He'd danced with her that night. And at 11:59, Dustin Colter gave Jade her first kiss.

At the moment, she wanted to be near his familiar warmth, to hear his laugh, to forget about death and infidelity.

She wanted to feel sixteen again.

Jade wrapped her fingers around the door handle. *God, if I shouldn't be here, tell me now.* After a second's hesitation, she jerked the chrome lever and stepped out on the gravel ground.

The rhythm of an air tool *zrrp, zrrp, zrrping* was the song in the air. Jade peered through the opened doors as the late evening breeze nipped at her cheeks and nose.

Dustin worked on a stripped-down car that might have been a Camaro in another life. His faded jeans, with holes at the knees, were his trademark.

He exuded a certain kind of laid-back charm infused with confidence. Like he could handle any crisis or surprise thrown his way. Nothing was worth getting ruffled over.

Dustin caught her watching and did a double take. He grinned. "Come to watch a master craftsman at work? See how *they* do it?"

She laughed, but her heart stumbled a bit at the reverie in his tone. "Before you get famous and lose all my calls and messages."

His quick smile accented the curve of his jaw and reminded Jade of the many reasons she fell in love with him in the first place.

"Dustin, I think—" Carla Colter popped out from behind the Camaro's open hood dressed in coveralls and ball cap. "Jade, honey, what are you doing here? Is everything all right? How's Beryl?"

"Fine, fine." Jade cleared the lie from her throat, shifting her eyes from Dustin to Carla, who shoved her curls away from her face, exposing her kind expression. "Mama's fine."

"Listen." Carla walked over and cupped her hands around Jade's face. "I'm here for you. Call if you need me. I am so sorry about your mama. She's become a good friend."

Jade nodded, keeping her posture stiff. If she spoke, she'd crumble into the woman's arms.

Carla kissed Jade's forehead as if she belonged to her, to the old barn, to the family. Her touch seeped clean to Jade's bones and calmed the storm brewing beneath her chest.

"How about a pop? Jade? Dustin?"

Carla tugged open the old fridge in the shop's corner. Dustin hugged Jade with his eyes. For that moment, she was sixteen, secretly married and waiting for Carla to leave so they could make love in the loft.

She was home. She belonged.

"This is my best batch of root beer yet." Carla handed Jade a cold, opened bottle of her homemade soda pop.

"I remember these." Jade's vision blurred with tears as she took a long, deep drink. "Oh, sweet sassafras."

"Used the actual root this time, not an extract."

"Best yet, Mom," Dustin said, lifting his bottle to his lips while keeping his eyes on Jade.

"Are you holding up, Jade?" Carla leaned against the Camaro and crossed her ankles. She had a youthful air about her, not one of a woman widowed.

"It's hard. Lots of things are hard right now." Jade raised her bottle. "But I'm holding up, Lord willing and the creek don't rise."

"Your husband is doing well?" Carla barreled right past the No Trespassing sign.

"He's got some issues, Carla." Home was where a girl could bear her heart, right? Find comfort, peace, and wisdom.

"I'm sorry to hear that, Jade. I'll pray for him." Carla shook her head, gazing toward the far wall. "I've so learned the value of prayer. You can do more by talking to God about folks, than talking to folks about God." Carla patted the Camaro. "So, Jade, how do you like my car?"

"*Your* car?" Jade walked around it, whistling low.

"Mom decided to join the family business," Dustin said. "Wanted to build her own car. I found a beat-up '68 Camaro, and well . . ." He gestured to the work in progress.

"I'm slow, but learning."

"I told you, Mom, you're a talented mechanic." Dustin winked at Jade. "She's good."

"I'm not surprised. Look at her son." Jade stopped a few feet from him, wrestling with the urge to fall into him.

"This baby's going to be fast with a 383 stroker engine."

"Whatever that means." Jade smiled and leaned against the workbench next to Dustin.

"It means I like my cars like my men, with some muscle." Carla laughed and jutted out her hip. Dustin's cheeks tinged pink.

"Yeah, okay, Mom. I told you, I don't want to hear about your love life."

"At least I have one." Carla held her eyes on her son as she swigged her pop.

"Isn't it time for you go inside? Watch the news or something?" Dustin shuffled his feet, tucking his hands into his pockets. "Call your boyfriend?"

"Fine, I know when I'm not wanted." Carla tapped her son on the shoulder before gripping Jade's shoulders. "And you, hang in there. I mean it, you need anything, call night or day." She kissed her again before disappearing into the shadows beyond the garage light.

"Your mom, she—" Jade couldn't speak. She'd lose her last ounce of composure.

"Yeah, she is. I'm proud of her. After Dad died, she was really lost, but she found herself and the meaning of life again. Church. Faith. Love God. Love others. Moving home helped too." Dustin eased his pop bottle into a bottle crate at the end of the worktable. "So what's up, Green Eyes?" He touched the tip of her chin.

She shrugged, searching for words, noticing the pink Cadillac in the other bay. "How's the old girl?"

"Good. They shipped the wrong top, so we had to send it back. The new one should be here in a few days. I installed the new hydraulic and motor." He ruffled her hair, then gave her a side hug. "Next time, no jumping on the top if the motor freezes."

"Next time? There better not be a next time." Jade swigged the last of her pop and set her empty one in the crate next to Dustin's.

The floating, burnt amber sensation hit out of nowhere. Zaps of anxiety taunted her insides. Her abs tightened as her pulse fired. Dark purple dread attached itself to Jade's thoughts.

What was she doing here? *Run.* But she kept her feet planted and concentrated on Dustin's voice.

June's car . . . White, custom leather seats . . . Pink paint job . . . in-dash GPS . . .

The amber faded. The purple swirls let go. Jade breathed in deep.

"Jade?" Dustin gripped her arms. "Are you all right?"

She peered into his eyes. "Oh, Dustin." Jade collapsed against him. "It's all screwed up."

"Shh, shh, Jade, babe, it's going to be all right." He embraced her, fitting her to the contours of his lean torso and brawny arms. His familiar hands moved around her familiar curves. "Nothing can be *that* screwed up."

"Y-you don't know. I married into a Southern soap opera." She didn't mean to cry, but the combination of weariness, hurt, loneliness, and remorse had taken its toll. Dustin was the wall she needed. But this far and no more.

"Tell me, what's going on?" His lips were soft and warm against her ear. Gently, he rocked her side to side.

"What's *not* going on?" Jade wiped her face with her fingers and cradled her head against his chest. "Do you have a tissue?"

"Here." Dustin grabbed her hand and walked her to the back of the barn. "Bathroom's in there. Jade,"—he trailed his finger along the hairline around her face—"it's going to be all right."

"Promise?" She looked around a boarded-up stall. "In the cow stall?"

He grinned, winked, and her belly flip-flopped. "The cow stall with a sink and toilet." The fire of his wink traveled all the way to her toes.

The floor was carpeted with hay, but the toilet and sink were porcelain, the shower constructed of tile, glass, and brass.

"Glass and brass? Out here?" she called. "A bit nice for a barn."

"Hartline has connections."

Splashing water in her face, Jade reached for the thick cotton towel and studied her reflection in the mirror. What was she doing here, crying in Dustin's arms at ten o'clock at night? She was married. And way too emotional to be drifting down this river.

She leaned against the sink and spoke to the mirror. "You need to go home, Jade Benson."

When she came out Dustin was at the stainless steel worktable, putting his tools away.

"Why'd you come here, Jade?" His blue eyes pierced right through to her core as if he read her private emotions. Seems he'd wised up during the bathroom break.

She stared at the floor. "No place else to go, I guess. Just so much craziness."

"What'd he do?" Dustin began to wipe down the table. "Max?"

Jade wound the strap of her handbag around her fingers, letting it dangle against her leg. "He—he has a son."

"A son?"

"He's a year and a half. His mother is Max's ex-fiancée."

"You just now found out?"

"Yes. She was killed a few weeks ago, making her first solo flight across the country in a small Cessna."

Dustin studied her, then replaced the last of his tools without a word. The skin covering his jaw drew tight.

"It happened . . ." Jade pressed her fingers into her forehead, hearing the confession in her head. Could she verbalize it? Give it life through her words? "Right before we were married. One dumb night . . ."

"One dumb night." Dustin faced her, hands behind him, gripping the table's edge. "You deserve better."

"Do I?" She rearranged withered straw with her boot. "I've done worse than Max."

Dustin's scoff echoed in Jade's chest. "Hardly."

If he only knew. But tonight, she couldn't confess. Weren't there enough emotional balls in the air? Why toss in the one she'd dropped fifteen years ago?

"You deserve better, Jade. Than Benson, than me."

"Dustin, it's okay . . . what happened between you and me. It had to be."

"Are you going to leave him?"

"I don't know . . . I shouldn't have come here." She headed for the door without a glance toward him. What right did she have to invade his life? Walk onto his emotional plain and stake a claim? Especially for her own comfort.

Dustin caught her arm. "Whoa, where you going?"

"Home. Dustin, I can't barge in here like we hung out last week, crying on your shoulder like you're my best friend. Do you date? Have a girl? I don't even know anything about you anymore."

He lowered his face to hers. "You know everything about me."

One long inhale and his lips would be on hers. "Dustin, I'm—" Her body trembled.

"I'm achingly aware, Jade." He released her and stepped back, gaining his composure. "You can impose on me anytime, Jade. I thought that was clear when I showed up at the hospital." He regarded her for many heavy heartbeats, then whipped his phone from his shirt pocket. "You know what time it is?"

"What time?" Jade pinched her brow. "I don't know, around ten thirty." What was with the slick grin? "What are you . . . Oh no, Dustin, no, it's not *that* time. Come on, you're kidding."

"Jade-o, I *never* kid . . ." With the phone to his ear, he searched the shelves along the wall. "Hartline . . . do you know what time it is?"

A football spiraled toward Jade. "Ack! Dustin." She almost ducked, but dropped her purse on reflex and snatched the ball in midflight.

"Way to go. I thought you were going to miss, Fitzgerald." *Benson, Dustin; my name is Benson.* "But it's all right. You're a little out of practice. We can work with that."

He dialed another number. "This is exactly what you need, Jade-o. Get rid of the weight of the world. Put the light back in your eyes. Help you forget about your husband, your mama . . . just for tonight, it's game on. Midnight football. All that other crap doesn't exist. Brill, man, it's midnight football."

The idea appealed like Christmas morning. No troubles. No worries. Peace on her earth. If only for a few hours. She passed him the ball.

"Game on."

Midnight football was Dustin's invention, and the reason Jade understood what it felt like to laugh until it hurt.

He cradled her with his shoulder. "In the bright light of morning when your body is so sore from using muscles you forgot existed, your brain won't care about all the problems, Fitzgerald." Dustin warmed her temple with a kiss.

Benson, I'm a Benson. Still chatting with Brill, Dustin dug around in a metal cabinet. Flags and cones and one muddy set of cleats flew out and hit the floor. "Yeah . . . call Spence . . . okay, but tell Susie she can't call time-out because she broke a nail . . . I know, but once is one time too many. No . . . Jade. Yeah. Jade. Fitzgerald. She's in town."

"Benson," she said out loud this time.

"Good." Dustin gazed over at her. "Yeah, she's really good. Okay, see you in twenty. And bring the Boss." Dustin ended the call, grabbed a gym bag, and stuffed the flags and cones inside. "I'll drive you to your house to change; then we can go out to the field. Bring you back here for your truck."

"Sounds like a plan. Convoluted, but a plan." She followed him, carrying a set of cones to his truck. "Dustin, aren't we too old for this?"

"Hush. We are never too old for midnight football." Dustin opened the passenger door and gave Jade his football face—narrowed eyes, tight jaw, jutted chin. "Get your head in the game, Fitzgerald, and let's play some smashmouth fooootballlllll!"

Twenty-Two

June hovered by Jade's bedroom door, arms folded over her waist, wearing a charmeuse robe. "Where are you going so late?"

"To play." Off with the nice top and sweater, on with the T-shirt and UT sweats. "How's Mama?"

"Sleeping. Play what? With who?"

"Football. With old friends." Jade tied on her first sneaker.

"Football? At this hour? It's nearly eleven o'clock."

"Midnight football, June. It's played at night. The later the better. Thus, the name, 'midnight football.' Dustin is waiting for me downstairs." With her second shoe on, Jade straightened the legs of her sweats and situated the gathered hem over her socks. "Where's Reb?"

"Flew back home. Jade, is it wise to be going around with—"

"My ex-husband?" Jade searched her toiletries bag for a ponytail holder. "We're playing football on a public field with other people. I want to laugh, scream, run around, smash some heads, score touchdowns, and forget."

"Forget Max? Your responsibilities? You're not a kid anymore, Jade." June leaned against the door frame. "Mercy, so you've had a bad few weeks. So what? You have a husband who loves you, and—"

"Loves me? Like Rebel loves you?" Her ponytail was too high and tight. Jade loosened the tie and started over. "All the misery he's put you through because he wasn't a hundred percent sure Max was his son."

"You heard." June's voice was flat and thin.

"We can hear the ants picnicking in these walls."

"Max doesn't know, Jade. About Bill." The soles of June's slippers scraped over the hardwood, then the area rug, as she entered the room.

"Of course he doesn't. Your family is all about secrets. Why would any of us want to know the truth?" Jade tossed her hairbrush to the dresser.

"There's no reason for him to know." June's features were taut and dark.

"Except another man might be his father." Jade snatched her jacket from the bed and stepped around June for the door. "A paternity test could put it all to rest, June."

"Rebel doesn't want it. Look down your sleek nose all you want, Jade, but for all Reb's faults, he raised Max like his own flesh and blood and never once wavered. If it took enduring years of infidelity to be the brunt of his anger about Bill Novak so he could embrace my son as his own without prejudice, then so be it. It was worth it."

"I guess I'm not the martyr you want me to be, June." Jade exited into the hall, then paused to face her. "I'm not going to live like you. Life is too short. And I don't have a son to consider. This is about Max and me, not you and Reb, so don't pull me down into your brand of crap. Now, if you'll excuse me, my friends are waiting." Jade jogged down the stairs.

"If you fall in love with that boy again, Jade"—June trailed her—"you won't know which way is up. Tonight it's football, tomorrow a lunch. He'll get close . . ."

Jade jerked open the front door. Lights from Dustin's truck reached across the ground, barely touching the edge of the porch. "Don't you dare make me out to be like you."

"You think I planned to fall in love with Bill? Planned to have an affair? When I married Rebel, it was for life. I'd be faithful and true-blue. I was a Christian woman, for pity's sake; how on earth would I ever find myself in another man's bed? But I did, Jade."

"I'm not going to Dustin's bedroom."

"Really? Just how did you end up at his house in the first place?" She took hold of Jade's shoulders. "Think about what you're doing, Jade. You're mad, upset. Things are messed up. Your in-laws have secrets. Your husband betrayed your trust. Your own desire for children has borne emptiness. But going back to Dustin isn't going to make it right. It will only make it worse."

"You think you know me, June? Think you can understand what it's like to be barren? To discover your husband gave another woman the one thing you wanted most? Oh, wait, you did that to Reb. Gave another man the son your husband wanted."

"Max is Rebel's son. Goodness, how can you not see it?"

"On top of it all, my mother is dying." Jade snapped her shoulders out of June's grasp. "So I'm ending this conversation and going to play football. And if Dustin happens to flirt with me, I might just flirt back. But I won't end up in his bed."

June crossed her arms, arresting Jade with her steely glare. "Well, since you're so good at breaking down everyone's issues, are you planning on telling Dustin the truth about you?" She lifted her eyebrows. "That you aborted his child?"

"I don't think it's any of your business, June." Jade stood on the threshold. "Do you live to make people as miserable as you, June?"

"Who says I'm miserable? I'm just asking a question. You accused me of secrets in such a self-righteous tone. I'm merely reminding you of your own."

Did she find pleasure in this? Chaining Jade to her pitiful wall? Jade glanced toward Dustin waiting in his idling truck. "I just want to play football, June. Maybe when my present makes sense, I'll be able to bear the burden of my past."

~

"Before we play, we'll review the rules for Jade." Dustin motioned to the fifty-yard line as he walked toward the end zone. The PCM Mustang's floodlights lit up the field. "And for Susie, because she forgets the rules from week to week."

"Don't talk smack to me, Colter." Susie walked under Dustin's nose. "You change the rules every time we play. However, I can recall the periodic table and recite pi out twenty decimals. Can you?"

He smacked her head with the football. "Geek."

"Blockhead."

Jade laughed, feeling both shy and elated to be with friend-friends. Any jitters about meeting Hartline's math and science teacher girlfriend ceased with Dustin's teasing and her rebuttal. She could hang with Susie, a petite brunette with long, dark hair flowing out from under a wool cap.

"Susie, this is Jade." Dustin walked backward toward Hart's truck. "Jade, Susie."

"So you're *Jade*." Susie offered her cold hand, shivering.

"The one and only." Why did she say *Jade*? Like she knew a secret.

"I'll say." Susie smiled as she stared to where the boys worked to light a fire in the fifty-gallon drum, her arms still wrapped around her torso as she shivered. "Dustin talks about you like you're still in his life."

The Boss, Springsteen, blasted from Hartline's truck parked in the home team end zone.

"Baby, come on, let's get playing. I'm freezing." Susie bounced around, curling her arms up tight.

Ben Hartline fired another log from the bed of his truck into a barrel, feeding the struggling flames while Brill, Spence, and Dustin set up the field cones.

"Watch." Susie motioned toward the barrel and flame. "See Spence? Hart will probably catch him on fire." She laughed easily.

"Wouldn't surprise me." Spence leaned tentatively over the flame just as Brill aimed some kind of bottle that shot liquid.

"So Dustin . . . he talks about you mostly when he's tired, had a beer or two, when the guys start reminiscing. I tease him, tell him you only exist in his dreams. But now, here you are."

"Live and in person." *Dustin, what are you doing?* Worse, what was she doing? Why did Susie's confession wrap around Jade's heart like a velvet glove? June's warning was a thousand miles away.

Jade watched the flame in the can kick up and lick the night. Dustin was easy to spot among the guys with his broad, upright posture. The truck lights mingled with the growing fire highlighted his face and the ends of his waves.

So Dustin carried a small torch for her. Maybe? Didn't mean he'd seduce her or that she'd end up in his bed.

She was playing football with him. Not much romantic about a cold, muddy field.

The Boss's song faded, but in the next heartbeat started again with Springsteen lauding the "Glory Days."

The guys cheered when a flame shot out of the barrel. Again Hartline showered it with fluid. Sure enough, the flame licked up just as Spence checked the barrel a second time.

"Told you." Susie laughed, shaking her head.

Watching Spence jump away from the igniting flames sparked a vivid image in Jade's mind. Dustin's flame already felt lovely to her cold heart.

But she was married. She'd stood before the Lord and made a vow.

"S-so, Susie." Jade gathered her emotions, shaking the fiery image and touch from her soul. "How'd you and Hart meet?"

"How do you not meet someone in this town? Brill had a party, invited all the teachers, and I went. Ben Hartline was handsome, charming, if not a bit brutish, and I had to have him."

The guys jogged toward them. As Hartline approached, Susie called, "Didn't I, baby?"

"Didn't you what?" He scooped her in his arms, kissing her cheek.

"Have to have you?"

"How could any woman resist?" Hartline winked at Jade. "Except you, Jade. The only girl in school who wouldn't give me a second look. Jade only had eyes for Dustin."

"Only girl in school, Hart?" Jade laughed. "Aren't you a legend in your own mind."

"Woo, she's got your number, baby." Susie slapped Jade a high five.

"Okay, the girls can't be on the same team." Hart tugged Susie away from Jade, whispering in her ear, making her laugh.

"Hey, Hart, knock it off. We came to play football." Dustin tucked in next to Jade and the last of her strength left her knees. Too much testosterone and estrogen in the air. "Brill"—Dustin pointed the football at him, his oversize Northern Iowa Wrestling sweatshirt swishing around his waist—"you and I will captain."

Brill stepped across the fifty-yard line and stood opposite Dustin. He was Prairie City's newest football coach, massive and muscular. The strength of his arms and chest challenged the limits of his sweatshirt.

"The game"—Dustin glared at Susie—"for those of you who like chemistry more than sports . . ." Susie swatted at him. He ducked, laughing. "Is midnight football. Three on three. If a team scores in four downs or less, you keep the ball and go again. If your team fails to score in four downs, you punt."

He paused, perusing all their faces. Hearing the rules made Jade's legs ache with anticipation. She was ready to run.

"The QB hikes to himself"—Dustin demonstrated—"and passes to one of his receivers. Receivers, you cannot back up any more than five yards to make a catch. You have to run forward. You can pass to another team member in order to keep the ball alive. You drop it or throw an interception, the other team takes over. We start play at the fifty-yard line. No tackling, I don't care how gorgeous the girls are. And in your case, Spence, how gorgeous Brill is to you. Any questions?"

"Brill? Please, give me some credit." Spence recoiled from his friend. "I'd rather go for you, Colter. You're unattached, aren't you?"

"Over my dead body, rotted beyond recognition." Dustin conked Spence on the head with the ball.

Spence and Brill jigged to the Boss, who now sang "Dancing in the Dark."

"Let's choose up. I got Jade." Dustin grabbed her hand and pulled her over the fifty-yard line and into him. His arm hooked around her waist. It was intimate. The gesture whispered, *Wanted*. Jade heard the crackle, felt the heat of the fire in the barrel.

"I got Susie." Brill wiggled his fingers at her.

"Well"—Spence turned to Hartline—"here we are again, the nerds picked after the girls."

Jade laughed. She was done with being reserved and holding it in. Done with ridiculous muses about past and faded lovers.

These were her friends. And she was playing midnight football.

"Speak for yourself, Spence. I'll team with Brill," Hartline said. "Can't run against my girl."

"Spence, you're with us." Dustin backed up a few yards, dragging Jade with him, his arm around her, not letting go. His fragrance of soap on warm skin awakened her scent memories—the night he asked her to homecoming, the night he proposed.

He lowered his lips to her ear. "Watch Susie; she looks ready to knock some heads."

"Dustin, if pent-up emotion is rocket fuel to the human heart, I have enough to fly to the moon."

He laughed and kissed her cheek. "I knew you were the girl for my team."

She stared after him. Why did so many of his words carry a layered meaning to her heart?

"Let's play some fooootballl." Dustin smacked the ball on the scrimmage line and then backed up, motioning for his team to gather round. His body motion was smooth and exact, controlled.

Jade bent in the circle of Dustin and Spence, the churn of excitement meeting with the heat of temptation. But her desire cooled as she realized Dustin was just being Dustin. He'd always been physical and affectionate. Look at how he tussled with the guys.

You're seeing what you want to see, Jade. Escaping into another time and place.

"Spence, I'm going to pass to you."

"No, me." Jade touched her chest with her hand and the diamond she remembered to slip on today caught a corner of the stadium lights. In a single breath, she stuffed her silly-girl fantasies into place. She was *married*.

"No, they'll be looking for a girl first play," he said. "To Spence . . . on three."

"Dustin, please, to me. I need this."

He regarded her, then Spence.

"Fake it to me, Colter. Then hit Jade. She can do it."

"Hey, are you guys quilting over there or what? I want to play some ball."

Dustin rose up and faced the opposition. "Hold on to your knitting, Hart. You're going to need it to occupy your hands, since your team is never going to get the ball."

Jade snorted. Dustin ran his hand over her hair. She sobered. There, was she imagining the intimacy of his touch? "Spence, run short, down and in. Jade, go long—and I mean really long."

"No, I'm not doing the 'you go long' route."

"That's just it, babe." *Babe?* "They'll think I'm sending you out of the play. Cut toward the center at the twenty and I'll throw it to you. But do not stop running. I'll get it to you. On three?"

"One, two, three, break."

Dustin, Spence, and Jade lined up along the fifty, facing Hartline, Brill, and Susie. This was going to be fun.

The staccato drumbeat of "Born in the U.S.A." echoed across the field. The players dropped down to their knuckles, game faces on.

Jade's heartbeat drummed with the music.

On three, Dustin hiked to himself and rolled left. Jade ran down the right side of the field, going long, hand in the air. *Dustin, I'm open.* Susie ran five yards behind her while Hart and Brill had Spence completely covered.

Dustin pumped, faking it toward Spence. Since they double-teamed him, Dustin had all day to pass.

Spence was agile and quick, running a sideways crazy eight, laughing, scrambling to keep away from Hartline and Brill.

"Get open, man." Dustin stayed fixed.

Breathing . . . running . . . feet pounding . . . Her pulse filled her ears. At the twenty, Jade cut toward the center, never breaking stride. Susie abandoned her assignment on Jade to triple-team Spence.

Her opponents counted her out of the game. She raised her hand. *Dustin . . .*

He cocked his arm back to throw toward Spence, but in one smooth step, twisted right and sent the ball toward her in a perfect spiral. Stretching her stride, Jade ran under the ball, laying out her hands. It hit her palms and she tucked it away. She hit the ground beyond the goal line, the ball in her arms.

"Touchdown! Jade Fitzgerald."

Benson, Dustin, it's Benson.

Dustin scooped her in his arms, whirling her around, celebrating.

For one glorious minute, her feet never touched the ground.

The crickets sang as Dustin pulled into his driveway and parked by the garage. Cutting the truck's engine, he turned toward Jade.

"Six touchdowns. I think that's a new midnight football record."

Jade pinched an inch of her muddy sweats. "I think everyone took pity on me."

"Hart, have pity? Never. He'd take down his own granny to win. No, girl, you had game tonight."

She lifted her eyes to his. "Because of you. I needed this. Thank you."

He gazed at her for a long time. "I can brew some tea or coffee if you want to come in."

"Better not. It's after one. I should get home. Get out of these muddy clothes." She wanted to go in, very much. Too much.

"I'm glad you came by tonight." He reached to tug a stray strand of hair from her lips and brushed her cheek with the back of his fingers. "You're beautiful, Jade."

"Dustin." She lowered his hand from her face. "I'm married."

"I'm painfully aware."

"Don't . . . we had this conversation when you showed up in Whisper Hollow before my wedding. We can't keep rehashing the past."

"The past? Feels very present to me, Jade. We had a conversation in Whisper Hollow about you marrying Max, but it doesn't mean my heart jumped into line because the circumstances weren't in my favor. Believe me, I'd love to move on."

"Then do it." Now Dustin's heart was her responsibility? Did she have to bear everyone's burden *and* load? "Move on. Doesn't Susie have friends? What about Shannon Bell or Kendall Hartline? Seems to me you were pretty sweet on her at one time."

"Shannon's married. Kendall is Kendall. Not for me. This is a small town,

Jade. It's hard to date a single woman over thirty and keep it casual. One date, and I'm suddenly Mr. Right."

"Come on, there has to be someone since me. It's been fifteen years."

"Again, I'm painfully aware." He faced forward, gripping the steering wheel. "I was engaged once, but . . ."

"But what?"

"She wasn't you."

Jade shoved open her door. "I can't do this, Dustin."

"I'm sorry. I'm not being fair." He stepped out of the truck and followed her to where she'd parked Paps's truck. "I'm just being honest, Jade."

She whirled around. "Be honest with your friends, your pastor, your mama, but not me, Dustin."

"If you leave him, I'm here." He gently gripped her arm, his hip pressed against hers.

She turned into him, and as his arms slipped around her waist, she drew his face to hers. At first, her kiss was tender and sweet, then he pressed her against the truck with a passionate hunger.

Kissing him was familiar and alluring. His touch quenched a deep thirst, and nothing else mattered but the staccato beating of their hearts.

His kiss deepened. His touch began to unlock the desperate yearnings of her heart.

"Dustin, no." Jade pushed away, stumbling from the truck, gasping. "I can't do this." Fumbling with her keys, she jerked open the driver's side door and hopped into the cab.

"Jade, listen—"

She fired the truck backward, skidding over the gravel and fishtailing toward the road. At the end of the driveway, she paused and glanced at the barn.

Dustin stood as a dark silhouette in the white beam of the utility lamp.

Jade gunned the gas as tears leaked from the corners of her eyes.

Shifting into second gear, her thoughts raced, seeing, feeling the kiss over and over.

Did she kiss him? Did he kiss her? It seemed to just happen.

Jade hated that June was right. A blip of anxiety settled over her soul. Kissing Dustin Colter was wrong, but Jade knew one thing, despite all the warnings. She wanted to kiss him again.

Twenty-three

Tripp's three kids played in the backyard with Asa. The two boys were organizing a wiffle ball game. The older one, Scott, a junior high track star, was down on his knees beside Asa, swinging at Geoff's pitch.

Swing and a miss. Max bent back, wincing. *Ooo, try again, son.* Asa looked up at Scott, his eyes wide, a slow grin sprouting under his round cheeks. *Welcome to sports, son, yes, welcome.*

Meanwhile Tripp's wife, Ginger, spun across the yard with hands-in-the-air, feet-in-the-air, teaching little Mimi how to cartwheel.

For the first time in his life, Max was jealous of his friend.

Behind him, Tripp was getting off the phone. "All right, the program starts a week from Monday, Max. If you're committed, he'll make a space. Be glad to have you, he said. He needs a man with your background to bring perspective to the others."

"You mean to show how a man born with everything can be as big a loser as the man who has nothing."

"Pretty much." Tripp tapped his pen against his home-office desk, pushing his thin wire-rim glasses up his narrow nose.

"Is there another option?" Max dropped down to the sagging sofa. "With Dad being appointed to the court, Jade in Iowa, my mother-in-law not doing well, I'd like to—"

"You start making excuses now, Max, you'll never kick this thing. No short-cuts." Tripp stood to check the activity going on beyond the window. "The boys are digging Asa."

"Yeah, he's having a good time." Max rubbed his hands together, working through his thoughts. "Jade claims I make everything about me, even loving her is about all me. If I go to this rehab while everyone is in transition, am I still making it about me?"

"Are you? Why do you want to go?"

Max hated how Tripp answered him with questions. "Because I nearly damaged my son's leg for life."

"The Outpost is hard core, Max." Tripp passed over an e-mail printout. "A ranch in the middle of Texas no-man's-land. No television or computers, limited cell access. You go into town once a week to check e-mail, make calls. There's a licensed nurse on staff who will get you through detox; then you'll work the ranch during the day, have group and one-on-one sessions in the afternoon. Axel Sanderson is a good man, but he believes strongly in hard work, building open, honest relationships, letting the guys work it out with each other. And he's a good friend of Jesus. He'll make you want to be one too. So does it sound like a selfish move?"

"To me? No." Max had been staring at the wall, but he shifted his attention to Tripp when he mentioned Jesus. "Can an ordinary man be a friend of Jesus?"

"If not an ordinary man, then who? We're all ordinary compared to Him.

Jesus called us His friends. John fifteen. Man, you've been in the church too long not to know this stuff."

Leaning forward, Max considered the reality of being a friend of God. "I've been faking a lot of things for a long time."

"When you're good at just about everything, it makes it difficult to admit weakness and ask for help." Tripp came around his desk and propped against the edge. "When you went into the hospital last year, you looked at me and Jade, and you promised with intensity you'd never go to the pills again. What made you break your promise? Your parents' issues? Finding out you had a son? Max, you have to figure out why you leap to a substance before you leap to Jesus."

Max went to the window just in time to see his son swing for the fence. A hit. *Run, son. Run.* Asa's little legs pedaled and stumbled as Scott half carried him around the bases, Geoff taking his time to fetch the ball.

Coming around the bases—third was a watering can—Asa squealed when Geoff threatened to tag him out.

"Safe!" Max and Tripp called in unison.

"The pills were easy. My connections were in place, ready to deal. Pills allowed me to keep working, to keep my life the way I wanted it. So I told myself." Max faced his friend. "But that boy changes everything. He deserves the best I have. Rice and I already handicapped him by the way he was conceived. In a lie which led to deception. Then when I saw the bruise on his leg after being stuck in his crib for who knows how long, the realization hit me in a place I've never been hit before. My negligence could've left him seriously hurt . . ." Emotion rose in his throat. "I live with a lot of things I'm not proud of, but I'd never forgive myself if Asa was scarred because of me."

"Who's going to take him while you're in Texas? Four months is a long time."

"I'm hoping Jade."

Tripp raised his eyebrows. "What do the McClures say?"

"At the moment, it's not up to them. I have a meeting with Gus today to ask him to call off the dogs. They're only fighting for custody out of grief, a way to get Rice back."

"Don't underestimate the power of a grieving mother."

"Believe me, I won't." What time was it? Four thirty already? "Can I leave Asa here while I meet with Gus?"

"Okay by me, but will he mind?"

"I'll be back before he misses me." Max's cell rang. He looked at the screen. Cara. "Benson . . . Hey, yeah . . . Excellent, excellent . . . Really? Did you draw up the guardian papers? . . . Okay, okay, don't get in a tizzy, just asking. Did I ever tell you how great you are, Cara?" He winked at Tripp. "Sure, I'll add it to your fee. See you in twenty."

"And what's that all about?"

Max tucked his phone back in its holster. Max grinned. "My ace in the hole."

~

"There he is, there, there."

Jade woke from where she'd been sleeping in a chair beside Mama's bed. The colors of the afternoon shaded and warmed the room. Sunbeams danced over Mama's bed.

Since her early morning kiss with Dustin, Jade had holed up in Mama's room, avoiding June's scolding gaze and sour expression when she wandered down to the kitchen.

Uncurling her legs, she crawled onto the bed beside Mama.

"Who is there, Mama?" She brushed back the frayed ends of her hair. Tomorrow she'd wash it for her. "Did you have a dream?"

Her eyes, wide and clear, were fixed on something beyond the window. "Jesus is here, on His donkey, waiting for me in the field." Her finger trembled as she pointed to the window, toward the bright light. "He's waiting for me."

Goose bumps trickled over Jade's skin. "Mama, you see Jesus?"

"Oh yes, He's waiting." Mama eased back down to the pillows, her eyes slipping closed.

"Mama," Jade whispered, "h-how do you know it's Jesus?" She could be seeing anything, anyone. The hospice nurse warned about hallucinations, and it was no secret Mama had gone on a few acid trips in her day.

"He's beautiful. Pure." Mama's voice purred. "Like nothing I've ever seen out there on any psychedelic trip."

"He's waiting for you?" She regretted her tone, incredulous and dubious. But it was Mama who once told her death meant she'd inherit her own planet with all male servants.

"I think so. But He won't look at me." Her voice weakened, and she gave up any trailing thoughts.

"Mama?" Jade shook her shoulder gently. "Why won't He look at you?"

"Waiting." She squeezed Jade's hand. "Holy."

In the next breath, she dozed, slack jawed, wind battling its way into her rattling lungs.

"Jesus, don't take her tonight." Jade bent to kiss Mama's temple. "Please wait . . . I'm not ready."

"He's calling you, Jade-o." Mama's voice was clear and strong. But her eyes were closed. She snorted between each word. "He loves you."

"Mama?" But she slept. Gentle jostling didn't rouse another word out of her. Jade crept over to the window and searched all the corners of Tank Victor's field.

In the back booth at Mae's, Max sipped black coffee, his hand resting on a sealed legal-size envelope. The idea of reasoning with Gus, alone, came to him during a moment of desperate prayer after he'd rescued his son from the baby-entangling crib.

He didn't hold much hope in winning Gus over until Cara called. The investigator they'd hired had earned his fee.

When Gus entered, Max caught his attention with a raised hand. Sliding into the booth across from him, Gus was somber, even worried.

"Coffee," he said to the waitress before she could even ask. "So what's this all about?" Gus touched the envelope with his fingertips.

"I want you to call off the dogs," Max said. "Stop the suit. This isn't good for y'all, me, or Asa."

"I got a woman at home who hasn't stopped crying since the judge awarded you custody. Then you won't let her see him. I had to call the doc for some tranquilizers. Can't say it's wearing on me well either."

"We were set for an amiable relationship until you decided to sue for custody." Max jammed his finger on the tabletop. "Sole custody . . . without giving me any rights at all."

"We're doing what's best for the boy."

"Call off the suit, Gus. And you'll be the grandparents of the century. I promise, y'all can see him whenever you want."

"Don't see how I can do that, Max. Bradley Richardson thinks we got an open-and-shut case." The waitress returned, set down a cup, and filled it for Gus. Then she set down a basket of biscuits. "On the house. Sorry about Rice, Gus."

"Thanks, Lindy."

"Call off the suit, Gus." Max laid his hand on the envelope.

"Can't do it to Lorelai." He stuck out his lower lip, shaking his head. "She's got her heart set on raising that boy."

"Gus, you're over seventy. Do you have the energy to raise a toddler?"

"We're in good health. We can hire help."

"Why'd you let her talk you into this? We could be sitting here right now, enjoying Asa together, remembering Rice."

A wet sheen covered the older man's eyes. He started to say something, but hesitated. "It's just best for the boy."

"You can't put the burden on Asa to take Rice's place."

"I said it's best for the boy." Gus blew on his coffee before taking a sip.

Max shoved the envelope across the table. "Then here."

Gus nodded with his chin. "What you got in there?"

"Just a little ammo."

The veins in Gus's neck throbbed. "Is this how you want to play it?"

"Seems you set the rules, Gus. You and Richardson. This is fair warning of what's to come if you keep going. Come on, this whole thing is ridiculous, and you know it. Rice would never want this."

"I don't know any such thing." He opened the envelope and scanned the pages. His expression revealed nothing. When he slipped the papers back into the envelope, he peered at Max. "This isn't proof. They've never found any evidence."

"DNA testing has come a long way since the '60s, Gus." Max slid out of the booth, dropping a ten on the table. "If the media gets wind of this and the DA is pressured to reopen the case . . ."

"I wasn't even involved!"

"Then you should have nothing to worry about." Max stood by the table for a second. Gus stared straight ahead. "Rice is dead, Gus. I'm hurting and grieving with you and Lorelai. End this, and let her rest in peace."

Sunday morning dawned with a new warmth. Finally. Jade woke with a hunger for worship. When the church doors opened at ten o'clock, she planned to be there.

Showered and dressed, she sat on the Iowa burial mound snaking along the back of the yard and lifted her face to the rising sun.

"It's finally getting warm." June appeared between the weeping willow and the side of the garage, arms crossed, her eyes scanning the horizon. "Beryl's sleeping. I hooked her up to the oxygen and she went right out."

"Thank you." Jade regarded her mother-in-law. Their conversations were cordial but tight since the Dustin argument. "Something on your mind, June?"

"Carla Colter called."

"Did she now?" The wind skipped past the ends of Jade's hair, tugging and twisting. "Say what you have to say, June."

"She saw you, Jade. When you came home with Dustin after the football game. She heard the truck and got up, thinking something was wrong, and well—"

"So she had to get on the phone and call you? What is it with you church ladies and gossip?"

"She didn't call to gossip. She was concerned. For some reason, she's under the impression you and I have a good relationship. Carla thought you might need to talk."

"If I needed to talk about kissing Dustin, I don't think it would be to you, June. It's none of your or Carla's business."

"It is my business." Her blue eyes snapped to Jade's face. "You're married to my son. I told you this would happen."

"Nothing happened." Jade scoffed. "What gets me, June, is how when your son or husband lie and cheat, it's okay with you to twist the truth. But I kiss my ex one late night and *bam*, the whole world has to know."

"I hated keeping Asa from you." June sat on the mound next to Jade.

"But you did it anyway, didn't you? My husband had a son the whole time we've been married, and you couldn't break your asinine honor code? Look, June, Dustin is a friend. And Friday night, I really needed a friend."

June grabbed her chin. "I've seen this look in your eye before, Jade. The first time you came to dinner at Orchid House with Max. You were falling in love with him."

"There's no *look* in my eye." Jade freed herself from June's grasp. "Mama had it right about me. I cling too tight. I don't like rocking boats or having rugs pulled out from under me. I'm not an adventurer. Well, maybe it's time to change."

"You listen to me." June lowered her hand. "Think long and hard about the Y in the road you're about to take. Paying Max back for his indiscretion with Rice won't change what he did. Or the fact that he has a son. It won't make you feel better about the abortion or miscarriages. What if you get pregnant with Dustin's child?"

"Pregnant? From a kiss? Oh my gosh . . ." Jade jumped up with a hard glare at June. "This isn't about me; it's about Max. You're not sure if Rebel really is his father, are you, June?"

"I'm sure. I was already pregnant, barely, when I went to meet Bill. Maybe that's why I was so repulsed by our affair. The life in me was already speaking."

Jade stared out at the field. A redbird sat about ten yards past the edge, its brilliant feathers a stark contrast to the dark chocolate dirt.

"When I met Max, he was a knight on a white steed. He took away my fear of falling in love. So I gave my heart. All of it. Then I discovered he had a secret. A love affair with pain meds. I could weather that, help him through. But it also scared me. I saw how weak he was—not in a manageable, everyday way, but in a 'this could cost us everything' way."

"Max relies so much on his capabilities he's unaware when he's about to drive off a cliff."

"I don't want to be riding with him if he does. I'm sorry if that sounds mean. I can't trust him, June. I can't. I search my heart, tell myself I should go home. I do love him. But the one thing that holds me back? I can't trust him."

"If you sleep with Dustin, you'll despise yourself, and him, like I did Bill. Right now, he's a good friend. A place to feel wanted. Believe me, I know."

"I'm not going to have an affair."

June's touch was light on Jade's shoulder. "Shug, wake up. You've already started down the path."

Twenty-four

Asa screamed the last one hundred miles to Prairie City. Nothing Max tossed at him satisfied—juice, French fries, chicken nuggets, toys, books, DVD. Nothing.

The noise jabbed Max's skin like a million pinpricks. The phrase "getting on my last nerve" took on a whole new meaning.

The last ten miles, he just gunned the gas, set his jaw, and aimed straight for Beryl's place. Upping the radio volume, he zoomed in on the lyrics and bass beat.

He'd been resisting the urge to swallow a couple of Percs until he got Asa to a safe place. But sooner or later he'd have to deal with the shakes and vomiting. Detox would come later.

Once he signed on the dotted line to go to the Outpost, he felt relieved, a blend of peace and trepidation.

No fooling around this time. If he failed there? He shook off the idea. *God, what's it going to take for me to get serious about You, about my life?*

The prayer whispered across his soul, panic hit his heart, a certain dread and trembling. *The fear of the Lord is the beginning of wisdom.* But Max remained this side of stupid.

As he breached Prairie City's town limit, he slowed down, looking for the turn off to the old farmstead. Shouldn't be too hard to find. A white clapboard dwelling rising up from the budding Iowa prairie, situated beneath blue clouds, nestled between coffee-colored fields.

A half hour outside Prairie City, Asa finally fell asleep, spilling over the side of his car seat like a sack of bricks. Max exhaled. At last, peace.

When the house came into view, doubt stood front and center. Thirteen hours on the road, he'd not called Jade to warn her. If she said no, he didn't know what he'd do. While he deserved to be told no, he couldn't accept the answer. He had six days to convince her, if he had any power of persuasion.

He'd spent most of the drive time talking to God and musing on what he wanted to say to Jade, taking phone calls from his colleagues who'd agreed to handle his cases. Dad declared Max's move to be too dramatic and drastic. He rumbled and spouted, even hinted Max might not have a place at Benson Law when he returned. What kind of respect could Max command if he constantly ran when his problems became too large?

Dad could be really obtuse.

Nine hundred miles, six hours of sleep at a roadside motel, six McDonald's stops, twelve cups of coffee, and Max still had no idea what he wanted to say to Jade.

Except *please.*

The driveway gravel popped under the Mercedes' tires as Max pulled even with the house and parked. The place looked good, kept up, recently painted.

After parking and taking a moment to stretch and reckon with anticipation,

Max opened the door and stooped for his son. "Come on, Asa." He unbuckled the sleeping boy from the car seat and flopped him over his shoulder.

His little OshKosh jeans were stained and at the moment, soaked through. Max hadn't changed him since breakfast. Hey, why'd he pay top dollar for the fancy diapers if they couldn't do the job? As he flung the diaper bag over his shoulder and reached for Asa's bear, the boy woke with a jerk, screaming. How did he do that?

"Hey, son, it's okay, it's okay." Taking the porch steps, the door opened before Max could ring the bell.

Jade stood on the other side. Man, she was a sight for sore eyes. "What are you doing here?" She stood aside for him to enter as Asa continued squirming and screaming. "Is he sick? Are you all right?"

"We're fine, other than a very long car trip." Max slipped the bag from his shoulder to the floor.

"What is going on in here?" Mom came in from the kitchen. "Max, what in the world?" She reached for Asa without pause or question. "He's soaking wet." She glared at her son and picked up the diaper bag, murmuring to the little boy, "Let Grandma take care of things."

Mom disappeared upstairs, cooing and soothing her grandson. And Max was left alone with his wife. It'd been, what, eight days since he'd seen her, but it felt like a year. He yearned for her with a power that took his breath.

"You look like crap." Jade stood on the other side of the coffee table, arms folded, her posture defensive.

"Good. Matches how I feel." The living room welcomed him with a worn wingback chair facing the TV, a loosely crocheted afghan over the back of a mohair sofa, the aroma of coffee, seasoned lumber, and soap permeating the air. "And it's good to see you too." He collapsed in the chair, his back spasming as the tension released.

"Max, when did you feed him last?" Mom called down the stairs. "And what did you feed him?"

"Four hours ago, maybe? French fries." He bent over the chair's arm to see to the top of the stairs. She *tsk, tsk, tsked* him.

Jade slipped her hands into her jeans pockets. She looked to him like she'd lost a little bit of weight. "D-do you want some coffee?"

"Coffee? No." Max pressed his hand over his belly. His stomach burned at the sound of the word. "Water, please, a big glass. And food? Real food."

"Mama's friends have filled the kitchen with all kinds of stuff. There's home-made soup."

"Sounds good. Thank you." He appreciated her civility. He followed her into the kitchen and took a seat at the '50s looking red-ice table. "We should get one of these," he said, smoothing his hand over the surface.

"I have one. Right there." She peered back at him as she lit a fire under a large soup pot.

"I mean at our house."

"Max, why are you here? Why didn't you call?" She opened a drawer for a stir spoon. "Your eyes are glassy and bloodshot. How many?"

"Ten, maybe twelve a day." Their eyes met. "I have a lot to tell you."

She stirred the soup, not prodding for information. "Willow and Aiden are on their way. Mama's dying."

"Babe, I'm sorry." His hand shook as he lifted the mason jar of water to his lips.

Jade's back was to him, but he watched her wipe her cheeks with her hand. "She sees Jesus. On a donkey." Her shoulders rounded forward, shaking.

Max didn't care if she was angry with him; he pushed away from the table and gently touched her back. She turned and was in his arms, weeping.

"I'm so tired," Jade said.

He wrapped his arms around her back and kissed her forehead. He stroked her hair and exhaled past his first barrier. Holding her. The situation with Beryl was going to make what he had to say even harder.

"Anyone home?" The kitchen door shoved open, and Dustin Colter stepped inside.

Jade jerked out of Max's arms, her face red and wet. "Dustin, hey, come in."

His eyes locked onto her, then slithered over to Max. "Dustin Colter." He offered his hand. "You must be Max?"

Max's palm slapped against Dustin's. "Yes, I'm Jade's husband."

Dustin held his gaze for a long moment, then looked toward Jade. "I brought the Cadillac back." He dropped the keys to the table. "Good as new. The bill is taped to the wheel. She can pay us whenever she's ready."

"Actually, it's my bill. I'll bring the check around later, Dustin. Thanks."

The tenderness of her tone hardened in Max's gut. "What happened to Mom's car?"

Jade exchanged a glance with Dustin. *What? Did they joyride in it? Wreck while stealing a kiss?* "The top broke. I'll explain later."

"See you, Jade."

"Bye, Dustin."

The battle for Jade just entered a new plane, and Max rode into battle wounded, his hands tied by his own cords of sin.

~

Mama sat up in bed Monday afternoon, smiling, her green eyes alive for the first time since she'd come home from the hospital. "My babies are here."

With Aiden's arrival a few hours ago, Jade noticed a change in her countenance. She was happy. But she was letting go. Jade felt it.

"Beryl." Willow sat cross-legged in the middle of the room amid a pile of pictures, the floor lamp burning light over her shoulder. "There are no pictures of me until I'm like . . . graduating from high school."

"You're crazy, Wills." Aiden leaned over her shoulder. "I took a bunch of pictures on your first birthday."

"Really? You mean this one?" Willow handed a picture to her big brother. "The one where my hair is long enough for ponytails? I know age is relative to a man, but even you have to admit this is *not* me at age one."

"You choose to see what you want to see." Aiden landed on the floor next to her, reaching for a handful of pictures. "Look, here's one."

"I have braces. What is wrong with you?"

Jade perched on the end of Mama's bed, watching, grinning. Aiden showed Willow a picture of her as a baby, and she intentionally looked at one of her as a girl or preteen.

Aiden was lean and pale from a winter in Alaska. His coal-colored hair covered his ears and dipped into the collar of his pullover. He looked . . . like a hippie. A brother of the earth.

On the other hand, Willow was brown from the Guatemalan sun. She'd cut her long, sandy curls into short waves and Mama claimed she looked like Mia Farrow—the Sinatra years. Her eyes peered out from under her brow like evenly cut amber stones. The lucky girl had inherited Granny's aristocratic bone structure.

Jade ran her thumb over her dull, boring Tennessee-Iowa hued skin, proof of her lack of adventure, her enslavement to fear, that she was of the if-it-ain't-broke-don't-fix-it mold.

Take a closer look, Jade-o. Things are broken. Very broken.

She sighed. Aiden and Willow glanced up at the same time. "Nothing," she said.

"When are we going to talk about the elephant in the room?" Willow handed over a pile of pictures to Aiden, bored already. *See, this is why there aren't many pictures of her. She never sits still long enough.*

"Wh-what elephant?" Jade made a face as Willow hopped onto the bed next to her.

"The gorgeous one with a son." In an uncharacteristic move, Willow had kept her trap shut—mostly shut—about Max having a son. Instead, she played with Asa and taught him how to give high fives and "skin" and to thump his thigh with his fist and say, "Darn it."

Picturing him made Jade smile. Hearing his little voice, seeing his funny face—wrinkled brow, pooched lips—and his skinny butt sticking out as he pounded his leg. *"Darn it."*

"What's the story?" Aiden closed the sewing box lid and stood, hands in the pockets of his cargo pants. "I take it you didn't know about him."

"Do I look like I knew? I just found out about two weeks ago. Rice is . . . was his mother. She was killed in a plane crash."

Aiden nodded, absorbing it all. He was like Dustin that way. A rock. Willow whistled and gasped, made a big show. *That* was her way. "Rice was killed. I can't believe it." She inhaled with a hand over her mouth. "Oh my gosh, Jade. Vegas. Did it happen in Vegas?"

"You knew?" Jade gaped and popped her leg with the back of her hand.

"I didn't *know* know. I just overheard Rice talking to her parents during the reception about being in Vegas over the weekend. And I knew Max was there for his bachelor trip . . ."

Oh boy. Webs and lies . . . weaving. What if Willow had mentioned it? None of this might have happened. No, forget it. Jade would've never confronted Max.

"Aiden," Mama suddenly piped up, "I'd like some pictures."

"Pictures?" His expression remained serious and contemplative.

"Yes, of you, me, the girls, June, Max, the family."

Mama, what are you up to?

"I'll get my camera." He left the room without another word, but Jade heard him sniff and cough down the hall.

"Pictures? Are you sure?" Jade preferred to remember Mama as young, vibrant and free, sitting on the Indian mound with her face to the sun, the breeze braiding her long strawberry hair behind her.

Instead, her cheeks were sunken under sallow skin, and her narrow frame barely showed beneath her clothes.

"Help me." Mama stretched out her arms, struggling to sit forward. "I want to get dolled up. And take me outside. Being cooped up in here will take me to the grave faster than the leukemia."

"Outside, Mama, I don't know . . ." Jade took hold of one arm, Willow the other.

"Jade, why not? I love this idea." Of course Willow would.

"This isn't my finest beauty hour, but here we are together. Other than Jade's wedding and Mother's funeral, when were we all in one place?" Mama's eyes shone. "And getting along? I want us to take pictures, even if I'm not around to enjoy them. Gives me a chance to make up for some things, and don't you dare deny me, Jade-o."

"Yeah, Jade-o." Willow shoved open the window. A cool breeze shot into the room along with the rustle of tree limbs and tweeting birds. "Bonita, muy bonita. Hey, let's use the old red felt chair of Granny's . . . the one with the wood frame."

"Good thinking, Wills." Mama struggled to her feet. "I think it's in the attic. Maybe Max can bring it down, help out, feel a part of this family. Jade seems intent on freezing him out."

"Mama?" Forthright to her dying day.

"Well, am I wrong? Ooo, my bones." She reached for Willow. "I'd like to be photographed on the Indian mounds."

"Beryl, fabo idea." Willow ducked into the closet to gather clothes.

Fabo? "Hold it." Jade held up her hands. "We're not taking you outside, Mama. It may be the first days in April, but it's still too windy, too cold. You just had pneumonia."

"Pick warm things, Wills."

Aiden returned to the room, his camera around his neck, his bag over his shoulder, and a tripod in his hand. "If we move quickly, the light is perfect."

"Absolutely not. It's too cold, Aiden." Did she want to die tonight? Well, Jade just wasn't ready. Everything in her life was unbalanced, out of control, walking along a high wire, and darn it . . . "No, Mama. Just no."

"What's going on?" June commanded the room as she entered. Behind her, Max waited in the hall with Asa in his arms.

"We're taking Mama outside for a photo shoot." Willow held up a couple of outfits to the natural light. "June, can you do her hair and makeup?"

"My specialty."

"What? Am I wood? Isn't anyone listening to me?" Jade said.

"We hear you and are ignoring you. It's what Beryl wants." When did kite-in-the-wind Willow become a general? "Max, can you get the red chair from the attic?"

"Sure." Max glanced at Asa, then up at the open attic. He started to set Asa down, but hesitated, looking for someone to hold him. All hands were occupied. Except Jade's. Her role of protester left her hands free. "He fell down the stairs this morning, Jade. Can you watch him?"

"Never mind, I'll get the chair."

"Jade, oh come on, that thing weighs a ton. Max will need Aiden to help him. Remember when we tried to carry it . . ." Did Willow have to remember *every*thing?

"Then how did it end up in the attic?"

"Linc and Chancy carried it up there," Mama said with soft laugh. "Used a pulley."

When Jade glanced back at Max, he tipped his head to one side. "If you hold him, you won't melt."

"And what does that mean?" She motioned to the floor. "Just put him down in here; I'll make sure he doesn't run to the stairs."

Asa wailed the moment his feet touched the floor, raising his arms to Max. "Hey, buddy, it's okay." He picked Asa back up, looked at Jade. "A lot of changes for him in the past few weeks. He's still adjusting, not sure what's going on."

"Jade, for crying out loud." Willow popped out of Mama's closet. "Hold the baby."

"If he's adjusting, he's sure as heck not going to want me." Jade glanced around. "June, why don't you take Asa? I'll fix Mama's hair and makeup."

Max was in front of her, passing off his son. If she didn't raise her arm, he'd fall. Jade cradled him in the crook of her elbow, pressing her hand to his back to keep him from tipping. "Smooth move, Benson."

"I had to do something to get you to shut up." Max went to the hall and tugged on the attic rope. "Aiden, you coming?"

So Max's son ended up in her arms for the first time. His hazel eyes scoured her face, curious, not afraid.

"H-hey . . ." *Cough.* ". . . you."

Asa had Max's expression. His fragrant, clean skin mingled with the Downy scent of his little overalls and slipped through her nose down to her heart. Emotion swelled in her throat.

The boy reared back, his spacious eyes taking in Jade's face. She braced for his panicked wail. But instead, he raised his little hand and gently touched her cheek, his fingers wiggling up to her eyes.

The sensation in her throat moved to her eyes and burned. *No, no, no.* A *bump!* from the end of the hall broke the spell. The red chair lay on its side with Max and Aiden hanging out of the attic opening.

"I could've done that," Jade said, walking toward them, laughing. "Just tossed it down."

Asa rested his head on her shoulder and gently wound his fingers through her hair.

"He looks good on you," Max said as he climbed down the attic steps. "I think he likes you."

Jade steeled every emotion. He would not manipulate her through her desire for a child. She turned for the bedroom. "Willow, did you find the old suitcase? There are some clothes in there that would be perfect for Mama."

"Beautiful." Aiden bent in front of Mama, holding the camera to his eye. The shutter whirred.

June had styled Mama's hair so the top didn't appear so thin, and brushed color onto her cheeks and lips. She wore the leather headband Jade found among her treasures along with the tattered moccasins with a pair of forty-year-old bell-bottoms and a yellow, embroidered tunic top. And Paps's old fatigue jacket.

She'd returned to her former glory. Her eyes shone like the surface of an Iowa pond reflecting the summer sun.

Poised and serene, Mama fixed her even smile for the camera. The budding green of the grass and trees meeting with the sky's blue and Tank's rich, textured field created a spectacular backdrop.

Jade watched Mama posing, so happy, so alive, laughing when she made a face just as Aiden snapped the shutter. With a glance over her shoulder, she found Max with the boy over on the bench swing. Asa climbed over him, sitting on his right side, then his left, then sliding off the bench and falling forward onto the ground. He popped up, patting dirt from his hands.

In the two days he'd been on the farm, Max had moved into the basement bedroom with Asa. Linc fixed a gate to keep the boy from climbing the stairs.

Max remained vigilant around Jade, but quiet, doing a lot of work on his iPhone, playing with Asa, and talking with June.

It'd been easy to avoid him, yet easy to observe him. He'd changed. Ever so slightly. Jade couldn't put her finger on how she knew, but Max had come to a new place in his life.

Rebel's swearing in was on Friday, so Jade figured he'd leave by Thursday. Why he came in the first place and hung around was beyond her. Seemed he'd have a lot to do, preparing to take over Benson Law.

"Willow, get in the shot . . . stand over Mama's right shoulder," Aiden said.

But Willow could never do anything straight up and simple. Jade turned just as her sister flitted around Mama, striking an odd pose, bending backward over her lap. Aiden's shutter caught her every move.

Aiden lifted his eye from the viewfinder, laughing. "Willow, stand still and smile like you have half a wit in your head."

"Oh, leave her be, Aiden, and click the shutter." Dying had done nothing to Mama's spirit.

Willow flitted and the shutter whirred.

"Jade." Aiden motioned for her to get in the shot with Mama. "And, I guess, do whatever you want."

Jade knelt beside Mama and rested her head on her shoulder. She didn't want goofy or posed. She wanted heart. She wanted to remember Mama's shoulder, how broad and strong it was even when Jade refused to place her burdens there.

Mama gazed at her, the gentle breeze lacing her hair across her cheek. Aiden whispered, "Beautiful," and let the shutter fly.

Right in the middle of Aiden posing all three of "the girls," the redbird Jade had watched the day before fluttered to the ground at Mama's feet. He peered up at her, then hopped once, landing just beyond her toe.

Aiden lifted his head from behind the camera. Willow stopped flitting and Jade forgot to breathe.

So brave and bold, this little bird, his black eyes on Mama, his tiny red head tipping to one side. Mama leaned forward and whispered, "What is it, little bird?"

Aiden dropped to his belly and squeezed the shutter release.

The bird seemed unaware of anything but Mama. He lifted his beak to the heavens, fluffed his feathers, and sang—a pure, clear tone with a guttural beat. His melody sweetened the breeze. The song ended with a sweet, high, lingering warble.

Tears streamed down Mama's cheeks. "Oh, little bird. You've sung for me."

The bird switched his gaze toward Jade and hopped toward her, fluffed his wings again, and offered a single, shrill twitter. Then he spread his wings and caught the current and soared. After a few moments, he'd completely disappeared into the sunlight.

A heavy hush remained on them. June's arm linked with Jade's. "I do believe God was just here."

Mama brushed her hand over her cheeks. "And He sang to me."

Twenty-five

At the kitchen sink, June washed the casserole dishes, empty now after feeding the brood. She'd done more dishes in the past week than a year in Whisper Hollow. She'd forgotten the comfort of soaking her hands in warm, soapy water.

What a beautiful day. June liked the hum and fullness of kids being in and around the house. Even if two of the kids were at odds with one another.

After taking pictures, Aiden and Max dragged out the lawn furniture, cracked open a couple of beers, and sat on the picnic table talking. When June brought out the chips and dip, all of them, Jade included, gathered around, laughing and munching.

And that Asa. What a charmer. Like his granddaddy and daddy.

Warm water rushed over June's hands as she absently cleared away the suds, gazing out the window, night gathering round. Max was a good son. A good man. And he belonged to Reb.

But the truth? She didn't know for sure. She told Jade she was already pregnant when she met Bill, and she had made love with Rebel a few nights before. Spent the night with Bill. Made love with Rebel when she came home. So passionately that night. The next month she was pregnant. Reb had to be Max's daddy. Had to be.

But doubt remained in the fruit.

June had heard through Queenie that Bill had five children and three times as many grandchildren.

June and Rebel had one. Then none. With a heavy sigh, she placed the dish in the drainer.

Carla said she'd come by after her book club and pick up the dishes.

A flame flickered. Look there, Linc had brought over tiki torches. *Well now. How lovely. And there goes Max with Aiden and Linc. What are those three about?*

Jade talked with Beryl and Willow.

Seeing her with Asa earlier about had June in tears. If her daughter-in-law would just let down and stop holding on to her right to be angry. Though, mercy a'mighty, that crazy boy deserved to have nails spit at him. What was he thinking bedding Rice the week before his wedding? Couldn't even claim he was drunk.

Just stupid.

The fellas came around the barn with shovels, Linc with an armload of wood, and aimed for the fire pit. Beryl's smile was brighter than the tiki flames.

June dried her hands and headed upstairs for her jacket and a blanket for Beryl. They could scoot her close to the fire, but not too close . . . the smoke would be too much for her lungs.

By the time she came out, Beryl was by the fire pit. Jade took the blanket and wrapped it around her mama while giving Linc and Willow drink and food orders.

"Marshmallows, graham crackers, and Hershey's?"

"Yeah, we know how to make s'mores, Jade. What else?" Willow bumped Linc with her hip. He bit his lips trying to hold in his smile. Seems somebody was smitten.

"Mama, do you want a chocolate shake?" Jade knelt in front of Beryl. She loved shakes.

"I believe I do. But a small one, Willow. Not a medium, a small."

"Got it." Willow turned to Aiden and Max. "Want anything?" The boys claimed to be "all good."

As Linc and Willow hopped in his truck, Jade called after them, "Hey, no stopping to mess around."

June gave her a wide-eyed what-in-the-world look.

"They used to have a thing."

"Oh my."

"Jade, hush," Willow called. "I'm not like that anymore." She ducked inside the cab, but land sakes, didn't June see Linc pause, glance through the window at Willow, and let his shoulders droop.

Good for Willow. Part of maturing is changing. Stop leading with one's heart. One's lusts. Choosing self-control over wanton desire.

"You doing okay, Beryl?" June fixed the blanket around her legs.

"I'm doing better than okay." Beryl's hand patted June's. "I'm perfect."

As Aiden and Max stoked the fire, Carla Colter parked by the house, shouting a "hey there" as she came across the lawn.

"I skipped book club." She dropped to her knees and wrapped Beryl in a lingering hug.

Sharon and Elizabeth drove in next with a pot of lilies and set them at Beryl's feet. June sat in the Adirondack chair next to her, feeling every bit like a lady-in-waiting to the Queen of the County.

As the fire and conversation grew, one by one, cars turned into the Walker-Fitzgerald place. Old friends of Beryl's. Coworkers. Newer friends of Beryl's, friends of Aiden, Jade, and Willow.

Dustin and the boy he works with, Hartsomething, pulled in with a hoopla, parked a big truck, and then set up speakers on the edge of the bar and blasted an oldies station over them.

June watched Jade as Dustin joined their crowd of friends. He stood next to her, tracing his hand down her back. She caught it with hers, holding on for a long moment before letting go.

Jade, wake up, sugar.

"June, this is my old Midwest Parcel boss, Rolf," Beryl said, greeting a pencil-like man with too much mustache under his nose.

Rolf bowed to the Queen and her lady. "It's a pleasure."

The melancholy and golden scene expanded as more cars turned into the drive. So this was Beryl's going-home party.

What joy and sadness to witness. But June wanted her time to be just like this. And she would always believe Beryl's good-bye began with the song of the redbird.

~

The house was quiet except for the clink of dishes being put away. Max slowly ascended the basement steps.

At nine o'clock, Asa was out cold. The Iowa air and running wild over the grass was good for him. He'd had a blast tonight, eating more marshmallows than a nineteen-month-old—look at that, he knew his son's age off the top of his head—should eat before bed.

Asa was the star of the party besides Beryl. Bookends. The one just entering their world and the one about to exit. The unspoken balance comforted them all.

One minute in the warm bath, and the little boy's eyes drooped. Mom diapered him and he was asleep before she could slip on his pj's.

Max found Mom alone in the kitchen. "Hey, where is everyone?"

"Willow and Linc are out by the fire, making sure it dies down. Aiden went off to bed saying his jet lag was still messing with him. How're you, darling?"

Mom wiped a large bowl and tucked it into a bottom cabinet, then smoothed her hands over her jeans.

"I'm hanging in there, Mom." He wrapped his arm around her, kissing her temple. "How about you?"

"I'm doing all right, son."

"Are you going home for the swearing in?" Max leaned against the counter.

"Thinking on it. But I'm doing kind of fine up here on my own. I might want to stick it out for a while." June reached for the next dish to dry.

"I'll support you, Mom. But I love you both. And, for the record, I'm not too happy about this thing with you and Dad." Max took the dry dish from her and followed her pointing finger to the right cupboard. "Guess I'm not a rose without any thorns myself."

"I suppose none of us are." Mom handed him another bowl. "Have you told Jade?"

"About my plans? No, not yet." She barely gave him room to say hello to her.

"I'm proud of you . . . This is not an easy step."

"The alternative is worse."

June handed him a plate and pointed to the next cabinet. "You can do anything you put your mind to, Max. It's why the pills always puzzle me."

He settled the plate on top of the stack, then peered down at Mom. "When I find out why, I'll let you know."

June patted him on the back. "I bet you didn't come up those stairs looking for me." She motioned with her eyes toward the ceiling. "She's upstairs."

When Max hit the top step, Jade was coming out of Beryl's room. A small yellow light trimmed the dark space between the door and the frame.

"How is she?" He stopped on the top step, his hand on the banister.

"Sleeping. She loved the party, but it wore her out." Jade leaned against the wall, fingers in her pockets. "Don't know what it is about the prairie night and a bonfire, but . . ." She pinched her lips shut. Yeah, he understood. She didn't want to open up to him yet.

"Are you too tired to talk?"

"No." She shook her head. "I can talk."

Max was grateful the bonfire had made her mellow. "I saw a place down the road. The Hoss? Want to go there? I'll ask Mom to listen for Asa."

She hesitated, thinking. "Let me wash up."

The ride to the Hoss was quiet, but the kind of quiet that comes from two people who knew each other well. Did she sense it too?

"You holding up okay?" Max finally asked when he parked in a spot by the front door. The Hoss was an old warehouse with a neon sign blinking red, blue, and green onto the hood of his Mercedes.

"I am." Jade leaned forward a bit, squeezing her hands between her knees, sighing. "I'm getting used to the idea of her dying."

"She looked really happy tonight." Max wanted to brush his hand against her neck, but kept it resting on the console. "You're making her final days good, Jade."

"Doing the best with what time I have." Her sigh broke his heart. "Ready?" She popped open her car door.

The Hoss was a country-western establishment with a big dance floor in the middle, booths and tables along the side, a Budweiser sign blinking over the bar.

Tonight the place was mostly empty. A western song blared from a jukebox, and two guys with John Deere hats played pool in the front corner. The crack of balls was dissonant with the music.

A booth halfway down on the right-hand side was occupied, but otherwise, Max and Jade had the place to themselves.

"Hey, Jade."

"Hey, Sticks." She motioned to Max. "This is my . . . husband. Sticks and I grew up together."

"Good to know you, Jade's husband." The round man with big teeth nodded at them. "You guys take any booth, Jade. I'll be out with menus."

"The food is really good if you want something, Max," she said, leading the way to a booth in the back corner, passing the only other occupied seat.

Max looked over. *Great.* There was Dustin. And his redneck buddy who went by his last name. Fortunately, they were with two lovely ladies.

"Jade." Dustin hopped out of his seat.

"Hey y'all." She stopped, leaning to see who sat with her ex.

"You remember Katie," Dustin said, head down a bit. Max recognized the posture. The one of a man being in love with another man's wife.

"Katie, yeah, great . . . to see you."

"Fun bonfire, Jade," Hartline said, his arm around an intelligent-looking brunette.

"I'm so grateful y'all came out. Mama loved it. Really made her day."

"I remember she used to have some wild parties in, what, junior high?" Dustin slid back into the booth next to Katie.

Good, move on, man. The one you love is taken. The one next to you is pretty. She seems bright enough.

"Oh yeah"—Hart pointed, grinning—"and her friends pitched tents."

"Can't deny the fact Beryl loved a good time," Max said. Jade looked up at him. Well, did she expect him to stay out of the conversation? He needed to act like a husband here.

After a few more pleasantries, Max and Jade sat in a booth in the back. One away from the "gang." Sticks came around with water and menus.

"I'll just have coffee. Decaf," Max said.

"Diet Coke for me, Sticks. Thanks."

"Coming up." He headed back to the kitchen by the way of Dustin's table, saying something that got them laughing.

"Prairie City's a neat place, Jade." Max arranged the salt and pepper shakers.

"It's home."

"And Whisper Hollow?"

"Home, Max." The sheen in her eyes reflected the light hanging over their table. "But both have their lovely and dark memories."

"I'm sorry, Jade. I was a jerk, *am* a jerk."

"Max, I kissed Dustin." She tore at the end of the napkin wrapped around the utensils. "The other night."

He sat back, gripping the edge of the bench seat. "I see." The confession rattled him, but he wasn't surprised. Much. "Are you in love with him, or just getting back at me?"

"I wouldn't do that to him. Or you." She unrolled the napkin to blow her nose. "I kissed him because I wanted to, because I wanted to feel cherished. And I'm telling you because I'm sick of all the secrets and lies."

Max sat back as Sticks brought their drinks. He didn't blame her. As much as it sliced his heart to hear she kissed another man, one she could easily love, he couldn't be angry. Not very, anyway. Jealousy stung like the dickens, though.

"Cherished, huh?" Desired? He could mount a case for desire. He wanted her all the time, but in light of her words, he'd not done such a good job of cherishing her. "I can't stop thinking about you, Jade," he confessed softly. "I've wanted you since the day we met. I love you. Don't you know I could lose myself in you, babe?"

"Until you lose yourself in something else, someone else. Yourself."

He reached for the sweetener container. "Touché."

"I'm Dustin's Rice, Max. His first love. His first wife. The one who is a shadow on his heart."

"Is that what he told you?"

"Not in those words." She sipped her soda, shaking her head. Even tired and in the dim light, Max was captivated by her face and the sheen of her hair as it fell over her cheek. "I can tell. In some ways it helped me understand why you were with Rice."

"But, Jade, *you* are my Rice. I never loved her like I love you. Like Dustin loved you."

"But she was your childhood friend and lover."

"*That's* what made the night in Vegas easy. The familiar. Not because I still pined for her or because she cast some large love shadow over my life. She was a friend with benefits, if you know what I mean. And I'm sorry to admit it now. But when I dream of life, it's with you." Max peered into the dark surface of his coffee before lifting the cup to his lips. "What do you dream about, Jade?"

"Dreams . . . such a mystery." She peered into the empty room. The smack of pool balls had ceased. "I'm not sure what I want to dream about anymore."

One of the pool players dropped a quarter in the jukebox. A voice filled with longing and ache sang, "As the knot comes untied."

Between filtering through Max's platitudes and the tenor of Dustin's voice rolling over her shoulder, Jade was distracted. Did Dustin like Katie? Love her? Why should she even care?

Jade blinked, shook her head lightly, and tried to focus on what Max was saying.

"I'm sitting right here, Jade. I'm not walking out. I messed up, but let me remind the court it actually happened before our wedding." Excuses, always with the reasons and whys. "As for me and you, I'm not leaving, Jade. I'm all in, committed."

He looked strained, as if trying to run for the goal while a defender held on to his foot. Was he doing this for her? Or for himself? *Lord Jesus, give me wisdom.*

"Max, I don't know what to think other than I don't trust you." Her voice quivered as she stirred her drink with the straw.

"All right." He nodded. "That's fair. Very fair."

"Fair or not, it's true."

He shoved his coffee aside and stared at the bull-rider-clinging-to-the-bull mural reflecting in the mirror from the bar's opposite wall. "I'm going to Texas next week for four months. The Outpost. It's a ranch in the middle of nowhere where we work in the morning and have sessions in the afternoon and evening."

"When did you decide this?"

"Few days ago. With Tripp. This place is more like 'man up, you big baby.'" She knew he wanted her to laugh, but she continued to putter the ice around in her drink with her straw.

"What happened?"

"Ooo, lots of things. Starting with the McClures suing for custody of Asa."

"Your dad told me. So what happens with them if you're in rehab? Or this man-up ranch? Whatever." The ice watered down her soda, so she shoved it aside.

"The firm hired a detective to do a bit of digging."

"On the McClures?" Jade wrapped the straw paper around her finger, then looked up when Sticks set a new drink in front of her. "Whisper Hollow's Mike and Carol Brady?"

"Gus comes from a long line of moonshiners. Under his Southern gentleman veneer is a hard Appalachian man with a suspicious past. There's an open capital case that was never solved, and Gus McClure's name appears on the fringes. All we did was pull some files and evidence, show it to Gus, and ask him to drop the custody case. Otherwise, we might visit the DA to see if he'd wants to open a forty-year-old murder case. DNA testing has come a long way since the '60s."

Jade leaned back. "You would do that to him?"

"I'm not losing my son, Jade. Now that I have him, I'm not losing him. After all I've put us through, I'd be a fool to not fight for him." Max rested his arms on the table, his coffee cradled between his hands. Jade liked his hands. Thick, confident, tender. "The threat may have been part bluff on our part, but it worked. Gus's lawyer called the next day to drop the suit."

Just what went down in Whisper Hollow's hills? "So he's an accessory to murder?"

"I don't know, but he didn't want anyone investigating."

Behind her, a table squeaked. Footsteps echoed on the hardwood. Jade glanced back. Dustin was watching. He raised his hand. "See you."

"See you."

"Jade." Max grabbed her arm. "Look me in the eye."

She swerved around. "Keep your voice down."

"Listen to me. I'm not going anywhere. You want to run off with Dustin Colter? Do it, but I'll come after you."

"Interesting. He told me he'd be waiting for me."

"Jade, while I'm in rehab, anything could happen. But I'm going to be one lonely, praying, face-to-the-ground man before Jesus. I want what's best for both of us, and I believe"—he thumped his chest—"we belong together."

"I don't get this. What is driving you? The Outpost? Why are you suddenly getting your act together? Who's going to take care of Asa? Run Benson Law if your dad goes to the state supreme court?"

"Dad's turning over the firm to Clarence Chambers."

"No . . . I don't believe you." Would he? Rebel was coldhearted.

"Call him. Ask." Max tossed his phone to the table. "He said between the lawsuit, being a new father, the pill battle, and you running out . . ."

"I didn't run out." Jade sighed over the palette of her husband's life.

"He didn't think I'd have my head in the game. So I went out and proved he was right. Got mad, popped pills with a bourbon chaser, passed out in the den, and woke up to Asa screaming with his leg caught in the crib." Max demonstrated by twisting his arm back and around. Jade winced. "When I stumbled in to see what was wrong, he was wailing, in pain, naked, and covered with poop."

Jade eyed him. So he brought his brand of hurt to his own son. Maybe it was a blessing to be barren.

"I called Tripp and said, 'Let's go hard core.' I leave on Monday." Sticks appeared at the end of the table and freshened Max's coffee without asking. He took a big hot gulp, wincing. "I need to ask you something, Jade."

"Oh, Max." She denied him with a slow shake of her head. "Don't."

"Will you take Asa for me while I'm gone?"

"I said don't. Max, this is not fair, and you know it. What about your mom?"

"All is fair in love, Jade. I'm pulling a cheap trick in my fight for you. I saw your face when Asa touched your cheek."

"You can't manipulate me. I won't allow it."

"No manipulation, Jade. All my heart and my motives are on the table. Yes, I want you back, and if you spend four months with Asa, you'll fall in love with him. And maybe find it in your heart to forgive me. Want to be with me."

"I forgive you, Max. I do. I just don't trust you."

"Fair enough. But let me earn it back. Give me a chance. But either way, I need you to keep Asa."

"No, you don't. Your mom can keep him. Or the McClures."

He furrowed his brow, making a face.

"Okay, but your mom can keep him for four months. I'm sure you've hired a nanny." Jade slid out of the booth.

"But I want you to do it."

"How can you do this to him? To me? Force us to bond when you and I are not even sure we'll be together in four months? Max, it's always about you. Don't you care at all about anyone else?"

He was next to her, gripping her hands. "You are all I care about, Jade."

"Then how come it never feels like it?" Jade's cell rang from her hip pocket. She read the screen and peered up at Max. "It's your mom."

She listened for a second and turned for the door. "We're on our way."

Twenty-six

Jade stirred awake, her elbows slipping from the bent wood arms of the rocking chair. Two a.m. The golden glow from the small lamp on the edge of the dresser was the only light in the room.

Other than Mama's eyes. "You . . ."—she gasped for a breath—" . . . dozing."

"No, no." Jade shivered and crawled on the bed, curling up next to Mama. "Just taking a break from seeing." She checked the cannula hose running around Mama's ears and into her nose. "How are you?"

Dr. Meadows had come around eleven. He was one of the good ones. "Her system is shutting down," he said in a hushed tone, his sympathy going from Willow to Aiden, to June, to Max. Finally falling on Jade. "It won't be long. Keep her warm and comfortable."

On Mama's nightstand, he'd left a bottle of Ativan and another of morphine liquid in case air hunger caused her to panic.

"Some . . . party . . ." Mama struggled to breathe between each word. Even connected to the oxygen, her effort was laborious.

"Sure was, and you took our breath away, gorgeous." Jade attempted a smile.

Mama exhaled what might have been a laugh, but the rattle in her chest caught her wind making her choke and cough. Jade brought her upright, rubbing her back, coaxing, "Breathe with me, Mama. Inhale . . . good. Exhale. You shouldn't have stayed outside so long."

"Oh, Jade-o . . . my farewell . . . party." Mama held on to Jade's hand as she eased her back onto the pillow. "My farewell . . ."

"No talk of dying now, young lady." Jade fluffed the pillow behind Mama's head, wincing, nearly panicking herself as Mama struggled to breathe. Carbon dioxide, Dr. Meadow said, would build up and Mama wouldn't be able to expel it fast enough. "What will I do without you, Mama?"

Mama's smiled softly. "My Jade-o . . . capable, tender, kind. So proud, baby. So proud." Her forefinger lifted ever so slightly and pointed at Jade. "What you . . . became . . . did . . . without me."

A stream trickled down Jade's cheek. "You can't go, Mama, you can't. I need you."

"You *needed* me. Those days . . . gone by . . ." She faded, and for almost an eternity, didn't inhale.

"Mama?" Jade shook her into gasping for air. "Breathe. Keep breathing."

"So . . . tired." A deep, rattling cough exploded in her chest. Mama gasped and gagged, panic filling her eyes as her hands grasped the air.

"Okay, okay, here, Mama." Jade drew her upright again, making sure the cannula was in place. But the carbon dioxide was winning. "Breathe with me, Mama. In. Out. In. Out." Jade eyed the drugs on the nightstand.

The coughing-gasp subsided and Mama shivered, lowering back down to the plumped pillows.

"Hey, Mama, remember how you used to sit up with Aiden, Willow, and me on fall nights and tell us about traveling with Carlisle and the carnival? You told us stories of the trapeze artist and the runaway lion. Of the bulimic fat lady?"

Mama closed her eyes with a long sigh. "Circus . . . freaks . . . home." The end of her lips quivered as if she wanted to smile.

Jade brushed her hand over Mama's cheek. Her skin was so dry and sallow. "Everyone needs a place to call home."

"He's here," Mama said with a crisp clarity, her glistening eyes fixed on the window.

"Who's here, Mama?"

"Jesus . . . on His donkey."

"He's visiting again?" Jade tucked the blanket tighter around Mama's narrow frame.

"No, not visiting. Oh, Jade-o." She exhaled each word with a sense of wonder. Without gasping for air.

"Mama, do you believe?" Jade cupped Mama's face in her hands and turned her head until their eyes met. "Is He your Savior? I need to know. Will you be with Him on the other side?"

"It's . . . why." Mama struggled for a full breath. "He's come. But He waits."

"What's He waiting for, Mama?"

"You," she whispered.

"Me?" Jade peered at the window as if she might see Jesus with her own eyes. *What do You want, Jesus?*

"Let . . . me . . . go, Jade-o." She exclaimed a sharp, "Oh! He looked . . . at me."

"I can't." Buckets of tears filled Jade's eyes. "I can't let go. I'm scared."

Mama's chest slowly expanded, rattling and gurgling, then contracted. "I'm ready . . . peace."

Mama reached for the cannula, her hand shaking, tugging it free. Jade's tears dripped onto her hand. Mama's fingers shook and got tangled in the tube.

"Here, Mama, let me." Jade unhooked the hoses and turned off the tank. The silence echoed in Jade's ears. "Do you want the drugs Dr. Meadows left?"

"I want to enter . . . drug free." Her tender smile quickly faded.

"Even in death, you're doing it your way, aren't you?" Jade brushed Mama's cheeks with a kiss. Shaking, Mama puckered her lips. Jade's eyes filled as she lowered her lips to Mama's.

"I love you."

Mama tapped her chest. "Me too. Jade-o . . ." She coughed, working to draw air. "Max . . . it'll be . . ."

"Don't worry about Max and me." Jade dried her cheeks with her sleeve, then nestled next to her mother, tucking her arm under her shoulders. "We'll breathe together. In . . . good. Out."

"Sing . . ."

"Sing?" Sing what? No song came to mind, only fragments of melodies from the old tunes played at the party.

"A hymn."

A hymn? Jade scrambled for a hymn. Why couldn't she think of one? No words came. A hymn for the hippie . . .

Then she heard Granny's clear contralto. *Come home, come home, ye who are weary . . .*

Jade cleared the emotion from her throat. "Softly and tenderly, Jesus is calling . . ." She breathed in, breathed out with Mama. "Calling for you and for me . . . Breathe in, Mama. Out. Come home, come home . . . all who are weary come home . . ."

Jade breathed out with Mama. A serenity fell on her face. "Softly and tenderly, Jesus is calling . . ." Jade watched Mama. *Inhale, Mama, come on.* "Come home, come home . . ."

"Mama?" Jade squeezed her shoulder. "Mama, breathe in. Mama. Ye who are weary come home . . ." *Mama?*

She'd breathed her last. "Oh, Mama, Mama." Jade collapsed against her warm but still body, weeping, gathering the soft material of her gown in her hands.

Softly and tenderly, Jesus was calling.

~

God had painted cotton ball clouds across the cyan sky and set the day's thermostat to a warm and balmy sixty-two degrees. A perfect day for saying goodbye, for lowering Mama into the cold, dark earth.

Jade stood on the pale-green grass carpeting the burial mound that snaked around the old homestead with her back to the mourners gathering in the house, on the porch, in the yard.

The indistinguishable hum of voices married with the song of the wind floated toward her from the barn where a team was setting up tables. Willow wanted to celebrate Mama's passing with a barbecue. "That's what she would've wanted."

Jade inhaled the heady fragrance of roasting meat along with the warm, moist soil of Tank Victor's field.

For a moment she was eight, maybe nine, watching one of Mama's parties from her bedroom window, canvas tents pitched all over the yard, the green hose stretched through the grass for the makeshift shower. She ached to watch those parties again.

But the parties would be no more. Mama was gone. Jade's past was buried with her. She wrapped her arms around her waist, fighting the sense of loss that began swirling in her thoughts during the funeral.

"You doing all right?" Daphne and Margot appeared on either side of her. Daphne pressed Jade's shoulder with her hand.

"Yeah, just thinking." Jade shook her head and twisted Mama's jade ring around her pinky finger. "I wasn't a good daughter."

"Don't go there, Jade. You're mourning, not rehashing the past. It's over, book closed. You can't change anything back there."

If Daphne meant to comfort her, she missed.

"Come on, if you're being honest, go all the way. Your mom wasn't a stellar mom, remember?" Margot bent forward to see Jade's face.

"Margot." Daphne reached in front of Jade and shoved Margot aside. "You really shouldn't be licensed to stick sharp, moving instruments in folks' mouths. You have no compassion."

"I'm sorry, but the truth and reality are compassionate."

Jade shook her head. "I was just so mad at her for so long. I was the selfish one. So what if she married a few too many times? So what if she traveled for her job?"

"Traveled? Jade, she—"

"Margot." Daphne's interjection was piercing. "Jade, sweetie, none of us can see the past clearly. Good or bad. Be sad, be angry, cry, grieve, remember all the great things about your mom. And then, look to the future."

"My thoughts are stuck on how horribly I treated her. When I was packing to go to UT, she wanted to help. What'd I do? I ignored her, talked on the phone to my friends, who aren't even here today, and yelled at her because she had the nerve to *fold* my wadded-up tops."

"That was after the abortion, Jade. You were hurting." Daphne kept her voice even but firm.

"Right, but did I tell her I was mad? No, I just *showed* her. Acted like a two-year-old. Was I there for her when Bob Hill divorced her? When she got diagnosed with leukemia? She went through eight years of illness. Alone. A-lone!" The tears stung again in her tired eyes.

"It takes two to make a relationship, Jade."

"I didn't appreciate her. I didn't learn from her. I was too arrogant to think she had anything to teach me. And now, it's too late."

Margot gripped Jade's shoulders. "Jade, she lives in your DNA. She will always be with you."

"Am I interrupting?" Max took his place on the mound with the three of them.

"N-no, Max," Daphne said, unable to look directly at him.

"Can I speak to Jade alone for a second?"

"Sure." Daphne backed away.

Margot touched Jade's arm before leaving. "We'll be helping Willow with the barbecue. The dudes from the restaurant are very cute. A bit young, but *very* cute."

Jade smiled. Margot got her every time. "You do that."

"You holding up?" Max's voice was tender in her ear. He stood near enough for their arms to touch. His warmth penetrated through to her soul.

"Barely."

"Babe, I need to leave after lunch. If I don't get home in time to get organized, I won't be able to fly out to Texas Sunday night. I hate the timing of this—"

"When I was twelve," Jade started, "Mama split from Willow's dad, Mike. Mama had enough of men and marriage, of kids, so she took off with Carlisle and her carnival. She called Aiden out here, right where we're standing. Then me. She sat here with her face to the setting sun. Said she'd be gone for about four months, and I was to look after two-year-old Willow. Help out Granny. Not to fight with Aiden. Told me where I could find money and diapers." She looked up at Max. "And here I am again."

"I don't have to go to Texas, Jade. I can go later."

"Max, go to Texas." Jade patted his arm. "If you don't, this window will close forever."

"I don't want to abandon you."

"Your son needs a drug-free dad. I'm going to stay here for a while, at the house."

"What about the Blue Umbrella and Blue Two?"

"Just a couple of fancy junk shops."

"Stop. You worked hard to build those businesses. You're a respected—"

"Junk dealer. Sanford and Daughter." Her laugh was sardonic and cold. "Daughter . . . I could have a daughter now, but I don't. I killed her." Jade glanced up at Max. "How can you ask me to keep your son when you know what I did to my own child?"

"Stop." Max grabbed her and turned her to him. "Jade, this is a dark path. You don't want to travel here. You're being unreasonable."

She squared her shoulders, pressing against his hand. "Am I? Have I said anything untrue?"

"Factually, no. In tone and intent, yes. Very untrue. Jade, we can have Tom keep working the issue on the Blue Two insurance. Lillabeth can keep the Blue Umbrella going. Take time up here if you need it, but don't quit, Jade. It's not in you."

Jade stepped off the mound, heading for the cluster of cars sitting askew on the lawn by the barn. Dustin stood by his truck, hands in his pockets, ankles crossed. He was watching her.

Max regarded him for a moment. "Listen, Jade. Mom will take Asa, if you decide—"

"Good, good, I—I think that's best." Jade pressed her hand on his arm. "I'm sorry I can't be more for you right now."

He enveloped her in his arms. "It's okay."

They walked side by side to the house. In the kitchen, Carla and June had organized the paper goods and side dishes on the counter. Daphne and Margot, along with a small troupe of women, waited to march it all out to the barn.

"Jade?" June's hand brushed Jade's shoulder, her latest L.L.Bean sweater tied around her shoulders. Her blonde hair hung loose about her high cheeks and broad chin. "You doing all right?"

"As well as one can the day her mother is buried." At the sink she filled a glass with water and stared out the window.

Upstairs, Mama's room was empty. The bed made, the blinds open, the oxygen tank and medicines gone. And by this time tomorrow, the house, the lawn, Jade's life, would be quiet and alone. Stopped. Waiting for direction.

Her hand shook as she drank, but the water cooled her dry, hot insides. Her arms and legs wobbled with a hollow sensation, almost like they were detached from the rest of her. The burnt amber popped up over her thoughts, deeper, fiercer than before. The swirling purple rising from her soul was spotted with a penetrating black.

Batting her eyelids, she tried to clear away the blur and organize her thoughts. But they were caught in the gathering storm. She'd hoped she'd make it through the day without sinking into panic, without dodging anxiety. Grief had been a great anesthesia so far.

Yet in the span of a few seconds, Jade felt weightless, spinning, lost and adrift, like a ship at sea on a starless night.

Outside the window, Jade spotted Aiden and Willow on the lawn with Carlisle and Eclipse, who drove in from California and had to leave tonight. Mike Ayers and Daddy, who flew in today, joined their circle, looking as if they were reminiscing. Even in death, Jade let Mama down. Did she call Dad like she'd asked? No. Aiden had called. Daddy was leaving in a few hours. Rebel's plane waited to fly him home, but he was trying to convince June to go with him. His swearing in was postponed until next week. And June appeared to be weakening. And now, she apparently had guardianship of Asa.

In the morning, Aiden would be gone. Willow in the afternoon.

Jade gulped the last of her water. Mama was dead. In the cold ground. Reminiscing or staring at the pictures of her Aiden had enlarged and set on easels wouldn't bring her back.

Jade stumbled back from the sink, pushed by an internal pressure. Mama. She wanted her . . . Here . . . now . . . *I want you back, Mama.*

The bottomless sensation of aloneness doused her. Burnt amber collided with the purple swirls. She reached for the counter. She floated, the swirl lifting her soul from the kitchen. Jade's glass dropped from her hand, crashing but not breaking against the hardwood.

Mama . . .

The call echoed in her chest, but not from her voice. Max's boy wandered into Jade's view framed by the sink window. His little brown jacket hung loose over his shoulders. The tip of his nose was red and runny, while a tuft of his black hair stuck up from the crown of his head. "Mama?"

Why was he wandering alone? He could get lost. *Max? June?* No one trailed after him. Were they all in the barn? Did they just leave him?

Asa stopped toddling when he reached the edge of the grass and fell forward, catching himself with one pudgy hand to the ground. When he stood upright again, he stared at his hand, slapping away the dirt.

Jade figured he'd turn and do his little one-arm-pumping run toward the barn, but he remained still, staring at something Jade couldn't see. Then his head jerked toward the house, his bright eyes wide. He made a circle, looking. A pout weighted his little red lip, and even from the distance, Jade saw his brow tighten and tears emerge.

His lips moved. The wind captured his tiny, "Mama."

Jade fell against the sink's edge and stretched toward the window. Oh, his shoulders were trembling. Jade smacked the window frame with her palm, then shoved open the pane.

"Mama." His tiny voice broke through the screen. "Ma-ma." Asa tipped his head back. His wail hit Jade and trailed down her limbs to her toes. "Ma-ma! Ma-ma!" Tears sparkled on his raw, red cheeks. "*Maaamaaa.*"

Jade jerked straight, her middle constricting, her heart beating. *Mama.* Slowly, she collapsed to the floor, the boy's cry chasing her own wail. "Maaama . . ." She buried her face against her arms.

She wept hard. But when she heard voices, she raised her head, weak and drained. As if she'd cried for days.

June's voice skimmed passed, then Max's, comforting Asa. On her hands and knees, Jade crawled to the back door to peer out. Max was swinging Asa up in his arms, and the boy clung to his daddy's neck, shivering. "Mama."

Mama.

Jade crawled across the kitchen, burnt amber blinding her thoughts, rising to her feet as she reached the living room. Flutters filled her chest. Her thoughts fired without aim into a thickening fog. She burst out the front door and stumbled down the stairs.

Her body moved, but she couldn't feel her hands or feet. The only sound was the thrust of her breath in her ears.

Down the driveway . . . toward the road . . . She watched herself as if standing on the roof of the house. Slapping her hands to her face, her pulse surged. Her nose . . . her eyes . . . she couldn't feel them.

What if it was all a lie? If the man on the donkey was an evil, lying demon carting Mama off to hell. *No, no, no.* What if the whole big deal about God and the afterlife, going to heaven and meeting "on that beautiful shore" was a myth? A grand illusion?

What if there was no true hope? Jade ran, stumbling on the pebbled berm, gasping to fill her shallow lungs.

Did she let Mama go into nothingness? She might explode with a single scream. *Mama!*

A car horn shoved Jade from the side of the road into the ditch. She caught her fall with the heels of her hands. A rock had gashed her knee, so blood glistened against her skin and soaked into her skirt. Climbing out of the ditch, numb and detached, Jade bolted down the road, escaping from some *thing*, aiming at no *thing*.

Twenty-seven

Max heard shouts. He listened as he wiped Asa's mouth. More shouts. Jade, they were calling Jade.

Max peered out the barn door. Beyond the edge of the lawn, Jade was running in her skirt with Willow and Dustin chasing after her. Mourners began to cluster on the lip of the lawn.

"Mom." Max glanced around for her while tugging his Mercedes keys from his pocket. "Watch Asa."

~

Running stole her air but gave her some sense of being. Her heartbeat roared in her ears and shoved all the air from her fiery lungs. Twice she'd stumbled and twisted her ankle. But she couldn't stop . . . the darkness would win.

Beneath her skirt, her feet kicked, striding, and her hands pumped at her side, the scenario fixed in the gray plane of Jade's mind.

Footsteps hammered the pavement behind her. She fell again, face-first, into the pavement, screaming. Yet the sound in her throat never escaped her lips.

Jade. Stop. Jade-o.

Gripping the air, she struggled to her feet. *Run or the darkness will devour you.*

Then she heard it. A clear, pure voice slicing through the confusion and darkness.

I AM home. Come to Me.

She'd taken one step when a firm hand grasped her arm and whipped her around. "Jade, whoa, hold up, it's me, Dustin." He held her chin, his eyes trying to capture hers. "Talk to me, what's wrong?"

She tried to break free, but his grip bit into her flesh. "Let me go, Dustin." She huffed, gulping in all the air she could. Dustin's fragrance of soap and cologne burnt her nostrils. "Let me go."

The darkness was catching her. Where was the voice? Its clarion sound?

Burnt amber filled her senses. The swirling purple chained her ankles to the ground, then slithered up her legs and reached for her arms. She twisted with a huff. "Let me go, Dustin, let me go. I can't breathe."

But he refused. "Jade, stay with me . . . it's okay . . ."

"I can't feel myself, Dustin. Not my face, or my feet, just darkness, colors, evil colors . . . please, can you see me? Is my face there?"

"Yes, every beautiful part of you is there. Your face, your feet. Breathe with me. Deep inhale . . . exhale. Think peace. You're fine, Jade. You're fine. You're just having a panic attack."

"No, no." Jade gulped. "I've had those, Dustin, this . . . this is, is more. Terror. Tell me, please"—she fastened her hands on his arms—"that Mama is with Jesus, Dustin. He's real, right? Jesus, God? This whole eternal life. Who created Him? Who? I can't see it . . ." Jade heard herself rambling but couldn't stop. Her heart began to ache. "Tell me, Dustin."

"Your mom is with Jesus. God is very real. He's love. You can trust Him. Jesus said He is the way, the truth, and the life. Say it with me, Jade."

She swallowed, nodding, trying to remember . . . What did he want her to say?

"Come on, Jade." Dustin coaxed her.

"He is"—her eyes followed Dustin's lips—"the way, the truth, and the life."

The declaration inserted the first sliver of peace in her soul.

"Say it again. 'He is the way . . .'"

"The truth, the life. Jesus is the way, the truth, the life. No man comes to the Father but by Him."

She repeated the verse again with Dustin, her heartbeat slowing, the burnt amber fading, the purple swirls hissing and letting go, falling away. The fog clouding her mind dissipated. Sensation returned to her hands and feet. She touched and felt her face.

"How're you doing?" Dustin searched her eyes. "Better?"

She inhaled deep and brushed her hand over her damp forehead, shoving her bangs aside. "Yes, better. Better." The burn in her lungs began to cool.

She smiled at Dustin as Max's Mercedes skidded to a stop. He fired out of the door, leaving the car in the middle of the road with the engine running. "Jade, what happened? Are you okay, babe?" Max stepped around Dustin, slightly shoving him aside.

"I'm fine, Max." She peered beyond him at Dustin. "I'm fine."

───

"What can I get everyone? Sandwiches? We have plenty of leftovers. Barbecue, chips, beans and slaw, beer and sodas? Coffee? There's cake, my stars, enough to feed an army. For a small community, Prairie City can bring out the food."

June faced the crew in the living room, hands clasped, smiling. At least she felt like she was smiling, but she just couldn't stay somber any longer. It was driving her crazy. She had to do something with herself.

Max stared up the steps, hands on his belt, his back stiff. His signature posture of impatience. "What's going on up there?"

"Why don't you let Daphne and Reverend Teeter speak to Jade, Max? Have you fed Asa since lunch?"

Daphne, Margot, Max and Rebel, Aiden and Willow remained at the farm, changing their departure plans. Jade's daddy Harlan had already gone to the airport by the time Jade went running down the road.

Willow chewed the end of her thumbnail, and Aiden flipped through a magazine that June guessed to be a year old. He got to the end and started over again.

"What's going on with her?" Willow glanced from her brother to her brother-in-law to June. Rebel sat somber in the easy chair, hand over his lips. "We can't just let her sit up there and go crazy."

"The reverend is with her, Willow." June used her well-honed comfort tone. "And Daphne."

"She's been under a lot of pressure," Margot said. "Let's give her room, say a prayer."

"I haven't stopped praying." The whole room stilled at the tenor of Rebel's confession. June stared. *Oh, Reb, you are such a complicated mystery.*

After a second, Margot moved across the room and perched on the sofa next to Willow. "Daph is pretty sure she suffered from depersonalization or something stress related where she disassociated with herself." Margot peered toward the stairs. "Jade's strong, y'all, remember. She'll get through this."

June liked Margot. A good, commonsense girl. "Last call for food."

Margot slapped her thighs. "I guess I could eat something."

"Me too." Willow stepped over the coffee table. "Leftover barbecue is always good."

"I'm going to check on Asa." Max headed for the basement.

June brushed his back as he passed. Her boy looked so lost and sad. But the air of the room stirred. Hope filtered in. All with Rebel's single confession.

Aiden and Rebel started talking about Alaska, moving toward the kitchen. June paused at the base of the staircase. *Lord Jesus. Oh, Lord Jesus.*

The faint cry woke her. Jade sat up, holding on to Mama's bed with her free hand until the room stopped spinning. Silence rang in her ears. The clock by the bed flashed 3:00 a.m.

Shaking, she reached for the light, still gripping Granny's Bible. Her legs and back ached from running down the road in heels. June had bandaged the gash on her knee, but the torn skin throbbed.

While she felt one with herself again, the memory of what happened this afternoon caused her heart to double-beat and a sick sensation to sting in her belly.

There . . . the cry again. Jade stepped out of bed, listening. When the cry didn't repeat, she reclined against the pillows—still fragrant with Mama's scent—Oil of Olay and White Rain. She wanted to sleep again, escape death and fear, hear the clarion voice, but her senses were awake, disturbing her soul.

What was it Daphne called it? Depersonalization? Sounded too clinical for Jade.

"It can happen anytime, to anyone, but it can be triggered by stress."

"How long does it last?"

"Seconds to minutes."

"Can it happen again?" Jade caught a whiff of coffee, like Granny used to make. And bacon. She never wanted it to happen again.

"Can it? Yes. Will it, I don't know. We can take steps to help you."

Tears slid down her temples into her hair. *Mama, I need you.*

Dark . . . it all seemed so dark. And vivid. Daphne said the event had only lasted a few minutes, but in her mind it lasted for eternity. The aftershock rippled through her mind.

The wail hit Mama's room again. Jade bolted off the bed. Thin walls don't lie. Did a cat get in the house? Clutching Granny's Bible like a life preserver, Jade cracked open Mama's door. Darkness filled the hall along with an aching, thick stillness.

A whimper, followed by a cry, startled Jade's heart. Asa? Where was Max? She smacked on the hall light and angled over the railing to see down the stairs.

On the edge of her high-atop view, Jade saw a tiny leg curled under a crumpled body. What in the world? She started down. Max's son lay crumpled in the middle of living room carpet, sobbing, his tiny shoulders shivering.

"Hey, now, it's okay." Jade knelt beside him, patting his back, slowly pressing her palm down. Her hand nearly covered him. "How'd you get up here?"

He sat up at the sound of her voice. His face was worn with tears. "Want Mama."

Jade smoothed aside his dark, soft bangs, her eyes welling up. "Yeah, me too." So he'd gone looking for Rice. Escaped the basement. Maneuvered the stairs.

And she'd escaped the kitchen. Ran down a country road.

"Come here, baby." Jade lifted him and he curled into her, shuddering, his small fingers reaching into her hair.

She molded around him, breathing in his baby skin, rocking back and forth. "You and me, we're the same, Asa. Two lost souls without our mamas."

As she kissed his cheeks, his warm breath brushed the nape of her neck. His eyelids hung heavy as he gathered more and more of her hair into his hand.

"Your mama had dark hair like mine, didn't she? She was pretty. And so lively and adventurous. Did you know she was learning to fly a plane? My mama was amazing too. Hitchhiked across the country, went to Woodstock. Well, I guess that doesn't mean anything to you now, but one day I'll tell you about Granny Hill. Yes, I said Hill. Beryl Walker Fitzgerald Ayers Parsons Hill. I know, a law firm should be so prestigious. The woman had a string of last names, and she was full of . . . life."

Jade rose from the floor and eased into Granny's old rocker. Max stood in the doorway.

"Little bugger must have climbed over the basement gate." He eased into the room, bare chested, with the hem of his flannel pants dragging the floor.

"I heard him crying. When I came down, he was heaped in the middle of the floor sobbing for his mama."

"Guess it takes time, even for the little ones, to deal with death." Max dropped down next to the rocker and cupped his hand on Asa's head. "But he's getting better. Not waking as often, disoriented, looking for her."

"Today was about missing mamas."

Max shifted his gaze to Jade's face. "You two are kindred spirits right now."

Funny how right and perfect Asa fit into her arms. "What happened today was frightening, Max."

"Jade, say the word and I'll cancel Texas."

She rested her head against the top of the rocker. Despite all the pain and confusion of the past weeks, Max's raw emotion and honesty moved her. She wanted to tip forward and kiss him. "Go, Max. Get help. Asa needs his daddy clearheaded and strong."

"What about my wife? Doesn't she need me?" Max slipped his hand under her hair.

"Max, stop. You need to come to grips with the reality of broken trust. I don't hate you, but right now my heart is not safe with you either." A late tremor from her earlier emotional quake ran through her. "But I am willing, I think, to watch Asa for you, with June's help. If it's not too late." Jade gently kissed Asa, who was now sleeping peacefully in her arms.

Max rose up on his knees and covered her lips with his, then brushed his hand down her arm.

~

Along the first of summer, when spring began to lose its grip on Prairie City mornings and summer breezes circled the afternoons, the word *joyful* began trumpeting over the shadowy recesses of Jade's mind.

Sitting on the Iowa burial mound, Jade watched Asa pedal his Big Wheel through the thick grass. He'd begun to laugh a lot in the last week, and his vocabulary seemed to double every day.

What was it he said to June last night? Oh, she couldn't remember and she promised Max she'd record everything. *Everything.*

The golden sun hanging over her reminded Jade she'd wanted to plant some marigolds this evening. Just because.

Deciding to stay in Prairie City for a while shook her sense of order. She had two businesses to run back in Tennessee. A house. Friends. But here on the plain, Jade was learning to be at home with Jesus. No matter what her circumstances.

Lillabeth's semester ended, so she took over running the shops. She had Kip on a tight remodeling schedule. He'd called the other night asking Jade to call off her "dog."

Instead, she'd called Lillabeth and told her to growl and bark a little louder. She missed the shops. She missed her home. And for the past few days, she'd had a taste for Mae's cherry pie. But she wasn't ready to leave yet.

Asa growled as he aimed his Big Wheel right at her. She curled her body in tight. "Oh no, I'm going to get run over." He laughed and reverse-pedaled just before running over her foot.

When they buried Beryl, spring had just begun on the prairie. Now summer's green painted the horizon.

Jade spent April and May in counseling twice a week in Des Moines with Dr. Joe. Mostly reconciling her life. Talking out loud helped make sense of it all. But in recent days her inner changes came from her talks and prayers with Reverend Teeter.

At night, she holed up in her room with her Bible open and other books the reverend recommended. And she'd joined up with the women's prayer group. Only they called it a prayer furnace—stoking the fires for God. Carla

Colter was the leader, and those women were intense about the Lord's business and praying the Word.

Asa hopped off his ride and crawled into her lap. This was a new development with him, started about a day ago.

"Guess what? Uncle Linc is coming by tonight with a doggy. You want a doggy?"

"Doggy!" Asa punched the air with his fist. "Woof, woof."

"That's right, woof, woof."

Mrs. Lanker couldn't care for her chocolate lab any more, so Linc brought him out to the farm last night after Asa went to bed. Jade fell in love, snapped a picture with her cell, and e-mailed it to Max. He'd get it on Saturday when he went into town.

"Lunchtime?" June approached, casual and pretty in her khaki capris and white top.

"I suppose it is."

June stayed to help Jade, but now she was going home. After Mama's funeral, Reb changed. He'd finally agreed to counsel with Reverend Girden. There was a different light behind the lawyer's eyes. The fear of the Lord.

"Dustin called." June handed Asa the juice cup in her hand.

"Yeah, when?"

"Ten minutes ago."

"I'll call him after lunch." Light, airy tone, letting June know there was nothing to worry about.

"Have you heard from Max this week?"

"He called a few days ago." The wind blew stiff with a warm current. "He sounded tired. They work pretty hard. His latest e-mail said he was learning a lot." Jade peered up at June. "Asa said hi to him, called him Daddy."

June sat next to Jade, stroking Asa's head. "I love the smell of the prairie, but I'm ready to be in the Hollow again. I miss the morning fog clinging to the hills."

"And Rebel?"

June smiled. "We'll see. So far, so good. And what about you?"

"We'll see." Jade set her chin on her son's head. "So far, so good."

~

Approaching the brown mound of Mama's grave nestled in the shade of a maple, Jade held on to Asa's hand. Tufts of summer's green grass crept along the base of the tombstone.

Beryl Hill

At home with Jesus, finally free.

"We've come to visit your Granny Hill, Asa." Jade let loose the blanket in her arm, spreading it on the ground beside the stone.

The late-afternoon sun kissed her shoulders—she hated being inside on such beautiful days. She gathered her knees to her chest and tipped her face toward the light.

"Mama, good news: we've decided to keep the house, not sell it. At least not yet, anyway," Jade said to the air. She smiled as Asa scooted his truck over the grass and into the dirt of Mama's grave.

"Mama, here. Hold, please." Asa stuck out his hand, offering Jade his truck. Calling her Mama came from within him. She'd never coaxed him. Neither had June.

Satisfied his truck was in good hands, Asa climbed onto his small tricycle and reached his chubby legs out to the pedals.

She'd never tire of hearing her name—Mama.

If she'd had known what the start of the year would've been like, she'd have hidden behind the door of New Year's Eve and never come out.

But it was facing the pain, pushing through the heartache, that brought her to this moment of peace. Life had true hope for her.

Max was doing well at his Texas outpost, but digging up the wells of his past caused him to struggle with dark revelations. He questioned everything. Even his career. So far, he'd not mentioned their marriage. But Jade was glad. She had her own doubts to wrestle down.

When Max called, though, he sounded strong. His emails were filled with his easy prose, updating her on his progress, signing his notes with a simple, "Love, Max" as if he understood he didn't deserve her.

Jade exhaled. She wasn't sure he did. But no matter, she'd let none of it disturb her peace today as she sat on the mound next to Mama with the wind in her hair. She'd deal with Max when he came home.

The most surprising thing this year? Asa. How could such joy come out of such bitterness? Only God could do such a thing. When she held Asa the night she'd found him in the living room, she'd been overwhelmed with the sense of wanting to never let go.

He was her son.

The crunch of tires over the gravel added notes to the air. Jade tipped her chin north toward the heavens.

Footsteps swished over the grass and a warm, solid Dustin dropped to the ground next to her. "June said you'd be here."

"She said you called."

Asa pedaled past them on his tricycle, flashing a tiny grin at Dustin.

"I'm going to get you, buddy," Dustin teased.

Asa pumped his legs, ducking down toward the handlebar without a squeal or blip of laughter, and set his determination to flee. His blond head disappeared as he dipped below the rise of the knoll.

"He's doing good."

"I'm married, Dustin. I stood before God and man and made a vow." The confession released the balloon of pressure lodged in her chest.

"Hartline and I sat on the bleachers last night, talking until after midnight." The breeze inched between them, carrying the song and scent of the crystalline day. Asa emerged from the other side of the mound, driving straight for Jade and Dustin.

When he crashed into Dustin's foot, he laughed as if he'd won and knew it, then reversed his way back down the small mound.

"I take it you weren't talking about your business." Jade smoothed away the wisps of hair covering her eyes.

"We weren't." Dustin's arms rested on his raised knees, and the curve of the horizon—where blue sky met green earth—reflected in his glossy eyes. "We talked about you and how I should've never let you go." He peered at her. "I wish you were my wife and that little boy out there were mine. But I realized last night . . . I can't come between you and Max. I've made darn sure to stand in his shadow so when he hit the dirt, you'd see me waiting there." He picked at the grass, winding thick blades around his fingers. "And I've learned to live with woulda-shoulda-coulda, but I can't live with busting up a marriage. I'd hate myself, and ultimately, so would you."

Jade let his confession ride, the tenor of his words resonating with her own recent revelations. Asa sped toward them again, sweeping wide around their backs and gunning down the knoll.

"You saved me, Dustin, in so many ways."

"I also crushed you."

"Yeah, I guess you could say that, but I've finally moved on. I'm not sixteen anymore. I'm thirty-one, and a lot of life has flowed over my wounded soul. I'm stronger, healed. I did love you desperately, Dustin, but if someone handed me a magic wand right now to turn back time, I'm not sure I'd do it . . . I love Max, Dustin. God help me, I do."

Dustin's arm swung around her shoulders, and he pressed her into him. "Then you love him with all your heart, hear me?"

Her newly constructed wall of confidence cracked, and Jade sobbed against him. Dustin would be so easy to love. So easy to lie back in the grass and let the sunlight pass over them.

But Max was working hard, baring his heart and soul to strangers as well as to her. Jade needed to keep her pledge. She wanted to be there when he came home.

Wringing her sobs dry, Jade sat up, brushing her fingers over her cheeks, scanning the grounds for Asa. He'd paused to search the grass for something, bugs probably, his recent fascination.

"Will you be all right?" she asked.

"Absolutely. Doing the right thing isn't easy, but it's always good." He gazed toward the road, his Adam's apple dipping and rising with each swallow. "I have a date with Kate tonight. We have a lot in common, and I think she'll—" Dustin cleared his voice. "Hey, I need to get going."

His kiss lingered on Jade's forehead.

"Send me a Christmas card?" She stood with Dustin. The blue light of his eyes shone with backbone and belief.

"Every year." He backed toward his truck. "See you, Asa buddy."

The boy jumped off his trike and ran toward Jade, crashing into her leg. She swung him up into her arms as Dustin fired up his truck and aimed for the road.

Heading west, he drove toward the burnished blaze hovering above the bend in the road. Jade watched until a wash of light enveloped his tailgate, and everything that had been disappeared.

"All right, all right, you." Jade came into the moment, setting Asa on the ground. "I'm going to get you, son. Better run fast." She chased him over the Indian mound toward the trees.

Son. She had a son. As Asa's laughter buoyed in the air, it seeped into her heart, watered the dry places, and redeemed her barrenness with love.

Letting him run just beyond her grasp, Jade tugged her ringing phone from her pocket. The number on the screen arrested her forward motion. This wasn't his day to call. Jade answered, "Max, hello."

Acknowledgments

Thanks to all who helped the book come to life:

Our editor, Ami McConnell, ever wise, ever seeing, a talent at seeing the layers in story and drawing them to the surface.

The team at Thomas Nelson: Natalie Hanemann, Katie Bond, Eric Mullett, and Allen Arnold, for your work and faith in this project.

Jennifer Stair, for her insight and edits.

Al and Will Donaldson for insight on a '66 Cadillac.

Susan May Warren for keeping the candle burning during the drafting stage.

Ellen Tarver for reading the book in the early stages and offering ideas.

April Schaffer who jumped behind *The Sweet By & By* with enthusiasm and energy, and created such a great street team. You rock!

Reading Group Guide

1. In the opening scene, Jade thinks she might be barren. Other than being childless, what are ways her heart and life are barren? Have you had barren seasons in your life? How did God meet you?

2. June has known for years of her husband's infidelity. Is there a reason she's kept quiet? Are there issues in your life or your family's life that cause you to remain quiet for the good of the whole? When is this a dangerous thing to do?

3. Jade's mother, Beryl, was an absent parent during Jade's childhood. But now she's dying of leukemia and Jade is taking care of her. Why does Jade do this? Is there someone in your life who has hurt you but you repay with kindness?

4. When Jade discovers Max has a son younger than their marriage, she loads Beryl into a car with June and heads for Prairie City. It is a natural inclination to run from trouble and pain. What issues have you run from in your life? Would it have been better to stay, face the pain, and work it out?

5. Jade is tempted by her relationship with Dustin. He symbolizes her heart's longing to return to someone safe, and something familiar. Can you think of a time or incident where you wanted to return to something familiar as a source of comfort? Perhaps food or drinking, a relationship, or a place? What was the outcome?

6. Back in Whisper Hollow, Max is adjusting to instant fatherhood. His secret affair produced a beautiful boy. While God forgives us of our sins, we are often left to deal with the consequences of our actions. How does this impact Max? How has a similar situation impacted you?

7. Jade wants to have a connection with her Mama before she dies and looks through a box of her things -- memorabilia and pictures. Why is this important for Jade? Is there someone in your life you need to connect with before they move on, or perhaps die? Why is healing and forgiveness important in our lives?

8. During a spontaneous party for Beryl, a little red bird appears and sings her a song. Did you feel this was symbolic? Share a time when you heard God speak to you in an unusual way.

9. During the story, we see Jade suffering from panic attacks and fear. Are there times in your life when panic hits you out of nowhere? How do you respond? What hope do we have in Jesus, the Prince of Peace, to get us through those anxious hours?

10. After the funeral, Jade has a depersonalization moment. She loses all sense of self, panics, and runs down the road. Dustin is the first to catch her and she tells him to "let her go." What does this symbolize in their relationship and in Jade's Prairie City life? Is there something or some-one you need to tell, "Let me go"?

11. When Jade hears Max's son, Asa, crying in the farmhouse living room, she comforts him. How does this impact her heart? Share about a time in your life when God comforted you in an unusual way, or through an unlikely source.

12. By the end of the book, Jade has bonded with Asa. How does this answer her fear in the opening paragraph about being barren? How has God filled the barren places of your life?

From multi-platinum award-winning artist SARA EVANS with
Rachel Hauck, the novel that started the Songbird Series…

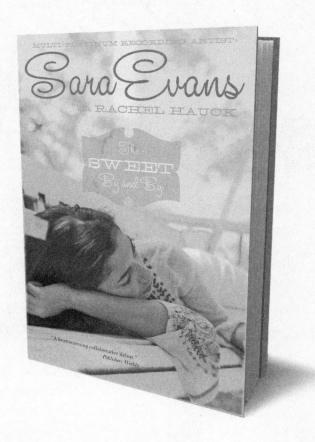

"HEARTWARMING"
—*Publishers Weekly*

"ENCHANTING"
—*New York Times* best-selling author
Patti Callahan Henry

"BREATHTAKING"
—*New York Times* best-selling
author Robin McGraw

"BEAUTIFULLY REAL"
—actress Eva Longoria Parker

Also from Rachel Hauck, co-author of

The Sweet By & By

Visit
RachelHauck.com

Experience
the inspiring conclusion
to the Songbird series.

Love Lifted Me

Available Winter 2012